THE WARRIORS

THE
WARRIORS

A NOVEL

PAUL BATISTA

OCEANVIEW (PUBLISHING
SARASOTA, FLORIDA

ISBN 978-1-60809-318-2

Cover Design by Christian Fuenfhausen

Published in the United States of America by Oceanview Publishing

Sarasota, Florida

www.oceanviewpub.com

10 9 8 7 6 5 4 3 2 1

PRINTED IN THE UNITED STATES OF AMERICA

To Betsy McCaughey, with all my love.

THE WARRIORS

CHAPTER 1

RAQUEL REMATTI—TALL, VIGOROUS, dressed in black—was on her feet as soon as Judge Naomi Goldstein said, "Your witness, Ms. Rematti."

Even before she reached the podium next to the seventeen men and women in the jury box, Raquel asked Gordon Hughes, "How long did you work for the Senator?"

"Seven years, Ms. Rematti."

"From the time she ran her first race for the Senate, correct?"

"Just before, that's right."

"And you had worked for President Young before that, correct?"

Gordon Hughes had been taught by the prosecutors that it was important to lean slightly forward and look at the jurors when he answered every question: it gave him, they said, a rapport with the men and women in the jury box. It would also, they said, make him seem less impressed and intimidated by the legendary and striking Raquel Rematti. And it also gave him those crucial moments to think about the question and the answer instead of just reacting. He said, "I did."

"You were with the Senator when her husband was assassinated, isn't that right?"

"I was."

"In fact, you were in that hotel room in Seattle with her when the Secret Service called to tell her that President Young had been killed by a suicide bomber?"

"That's right."

Raquel had come to know her client well in the months after the Senator first learned she was under investigation for fund-raising fraud, theft by her of campaign contributions, money laundering, and tax evasion in connection with the early stages of her race for the presidency. Now five feet away from Angelina Baldesteri as the Senator sat impassively at the defense table, Raquel sensed the almost imperceptible tension in this coolest of any person she had ever known. For years she had used the words *stone-cold killer* to describe some of her clients who were, in fact, *stone-cold killers*. She had come to believe she had encountered in Angelina Baldesteri somebody who was *stone-cold*, even though she faced life in prison and the complete destruction of her reputation. Yet this was the first time Raquel had picked up any sense of tension in her client.

"And in that room in Seattle, on that awful night, you cried when you heard the news about the President's violent death?"

"I did."

"And the President's wife cried, too, correct?"

"I honestly don't remember that, Ms. Rematti," Gordon Hughes said. "Senator Baldesteri, even when she was the First Lady, was a stoic."

"And you're not a stoic, are you, Mr. Hughes?"

"No."

"And we all know that because when the prosecutor asked you two days ago how you feel now about the crimes *you* committed, you cried, didn't you?"

"Yes."

"For all of us to see, correct, sir?"

"It wasn't my intention to cry. It just happened that way."

"Just like that night in Seattle when word came that the President was killed, correct?"

"Yes."

Raquel was now at the podium. Although she had listened to Gordon Hughes testify against her client for two days, Raquel didn't have a single note in front of her. She knew exactly what she intended to do.

"Let me ask you this, Mr. Hughes: When FBI agents knocked on your door in your townhouse on DuPont Circle in Washington at six in the morning, did you cry?"

"No."

"When they told you that you and Senator Baldesteri were the target of a criminal investigation for tax evasion and fund-raising fraud and money laundering, did you cry?"

"I was upset, I think."

"You *think*? That was nine months ago, wasn't it? You remember crying when the Senator's husband was blown up years ago by an ISIS suicide bomber in Manhattan, but you don't remember crying when seven FBI agents arrived at your home at six in the morning and told you that they and the Justice Department believe you concealed twenty-six million dollars in payments and never reported that to the IRS or to the Federal Election Commission? And you can't today remember how you reacted to that, is that right?"

"I told them they were wrong. It was a mistake. They had the wrong person. Their views and impressions were wrong."

"When you said all that, sir, you were lying to federal agents, isn't that right?"

"I was."

"And you are a lawyer, aren't you?"

"I was then."

"And you know that lying to federal agents, even when you're not under oath, is a crime, correct?"

"I wasn't thinking about that. I was thinking about how best to protect Senator Baldesteri. She had just started serious meetings to talk about running for President."

Hughes was a large man, a onetime college football player. He looked like a solid Midwesterner, the kind of man who might inspire confidence in places like Oklahoma City, Minneapolis, and the myriad other cities in which Raquel over her three-decade career had tried cases. But this trial was in Manhattan, and most of the carefully selected members of the jury, five black men, four black women, three Jews who were New York natives, two WASPs from the Upper East Side, a Chinese grocery store-owner, a Muslim college professor, and a beautiful Latina from the Bronx, were not likely to have the same warm, trusting reaction to this blond man that jurors in a city like Indianapolis might have.

Raquel, who had often wondered why the shrewd Louisiana-born and Wellesley-educated Angelina Baldesteri had ever brought a man like Hughes into her innermost circle, wanted to transform this bland Midwesterner into a snake oil salesman, a huckster, a modern-day Elmer Gantry.

"How much time did you spend, sir, wanting to protect the Senator after the FBI came calling on you?"

"I don't remember."

"Was it as long as a day?"

"I'm not sure. It made me uncomfortable to lie."

"Lying makes you uncomfortable, Mr. Hughes? Is that what you are telling us?"

"It is."

To Raquel's left and next to the jury box was an easel with large sheets of white paper, a relic of old elementary school classrooms.

"You told Mr. Decker on direct examination that you signed a cooperation agreement with the U.S. Attorney's Office three days after the FBI first visited you, isn't that right?"

Hunter Decker, now seated motionless at the prosecution table, was the lead Government attorney.

"That's right," Hughes said.

"And in that cooperation agreement you promised to tell the Government everything you now say you knew about the process of the funding for the Senator's campaign, correct?"

"Yes."

As Raquel saw, Hughes gave that confidential, *you-can-trust-me* glance at the jurors. Covertly glancing at the two rows of people in the jury box, she was pleased to see that, unlike at the outset of his testimony, some of the jurors deliberately did not return Hughes' *trust-me* glance.

"And when you signed that agreement with the prosecutors to cooperate against the Senator you also agreed to tell them about every single crime you ever committed?"

"I did."

"And you let them know about your crimes, didn't you, because you're a man of your word?"

Raquel spoke quietly but distinctly. Even the dozens of spectators in the fully occupied gallery, many of them reporters from the *Times*, the *Washington Post*, Fox, and CNN, heard the clarity of her distinctive, measured voice.

"I did," Gordon Hughes answered. "I did what I said I would do."

"And yesterday you told Mr. Decker, the judge, and the jury what your crimes were, correct?"

"Yes."

Raquel took a black Magic Marker from the narrow shelf on the easel that faced the jurors. She wrote rapidly at the top of the white sheet, *Gordon Hughes' Crimes*.

"And the first thing you said was that you haven't filed tax returns for three years?"

"I'm late."

"Unlike the people on the jury, you don't have to pay taxes on time, do you?"

For the first time since Raquel started her cross-examination, Hunter Decker stood. "Objection."

Judge Naomi Goldstein, seventy-five and appointed by Ronald Reagan, didn't hesitate to say, "Overruled." No elaboration, no discussion. She rarely spoke. She was a minimalist judge.

In big, block-size letters Raquel wrote, in her best parochial school handwriting, *Crime 1: Tax Cheat.* "You see those words, Mr. Hughes?"

"I do."

"And you are a tax cheat, correct?"

"I was."

"You pleaded guilty to that?"

"Yes."

"Incidentally, sir, have you paid any of the taxes that you owe?"

"No one has asked me to."

"You have to be asked? Do you have some sort of special status that requires somebody to ask you before you pay?"

"No. I just don't have the money."

"Let me ask you this: You testified yesterday, didn't you, that you were in the Fairmont Hotel in San Francisco a year ago with Dr. Joseph Chuang?"

"I did. That was one of the questions I was asked by Mr. Decker."

"And you told Mr. Decker that Dr. Chuang was a high-level executive of the Sino Oil Company in Shanghai, correct?"

"Dr. Chuang told me that. I said it to Mr. Decker."

"The biggest oil producer in China, isn't that right?"

"I had been told that. I can't be sure. But it's big."

"And Dr. Chuang came to the meeting with two Chinese associates, correct? Mr. Wan and Mr. Tin?"

"Yes. The Chinese are like nuns. They travel in groups."

Raquel had one of those fleeting moments of pleasure any trial offers up for a lawyer: Hughes had just insulted the Chinese juror. "And that group, as you told Mr. Decker, left Tumi suitcases with you that contained two million dollars in used one-hundred-dollar bills, correct, sir?"

"Yes."

"Did you use that money to pay your taxes?"

"Obviously not." Hughes paused, glancing at the jury. "In any event, it wasn't my money. The money belonged to Senator Baldesteri."

"Belonged to Senator Baldesteri, is that right, sir?"

"That's right."

"What does *belong* mean to you?"

"Belonged means belonged, Ms. Rematti."

"She owned it?"

"That's right."

"Was she in the room when Dr. Chuang and his friends were there?"

"No."

"Was anyone else in the room when the Tumi suitcases were given to you?"

"No."

"Did you ever hand the money to the Senator?"

"No."

"Yet she *owned* the money, the cash *belonged* to her, is that your testimony, sir?"

"It was for her campaign. Her use."

"And we know that because you tell us that, correct, sir?"

"I was her campaign manager. So I knew that."

"And you're a liar, aren't you?"

He answered that question just as the prosecutors had instructed him to answer it: "From time to time."

"And this is one of those times, correct?"

Hunter Decker, a handsome man in a blue suit, stood. "Objection."

Barely audible even though she wore a tiny microphone on the white collar of her black robe, Naomi Goldstein whispered, "Overruled."

Gordon Hughes leaned toward the jury. "No, not this time. Everything I've said is the truth."

Without hesitating, Raquel wrote on the big sheet of paper, *Crime 2: Bankruptcy Cheat.*

"You see those words, Mr. Hughes?"

"I do."

"You were in the casino business, Mr. Hughes, is that right?"

"Not for long, but yes, I was."

"And before the FBI made its visit to you, you were once a part owner of a casino in Atlantic City, am I right?"

"Yes, along with other people."

"And you filed a bankruptcy petition, isn't that right?"

"Yes. The casino was in trouble. Gambling in Atlantic City was unraveling. Ask Donald Trump. He tells everyone the same thing."

"And on that filing you made in bankruptcy court for your casino you lied about who its real owners were?"

"I did."

"And you admitted that to Mr. Decker and the FBI so that you could get the benefits of leniency under your plea agreement to testify against Senator Baldesteri, correct?"

"That was a crime I committed, Ms. Rematti. So, just as I was required to do, I came forward and volunteered the information that I had lied in the bankruptcy proceeding. Before that, no one knew that I had. I could just as easily have kept it to myself."

"My, that was considerate of you. But you didn't tell the whole truth even then, did you? And you're not telling the whole truth about the bankruptcy cheating even now, are you?"

Angelina Baldesteri during one of her first meetings with Raquel had described Gordon Hughes as "powerful, loud, hard-driving, and effective." But those words had not yet described the mild-mannered Midwestern man on the stand for the last two days. "He must be on lethal quantities of Valium," the Senator had said to Raquel after the first day of Hughes' testimony to explain his subdued demeanor.

"That's not true, Ms. Rematti. I disclosed the names of all the partners in the casino, and I pleaded guilty to lying to the Bankruptcy Court, and at some point after this trial—Senator Baldesteri's trial—I'll be sentenced for that crime, too."

"Isn't it true you are still leaving out the name *Oscar Caliente* as one of your partners in the casino?"

"No."

"No? You know who Mr. Caliente is, don't you?"

And, as Gordon Hughes took a longer pause than usual, Raquel detected, by the instincts formed after years as a trial lawyer who was now renowned as one of the four or five best criminal defense attorneys in the country and the only one who was a woman, the emergence of that hard edge the Senator had described. This time Gordon Hughes stared with a tough-guy, supercilious edge at Raquel without glancing at the jury. "You know him better than I do, Ms. Rematti. Just put your name on Google and the words *Oscar Caliente* appear in dozens of matches with your name."

Raquel knew how important it was never to let a witness take control. "Listen carefully, sir: You know who Mr. Caliente is, correct?"

"Google tells me he's the head of the Sinaloa drug cartel in the United States and that just two or three years ago you represented someone—I think he was called *The Blade of the Hamptons*—who worked for Oscar Caliente."

Years earlier, Raquel would have looked at the judge and said, "Your Honor, move to strike the answer as non-responsive." But by now she'd learned that too-formal sounding statements not only made her seem defensive and anxious to hide something from the jurors but were also futile: even if the judge agreed and instructed the jury to disregard the challenged answer, the bell couldn't be unrung.

Raquel asked, "Did you ever meet with Oscar Caliente?"

Remembering the instructions given to him by Decker and his assistants, Gordon Hughes now softened his expression, leaning confidently toward the jurors, and said, "I did."

"Who did you understand him to be?"

"One of my other partners, the late actor Philip Seymour Hoffman, told me he was a wealthy Argentinean who had become a naturalized U.S. citizen and who wanted to be a silent partner in the casino. So the name Polo Grounds, LLC was used on all the documents. I was told Mr. Caliente liked to play polo. He owned polo horses."

"But you knew that only Oscar Caliente was Polo Grounds, LLC, correct?"

"I never dealt with anyone else from Polo Grounds, LLC."

"And you knew Mr. Caliente was a leader of the Sinaloa cartel?"

"I do now. So do you. I didn't know that then. I had no idea at that time. I never would have spent a second with him if I knew that. But I didn't, and I still don't know that for sure."

"And you know the Sinaloa cartel is the largest, most violent drug cartel in the world, right?"

"I read that in the newspapers. And it's mentioned on some of the entries I saw under your name on a Google search. In fact, as I recall it, those were words you used."

"How often did you meet Mr. Caliente?"

"Only once."

"At the Peninsula Hotel in Manhattan?"

"Yes."

"For how long?"

"Ten minutes."

"What did he say to you and what did you say to him?"

"We talked about the fact that he had money he wanted to invest in the casino."

"Did you ask him where his money came from?"

"No." Hughes icily shifted his gaze from the jury to Raquel. "Where does your money come from?"

She ignored him. "And why," she asked, unfazed by Hughes' hostility, which she, in fact, welcomed, "didn't you put Mr. Caliente's name on the bankruptcy disclosure form?"

"The form asked who the casino's owners were. The shares had been issued to Polo Grounds, LLC. I checked with official New York State filings and saw it was a legally organized company, not just a fictitious name. So I thought at the time I was answering the question that the form asked."

Quietly, intently, distinctly, Raquel spoke, "You knew you were lying then and you know you're lying now, correct?"

"Forms can be ambiguous, Ms. Rematti."

"You graduated from Stanford Law School, right?"

"I did."

"And then you went to work as a young lawyer for Cravath, Swain & Moore, one of the oldest and fanciest law firms in the world?"

"I did. I was only there four years. I developed other interests."

"You were in the corporate department at Cravath?"

"Yes. I was young."

"But you knew that when forms like the bankruptcy filing used words such as who owns a company *beneficially*, *directly*, or *indirectly* they are looking for real information about who the real owners are?"

"If you say so."

"No, no, Mr. Hughes," Raquel said. "Just answer the question."

Almost meekly, he stared at Raquel. "You're right."

"So, you lied?"

"I concealed." Gordon Hughes glanced at the jurors. In that moment, he finally recognized he was rapidly losing whatever confidence and credibility and rapport he felt he might have developed with them in the last three days. The two older black women, one a cleaning lady and the other a high school English teacher, both prim, both from Harlem, both churchgoing Baptists, were no longer even glancing at him.

"Concealed?" Raquel Rematti repeated. "Doesn't that mean lied?"

"I had, or I had at the time I signed the bankruptcy court form, a wife and five children. I saw the casino opportunity as a way to take care of my family. I regret to say I had no interest in getting into the details of where any of my investors got their money. People are entitled to use corporate or entity names."

"Listen to me carefully, Mr. Hughes. You knew you lied on the bankruptcy form, didn't you, when you didn't disclose the name of Mr. Caliente?"

"You win, Ms. Rematti. I lied. Okay?"

Still without notes and still without pausing, Raquel said, "Let's draw a circle, Mr. Hughes, on the board. Do you see that circle?"

"It's a very good circle, Ms. Rematti."

"Let me write on this curve the words *Tumi Suitcases with $2 million from Dr. Chuang*. Do you see that?"

Hughes nodded.

Judge Goldstein said, "You have to answer with words, Mr. Hughes. The court reporter can't transcribe a nod."

"I see it," Hughes said.

"You testified that even though the $2 million *belonged* to Senator Baldesteri you didn't hand any of it to her, correct?"

"Not directly."

"Oh, so there is always a difference between directly and indirectly for you?"

Hughes was weakening. He shrugged.

"Words," Judge Goldstein said, "use words."

"You've been over that, Ms. Rematti," Hughes said.

With her black Magic Marker, Raquel wrote on the smooth crescent of the circle, *Oscar Caliente $500,000.* "You see that, Mr. Hughes?"

"Sure."

"How long after Dr. Chuang and the people you call his two nuns gave you the Tumi suitcases with the $2 million at the Fairmont Hotel in San Francisco did it take you to count out the $500,000 in hundred-dollar bills for Mr. Caliente?"

"Two, three hours—I was alone. I was told that Mr. Caliente was in a suite at the Stanford Court Hotel just a few blocks away from the Fairmont, that he knew Dr. Chuang had delivered the cash for Senator Baldesteri's campaign, and that he wanted at least part of his casino losses returned. And that he wanted it fast. It didn't matter to him where the cash came from."

"What did you do when you finished counting out the money?"

"I called a man named Hugo. He was the person I needed to speak to when I had a need to reach Mr. Caliente."

"Did you use your cell phone to call Hugo?"

"Good question, Ms. Rematti. I went to the lobby of the Fairmont and used an old-fashioned guest ground line to call Hugo."

"What happened next?"

"Fifteen minutes later I was in the lobby with a big Tumi suitcase. Hugo came into the lobby. He recognized me. I had never seen him before. He took the suitcase."

"And there was $500,000 in cash in the suitcase, correct?"

"Down to the dollar."

"Were you afraid of Mr. Caliente?"

"By that time, completely afraid of him."

"Are you still afraid of Mr. Caliente?"

"Absolutely." Gordon Hughes paused and cracked open the cap of a bottle of Evian water. It was at that moment the only sound in the classic, wood-paneled courtroom. "You should be, too, Ms. Rematti."

Judge Goldstein said, "That's enough, Mr. Hughes. You were once a lawyer. You know that comment is inappropriate."

Raquel Rematti asked, "And that leaves you with one-and-a-half million dollars in one-hundred-dollar bills, isn't that right?"

"That's right."

"And where did it go?"

"In every political campaign, Ms. Rematti, from a race for county railroad commissioner in rural Texas to President of the United States, there are thousands of little mouths to be fed. And those mouths need cash. They don't take checks or credit cards."

"And you testified when Mr. Decker asked you questions that you told the Senator that Dr. Chuang had given you $1.5 million in cash?"

"That's right. I saw her two nights later at a fund-raiser in Minneapolis."

"And you testified that she told you not to report the $1.5 million to the Federal Election Commission or the IRS, correct?"

"Correct."

"You testified she told you just to keep the cash in secure places and use it when you needed to? When the little mouths needed to be fed?"

"That's what she instructed me."

"And you told the jurors yesterday that she ordered you to give $75,000 of the cash to her?"

"Yes, she did. I did what she told me to do. She always took cash, for her own use, from campaign funds."

"And nobody else heard this conversation, is that right?"

"I'm certain of that."

"Are you certain of that because the conversation never happened?"

"No, Ms. Rematti." Gordon Hughes leaned forward again toward the jury. The two elderly black women continued to gaze into the dead space in front of them. The gorgeous, impatient Latina juror was staring at the black polish on her fingernails. "No one else heard it because the Senator and I were in the shower together when I told her. There was no one else in the shower."

Even Judge Naomi Goldstein, rigid, ossified, a woman who never once spontaneously called even a short bathroom break for herself, broke into the faintest expression of surprise when she heard Gordon Hughes' words. She actually glanced at him and, for an evanescent moment, at the suddenly alert jurors.

Raquel Rematti had long ago learned that, like great athletes, great trial lawyers needed luck at crucial times. She had one of those moments when she heard Judge Goldstein say, "I see that it's now almost four. As I told you, ladies and gentlemen, during jury selection, every day of trial will stop at four. I will, as I've told you, expect you all here at exactly nine tomorrow morning to resume. Ms. Rematti will pick up her cross-examination of the witness then. So we are suspended for the day and, as I've also instructed, none of the jurors is to discuss this case overnight, watch television, or listen to the radio, or look at any form of social media. No Facebook, no Twitter, not a single source of information until all of the evidence has been presented here in this courtroom and until you have finished your deliberations. Although I know it's difficult in this day and age to resist these temptations, you all promised during jury selection to do that."

When she spoke directly to the jurors, her voice was remarkably strong for a woman who looked ten years older than her actual seventy-five years. She was profoundly old-fashioned. She said, "I wish you all a good evening," as she waited for the men and women of the jury to walk like schoolchildren in a single orderly file out of the jury box to the rear door reserved for them.

As she stood and waited quietly at the defense table with the very attractive fifty-five-year-old Senator standing just to her left, Raquel thought, *Now what the fuck do I do with this?*

It was a challenge. She loved challenges.

CHAPTER 2

ANGELINA BALDESTERI WAS not only the widow of an assassinated President but also a sitting United States Senator with the
support of an incalculable but immense number of liberal suburban and urban women, blacks, Latino immigrants, labor union
leaders and union members, college students, and others who
wanted and expected her to run for President. And this was something the Senator, in her first meeting with Raquel Rematti, said
she was going to do. "Which is why you must win this trial," she
had told Raquel. "Not only win it. But get Harrington and his
puppets in the courtroom disbarred, destroyed, including, of
course, Hunter Decker."

When the indictment was announced at a press conference,
Hunter Decker, the United States Attorney for the Southern
District of New York, had stood behind Ralph Harrington, the
Attorney General of the United States. There were more than two
hundred Assistant United States Attorneys who worked for Hunter
Decker in Manhattan. Like all of the other ninety-three presiden-
tially appointed United States Attorneys in the country, Decker,
while he was a United States Attorney, never personally tried a case
or was even in the courtroom for a trial. He delegated all of that

work to the Assistant U.S. Attorneys. But he became the lead trial attorney for the prosecution in Senator Baldesteri's trial. Attorney General Harrington, who enjoyed being called "General Harrington" even though he had never spent a day in the military, had directed Decker to do that because George Spellman, the Republican President of the United States, insisted on it. "Somebody's got to stop that bitch," Spellman had said.

Hunter Decker, forty-eight, was unfazed, even flattered. Unlike many of the country's full-fledged United States Attorneys, most of them ambitious men and women with political connections but little or no trial experience, he had spent years as an actual trial lawyer in front of juries in complicated cases for the large law firms where he had worked. The Republican Party intensely wanted to prevent Angelina Baldesteri, the widow of a very popular and martyred Democratic President, from becoming President herself.

And, besides, Hunter Decker, who believed Senator Baldesteri was corrupt by her every instinct and, as he put it, "a walking crime wave," was pleased with the prospect of battle with the wily Raquel Rematti.

Raquel stared at the Senator at their first meeting when Angelina spoke matter-of-factly about her insistence on the disbarment and destruction of Hunter Decker. They were alone in Raquel's office on Park Avenue at 58th Street. It was a chilly late fall evening. "Senator," Raquel had answered, "you know the movie *Casablanca*, don't you?"

Baldesteri had many intricate qualities: the senses of humor and curiosity were two of them. She gave Raquel a faint smile and waited. Raquel had a sense of humor, too.

Raquel said, "There's the scene where Humphrey Bogart is at a table in his nightclub, Rick's Café, and listening to the Nazi Major

Strasser and the French Prefect Captain Reynaud as they're talking about the Nazis marching into Paris, London, and New York. Suddenly Bogart stands up and says, 'You'll excuse me, gentlemen, but your business is the politics of the world and mine is running a saloon.'" Raquel, her face shadowed by the dimming light in her office, had added, "Think of me as running a saloon. I have no interest in politics. You do. My business is to get you acquitted. Like Bogart just running a saloon. I'm not interested in destroying the President, Decker, or anyone else. Just running my own saloon."

The day after that first meeting, Leon Stanski, who was the head of a super PAC named *America Renewed*, had called Raquel and said, "The Senator has hired you."

"I'm glad to help," Raquel had answered. "But does she understand this is not just hard work for me but for her as well?"

"Never, Ms. Rematti, underestimate the Senator. She's the brightest person on the planet. And so the next question is how much money do you need as a retainer to get started?"

Without hesitating, Raquel said, "Five hundred thousand dollars. After that, one thousand and three hundred dollars an hour. I'll email you the wiring instructions for my bank account."

Stanski said, "No emails, Ms. Rematti. I never use emails. Just tell me now. I'll write the wiring instructions down on an old-fashioned piece of paper. And then swallow it."

Raquel recited the numbers of her account and her bank's routing number. Three hours later, using the app for her Citibank account, she saw that a wire transfer for five hundred thousand dollars had been received in her business account from Alexander Isaac Greenfield of Malibu, California. Raquel put that name into Google. There was no trace of any Alexander Isaac Greenfield in Malibu or any other place in California, or any other place in the world. This surprised her. But from her years of experience she knew that there was nothing illegal or even all that unusual about a client's payments coming from a source other than from the actual client, even if the source was anonymous. They even had the extraordinary, improbable name "third-party beneficiary" payments.

CHAPTER 3

IT WAS RAINING when Raquel Rematti and her client stepped out of the old federal courthouse at Foley Square onto the granite steps. As the former First Lady of the United States, Angelina Baldesteri had a permanent entourage of at least four Secret Service agents with her at all times. During trial days, the agents sat in the row of leather-cushioned chairs just behind the defense table. Even though no one was told who they were, it was obvious they were men and women protecting the Senator.

Two of the agents held aloft black umbrellas as the Senator and Raquel, both wearing high-heeled shoes, walked carefully down the stately courthouse's grand granite steps. As always, crowds of reporters swarmed as near them as they could reach. The agents, all in black suits, as was even the one taciturn woman who was part of this day's detail, and men in the uniforms of United States Marshals carrying M-16 rifles, kept the reporters and others at least ten feet away from the two women. Most of the reporters were shouting questions. There were bright television vans on the street, with flying-saucer-shaped discs on their roofs streaming rainwater in the downpour.

The three black SUVs that always carried and accompanied Angelina were parked on the sidewalk at the foot of the magisterial

courthouse steps where countless models down through the years
had been photographed for the covers of *Vogue, Cosmopolitan,* and
other glossy magazines. The side door of the vehicle in the center
slid open for the Senator and Raquel, as they, still protected by the
black umbrellas, stepped up into the middle seats. Their driver was
a woman in a uniform. The front door beside her opened and Alex
Swett, a fifty-year-old Secret Service Agent who had spent almost
three years with Angelina and was not only the leader of the crew
but the longest-serving of the ever-changing entourage that had accompanied her since her husband was shattered by a suicide bomber
in a crowd on the Avenue of the Americas, stepped into the front
passenger seat. He was soaking wet. Two other agents clambered
into the SUV and sat in the third row of seats behind Angelina and
Raquel. Except for the driver, every one of them carried visible pistols and rifles. Raquel was never sure whether this made her feel
more secure or more vulnerable.

The three SUVs sped rapidly onto Centre Street, which encircled
the old concentration of granite and marble courthouses and monumental, late-nineteenth-century municipal buildings, relics of the
Tammany Hall era. The vans' police lights flashed and illuminated
the wet roadway. Finally, Angelina exhaled, saying, "He's a lying
little bastard."

These were the first words she had spoken since Gordon Hughes
described the conversation in the shower.

Raquel said, "Angelina, you're forgetting Raquel's rule number
one. Remember? Never talk to me about anything other than lunch
when anyone else is around. We'll talk about this when we get inside
my office."

At the end of each trial day, Angelina and Raquel went to Raquel's
office to discuss what had happened that day in court and what
might happen the next day. They were always the only two people in

the room. Raquel at first had found a stubbornness in Angelina's unwillingness to understand a basic rule of the world in which Raquel earned her living: what a lawyer and client said to each other was always confidential, a secret, unless someone else who was not also a lawyer of the client was present. That was the essence of the attorney-client privilege, the *omerta* between lawyer and client; it was a private and insular relationship. The driver and the agents in the SUV were not Angelina's lawyers. They were her safe keepers. If they wanted to, or if they were somehow compelled to, they could freely repeat anything and everything Raquel and Angelina said to each other in the agents' presence.

Angelina, a highly accomplished woman who had a PhD in economics from Yale, always had difficulty in following Raquel's "Rule Number One." By instincts and by years in politics, Senator Baldesteri was a collaborator, although always the boss. Even when her husband was alive and during all of his political campaigns, she met and talked constantly with his and her aides, advisors, and consultants. When her husband was President, she was described by many as the sole member of a British-style Shadow Cabinet; others called her the "Princess of Darkness." She encouraged freewheeling discussions, the broaching of new or radical ideas and approaches. She always questioned and probed her and the President's aides as she and the President jointly worked their way to decisions. So the idea that she had to treat Raquel Rematti like a priest, the one person to whom she could not speak without losing the attorney-client privilege if anyone else was in earshot, was still alien to her. It still irritated her.

During the thirty-minute drive through rain-delayed traffic in downtown Manhattan to Raquel's Midtown office, Senator Baldesteri simply stared out the window, knowing that, while she could see people, umbrellas, storefronts, and New York's incredible array of stone buildings, no one from the outside could see her because of the deep tinting of the bulletproof windows. People stopped on the sidewalks in the rain as the black vans passed, with armed agents seated behind slightly open windows despite the rain as they scanned the walkers on the streets while the black entourage of vans passed. It was an impressive sight even for jaded Manhattanites.

* * *

Ever since she had started representing Angelina, there were always three parking spaces left open directly in front of Raquel's office building. They were cordoned off by yellow cones with orange police tape linking them. Immediately drenched in the downpour, one of the agents jumped out of the lead vehicle and moved the yellow cones to create an opening for all three SUVs to park as soon as the vans reached Raquel's office building.

As usual, there were several members of the Senator's staff waiting in the reception area of Raquel's office. They were all between twenty-five and thirty-five. They stood up when Raquel and Angelina walked through the glass door to Raquel's suite. And they all sat again when the two women walked into the inner office and that door closed.

"So," Raquel said as she sat behind her sleek glass desk, "what's the story?"

Angelina, now free to speak after being furiously pent up on the slow uptown drive, said, "Do you think I'd ever be in a shower with that guy?"

"I don't know. Stranger things have happened. These walls have heard some very odd and unusual things through the years. It's good they can't speak."

"He's lying. He made it up. Or that Decker bastard had him make it up. Any suggestions? I'm all ears."

"And I need," Raquel said, "to show that he made it up."

"Does it matter?"

"Of course it matters. I can see the editors in the *News* and *Post* right now coming up with the same front-page headline: *Dirty Money Shower Talk*."

Angelina was straightforward and blunt. "I didn't hire you to worry about the public relations aspects of all this. I hired you to be my lawyer."

Raquel leaned backward in her chair without speaking. Behind her, outside the large windows, the rain was now falling so intensely that, even though it was only five on a mid-May afternoon, it was dark outside. Dark, too, was her office: only a small lamp on a table next to her sofa was on.

"In fact," Angelina said, "it was *you* who reminded me that your business was running a saloon, like Bogart in *Casablanca*, not the politics of the world. I have people who know how to deal in public relations."

Raquel, early in her career, had made a conscious decision never to like or dislike her clients, although it was often impossible to ignore this instinctive human tendency to have favorable or unfavorable feelings about another person. During her popular seminars on trial practice at Columbia Law School, she always emphasized the importance of maintaining a distance from, but not an indifference to, clients. From time to time in her career, she'd broken her own rule, as she had during the long trial, several years earlier, of Juan Suarez, an illegal immigrant accused of killing the tenth richest man in the world, Brad Richardson, in East Hampton, at the far east end of Long Island. Juan was charming, charismatic, and utterly believable to her. Raquel had realized not long after she first met Juan, known as *The Blade of the Hamptons* in the world press, in his jail cell that she not only liked him, but as time passed, she had fallen in love with him without ever saying that freighted word *love* to anyone. The thought of him still sometimes preoccupied her although she had no idea where he now was. After the trial, Juan, whose real name as she came to learn might have been Anibal Vaz or something else, was deported when she miraculously won his release from the sentence of life imprisonment. Raquel was virtually certain that he'd returned to the United States, probably, in fact, to New York City. He had many reincarnations, many names, as she now knew. She found herself often looking for him in crowds, a sure sign of her lingering attachment, despite the simple fact that he was a consummate liar.

"I do have an idea," the Senator said. "Give me a second."

She opened the door to Raquel's office, that inner sanctum, the realm of secrets. Angelina said, "Laura, bring me the laptop."

A thirty-year-old woman rose from one of the cushioned seats in the waiting room. She carried a silver Apple laptop and handed it to Angelina, who closed the door. Angelina silently and intently spent three minutes scrolling through the picture section of the miraculous device. When she found the picture for which she'd been looking, she then slid the open laptop computer to Raquel.

"When was this taken?" Raquel asked after studying the vivid color picture.

"Three years ago. You see my face turned to the side. My name. The date. You see all that?"

"I do," Raquel said. "I also see the technician's name and the words Mount Sinai Hospital."

"You'd have no reason to know this," the Senator said. "But for two weeks three years ago I simply vanished from public sight. I wasn't walking the Appalachian Trail with Terry Sandford."

"Is this actually three years old?"

"Of course. Can't you see the date?"

At her Columbia seminars, Raquel had always stressed the importance of listening to clients, of letting them talk. After all, it was the client who was there when the events happened, the words were spoken, and the actions were taken. They later gave, or chose not to give, the lawyers the information. Lawyers could not, or at least they should not, make up stories for clients. *The art of listening*, Raquel told the students. *Lawyers talk too much*, she instructed them. *You don't learn by talking. You learn by listening.*

And now Raquel was not only listening. She was looking at the crucially important picture Angelina Baldesteri had just given her.

CHAPTER 4

Naomi Goldstein, at precisely nine in the morning, said, "Mr. Hughes, you know you're still under oath?"

"I do."

Raquel was already standing at the podium. Every one of the jurors had a computer screen in front of him or her. And there was a large computer screen to the side of the old-fashioned easel on which Raquel had started her black letter list of Gordon Hughes' lies and crimes. She was not a fan of computer screens. She thought of technology as a distraction in a courtroom, believing the best technique was for jurors to watch and listen, not to be distracted by the addictive wizardry of technological devices. But this was one of those times she knew she had to be flexible. At the outset of this day's cross-examination, all the computer screens were blank. But that would soon change.

"Listen to me, Mr. Hughes: When we ended yesterday, you described taking a shower with the Senator, do you remember that?"

Gordon Hughes had obviously slept well. He looked relaxed. Like most former high school and college athletes—for that matter, like most men—he had the confidence that anything he said about sex with a woman was accepted as true; it stuck, an assertion that could never be proven false.

"Yes, I do remember," he said, plainly satisfied with himself.

"Showers with another person are intimate events?"

"In my life they always have been."

"How many times did you shower with the Senator?"

"I can't be sure." Gordon Hughes, fresh and alert, had remembered to look at the jurors when he answered. Decker must have told him he needed to reestablish that rapport.

"Why did you shower with her?"

"Every time we had sex she wanted to shower."

"Did you soap and clean every part of her?"

"I did. Every part. Outside and inside."

"How often did this happen?"

"Often. Twenty times, maybe more."

"Did you wash her back during those showers?"

"Her back? Sure. I was usually behind her."

"And you've had showers with her recently, isn't that right? As recently as a month ago, is that correct?"

"Maybe more recently. Until she saw my name on the Government's witness list. Then it stopped."

"What is her back like?"

"Strong. Shapely. When she was a student at Wellesley College, she was on the female rowing team. You can still see the strength and shapeliness that created on her back."

Raquel paused. "How big are the scars on her back?"

Gordon Hughes took a sip of water from his Evian bottle. His grip tightened on the half-empty plastic bottle and the crackling noise of crushing plastic reverberated in the big ceremonial courtroom. His hand was too close to the microphone.

"Scars?" he repeated.

"You know what a scar is, don't you?"

"I do."

Raquel said to Naomi Goldstein, "May I have the technician put a single image on the screen?"

Naomi Goldstein said, "Certainly."

And then the image Raquel had first seen on Senator Baldesteri's laptop simultaneously filled the big screen and the laptops in front of each of the jurors.

"You see that computer image, don't you, sir?"

"I do."

"Who's depicted in it?"

"The Senator."

"You see her profile, correct?"

"I do."

"You see her name?"

"I do."

"You see the date?"

"I do."

"It's three years ago, isn't that right?"

"That's what it says on the photo."

"You see that running from her shoulder blades to her waist and following the sides of her spine are two prominent rows of healed-over scars, isn't that correct?"

"I see them," Hughes answered.

"They're healed but they're swollen, correct?"

"They look that way."

"They have that Frankenstein kind of look, correct, sir?"

"I don't know what that means."

"You see them clearly, don't you?"

"I do."

"When you soaped the Senator's back, you never saw those, isn't that right, Mr. Hughes?"

Gordon Hughes said nothing.

Finally, Naomi Goldstein spoke, "You have to answer the question, Mr. Hughes. You do understand the question, don't you?"

"Yes."

"You never saw those scars, did you, Mr. Hughes, during any of your twenty or more showers with the Senator, isn't that right?"

"That's right."

"And that's because you never showered with the Senator, correct, sir?"

Hughes, completely disarmed, didn't hesitate: "Never."

One of the lawyers at Hunter Decker's prosecution table audibly groaned.

Raquel asked, "And she never told you in the shower or anywhere else not to report the $1.5 million to the Federal Election Commission, isn't that correct, sir?"

"Yes. Never."

Raquel took the magic marker to the white sheet on the easel. She wrote, *Next crime of Gordon Hughes: Lied to the jurors—perjury at trial.*

Naomi Goldstein, almost in a whisper, said, "Do you have any more questions, Ms. Rematti?"

"No." Unlike most lawyers, Raquel knew the great skill of when to stop.

"Mr. Decker," Goldstein said, "do you have any questions on re-direct?"

"No."

"You can step down," Goldstein said to Gordon Hughes as if she were telling a smelly drunk to leave the room.

Clutching the now empty and crumpled bottle of Evian, Gordon Hughes left the elevated witness stand and passed by the entire length of the jury box. Not one of the jurors even glanced at him. Nor did Hunter Decker.

* * *

"Judge," Raquel said, "I'd ask at this point for a conference in your chambers."

"First come up here to the bench."

To keep the jurors from hearing the conversation, the court reporter, lugging her elaborate equipment, stepped up to Goldstein's elevated bench at the same time the lawyers did.

Naomi Goldstein's eyes had a filmy sheen over them, a symbol of her age. Raquel was so close to Goldstein that she smelled that outdated, slightly vanilla-scented perfume that her own grandmother used when Raquel was a child.

"Why?" Goldstein asked. "I have a jury here. Every minute of delay in this trial takes a minute out of their lives."

"We have just had a witness for the prosecution, its lead witness, who has just lied, and grossly so."

"I've been sitting on this bench for thirty years, Ms. Rematti. This is not the first time I've heard a witness lie." She stared at Raquel. "What is it that you want to discuss in my chambers? Why do we need to squander time? The jury has every reason to believe this witness is a liar."

"It goes beyond that," Raquel said. "Was it his idea to lie? Or did the prosecution instruct him to lie?"

Naomi Goldstein looked at Hunter Decker. "Do you want to say something?"

"What Ms. Rematti has just said, Your Honor, is without a doubt the most outrageous thing I have ever heard from a trial lawyer in twenty years of practicing law. She's accusing me and my associates of the crime of suborning perjury."

"Oh, I don't know about that, Mr. Decker," Goldstein said. "And describing something as outrageous is not a legal argument. It's an expression of hurt pride."

"If this witness has lied, and I emphasize *if*, I'll have the Attorney General undertake an investigation. At this point, I don't even know what Ms. Rematti wants."

Goldstein, with no change of expression, now looked at Raquel. "What is it exactly that you want? A mistrial?"

"No, this is the most publicized trial in the world today. A former First Lady, a sitting Senator, a potential candidate for President, is on trial on political charges on the orders of a Republican President, a Republican Attorney General, and a Republican United States Attorney."

"And your point?"

"I suggest you give a curative instruction to the jury now that if it finds a witness has lied in any one respect, it can find the witness has lied in all respects."

"No, Ms. Rematti, you know better than that. It's an instruction I give at the end of every trial, along with many other instructions, when all the evidence is in. I won't do that now. No matter how you may view what we are involved with here, it is no different from any other criminal trial."

"It is, Judge," Raquel said. "The world will think this is a court in a third-world country where the truth does not matter, particularly where the charges are politically motivated. This trial will take weeks. That instruction, when you give it at the end of the trial, will be buried in a host of other instructions."

As usual, Naomi Goldstein did not visibly react, but she angrily whispered, "Ms. Rematti, I've known you for years. Don't ever call my court a third-world country again, or one of my trials a show trial. I will hold you in contempt if you do. Your request is denied. Let's move on with the trial. You've made your record. You can raise this on appeal if there is a conviction. We have real work to do. Mr. Decker, send someone into the hallway and call your next witness. And be careful, Mr. Decker."

As Raquel and Hunter Decker left the bench, returning to their separate tables, he whispered to her, "You're a dead woman for this." He sounded serious.

Raquel smiled.

At the defense table, Baldesteri quietly said to Raquel, "What was that all about?"

"I was trying to get Decker disbarred," Raquel said, smiling. "Just like you wanted. It didn't work." The two women again shared their mutual sense of humor. "In fact, he just now said I was a walking dead woman."

"Bullshit, you're immortal," the Senator whispered.

CHAPTER 5

IT WAS NOT unusual in very major cases—and the case against Angelina Baldesteri was both major and in many ways unprecedented—to have two hundred names on the Government's list of potential witnesses. The list was almost always a "shock and awe" tactic, not a well-thought-out anticipation of people the Government actually intended to call. When Angelina first saw the list one week before the trial after Hunter Decker was required to turn it over to Raquel, the Senator had laughed sardonically, "What kind of sick joke is this? Some of the names here are people I went to high school with back in Louisiana. Their dads were oyster fishermen, just like my daddy. Some of these people were my classmates in high school. Did I do something wrong when I was elected class president?"

"These lists are always bullshit," Raquel had said. "They're meant to pull us off base. A distraction. They won't call a fraction of them. They have no obligation to do them all. I did the same to Decker."

Drily, Naomi Goldstein said, this time so that the jurors could hear, "Mr. Decker, your next witness, please."

One of the seven Assistant U.S. Attorneys who were seated at Decker's table walked briskly through the swinging doors that were part of the waist-high wall separating the packed gallery of observers and reporters from the courtroom well where the lawyers and the Senator sat with the rigid, silent Secret Service agents.

Slim and moving efficiently, the young woman reentered the courtroom with Leon Stanski, who, using a cane, walked slowly down the carpeted center aisle. This surprised Raquel, who was accustomed to surprises and spontaneity. But it shocked Angelina Baldesteri, even though she stayed motionless and, as Raquel sensed, disturbed, not as *stone-cold* as she usually was. Neither of them had actually expected Decker to call Leon Stanski as a witness. They thought that the appearance of his name on the witness list was a ruse.

Leon Stanski was well connected and sly. He was eighty-nine. As a young man, or at least investigative books and articles about the Jack Kennedy campaigns suggested, he had begun learning political craftsmanship by delivering cash to crucial local political leaders in states whose primaries Kennedy needed to win. He was known at one point as the "candy man." To friends when he was recounting his life story, he proudly proclaimed, "I was the first bagman, the original one. The Pharaohs created my line of work." Not once had he ever been indicted. By now, he had moved far beyond the cash-carrying era of his early education.

And he admired Angelina Baldesteri.

In a clear, commanding voice, Hunter Decker said, "The United States calls Leon Stanski."

Stanski was small and very well dressed. Just at the moment he climbed to the witness stand, Naomi Goldstein stood and, as she had with thousands of witnesses in her career, said, "Sir, do you swear or affirm to tell the truth, the whole truth, and nothing but the truth, so help you God?"

With his right hand held aloft, Stanski said, "I do," and sat down, so diminutive that he was almost hidden in the witness box.

"Mr. Stanski," Hunter Decker said, "have we met before?"

"Yes."

"How often?"

"Five times, I think. Something like that. You'd remember better than I can."

"When was the last time?"

"Yesterday or was it the day before?"

"So, it's fair to say you know who I am?"

"That's fair to say."

"How old are you, sir?"

"I was already an old man when you were born, Mr. Decker." Leon Stanski believed he was funny, in the Rodney Dangerfield–Jackie Mason style. "I'm eighty-nine."

"What was your occupation?"

"*Was?* I wish *was.*" He smiled. "I'm still a working man."

"In fact, you worked early on for the Kennedy patriarch Joseph P. Kennedy?"

"No. I worked for Jack Kennedy."

"All right," Hunter Decker said. "Now you work on fund-raising for the defendant, Ms. Baldesteri, correct?"

"Senator Baldesteri. I sure do."

"Are you paid for that?"

"Does the sun rise every morning in the east, or west, Mr. Decker?" He looked like he had wanted to say, *Do bears shit in the woods?*

"Are you paid for that?" Decker asked again.

"Sure, I'm paid. I'm bringing more than seventy years of experience to what I do. And to get to your next question, Mr. Decker, $20,000 each month. Seventy years of experience costs money."

"How are you paid?"

"Eleven thousand in checks, nine thousand in cash."

"Isn't it true that those payments are structured that way to avoid your obligation and the defendant's to file Currency Transaction Reports?"

"What in God's name," Stanski asked, "is a Currency Transaction Report?"

"You know, don't you, that for twenty years there's been a law that requires people who receive more than ten thousand in cash to file that information on a form with the IRS?"

"Don't know. I've reported every dime I've ever been paid, by cash or check or Pony Express, on my income taxes for one hundred fifty years. That's why I'm broke."

"You're not poor, Mr. Stanski, are you?"

When he was a boy, his parents, who lived in Jackson Heights in Queens, took him every summer to the Borscht Belt in the Catskills, that longtime but now almost defunct resort for working-class and middle-class Jewish families in New York City. It was in the summers in the Borscht Belt where he learned the faded art of one-line jokes from forgotten comedians. "No, broke is when you're dead. I'm still alive, I think. At least I was when I woke up this morning."

Hunter Decker, patrician and smooth, pretended to be impassive as he rearranged the yellow sheets of paper on the lawyer's podium in front of him.

"Six months ago, you arranged to pay by wire transfer $500,000 to Ms. Rematti as a down payment for her work for Ms. Baldesteri, right?"

Raquel, given all the trial experience she had, did something she rarely did. Standing, she said, "Objection."

Most experienced judges overruled objections. Naomi Goldstein was very experienced. But Raquel knew that most jurors in Manhattan, many of them retired men and women, would be overwhelmed and made jealous or disturbed by a number of that order of magnitude in legal fees. Besides, the amount of money a lawyer was paid was usually irrelevant, well beyond the boundaries of typical evidence.

"Overruled," Naomi Goldstein quietly said.

Raquel sat down.

With a sly smile on his deeply creased face, Leon Stanski answered, "That's the number. Five thousand C-notes."

"Is a C-note one hundred dollars?"

"Sometimes they're called Benjamins. That's the face on the hundred-dollar bill."

"How did Ms. Rematti get the money?"

"By a wire transfer, not a check. Wires," he added, "are real money, not like checks. Those are just pieces of paper. They can bounce."

"Who told Ms. Rematti she was going to get $500,000?"

"You're looking at him. I did."

"Did Ms. Baldesteri tell you to make that call?"

"No. Some guy at whatchama call it? A PAC man?"

"You mean a super PAC?"

"Maybe that's it. A few years ago, I think, some court said you could have a Superman PAC, or is it a super PAC?"

"Was that the Supreme Court decision in the *Citizens United* case?"

"Beats me. I never read Supreme Court cases. Not a hobby of mine."

"What," Hunter Decker asked, "is the name of the super PAC?"

"Not sure."

"Is it *America Renewed*?"

"Rings a bell."

"Aren't you listed as the Chair of *America Renewed*?"

Stanski asked, "Does the chair come with a table, too?"

Sounding annoyed, Judge Goldstein said, "Mr. Stanski, just answer the question."

"*America Renewed*? Sounds right. I'm the honorary chair of lots of organizations, I don't run any of them."

"Who told you to wire the $500,000 to Ms. Rematti?"

"Must have been the Senator, I think."

"Do you know?"

Leon Stanski glanced around the large, ornate courtroom with the confused expression of an octogenarian wondering whether he'd taken his medications that morning. And then, his voice suddenly sounding far clearer, he said, "No, it wasn't the Senator who told me to send the wire."

"Who was it?"

"I'm not good with names anymore. But it was a guy with a name like *Cantore, Conte, Valenti.*"

"Was the name *Caliente*?"

"Not sure. Could have been something else."

"Was the name *Robert Calvaro*?"

"Like that, like I said, something like that. I knew that whoever he was, he was close to the Senator. And that the Senator needed a great lawyer. And that this guy, whoever he was with the Italian or Spanish name or whatever it was, had the Senator's permission or approval or authority when it came to spending or sending money."

"What," Decker asked, "is the man's first name?"

"How would I know? Like I said, I'm not even sure what his last name is."

"Does the name Oscar ring a bell?"

"The only Oscar I ever heard of was Oscar and Felix. You know? The messy guy and the neat guy who were roommates in that movie by my old buddy Neil Simon." He looked at the jurors, actually winking at them. "Neil was a really funny guy even when he wasn't writing plays and movies. I told you that once upon a time I knew the first and last names of every alderman, selectman, county chairman, county commissioner, everybody in the country who could deliver votes. These days I have my name taped to the bathroom mirror so that when I wake up in the morning I can remember who I am."

Some of the jurors laughed.

Hunter Decker rarely laughed. His grandfather had been a United States Senator from Connecticut, his father a Secretary of State. He asked, "You remembered the name Oscar Caliente when you spoke to me yesterday, didn't you?"

Decker may have been the scion of a family of wealth and privilege but, as Raquel instinctively recognized, he had just made a potentially significant mistake. And, because of a slight change, a look of mild surprise in Naomi Goldstein's expression, Raquel believed the judge, too, recognized the same mistake. By asking that question, Decker ran the risk of making himself a witness. Old Leon Stanski was not Decker's client. Nothing they had ever said to each other was secret or privileged. And Decker had just put his own credibility on the line. He had opened the door to Raquel at some point calling him as a witness, if she decided to do that, to show he had unduly coaxed a witness, a form of subornation of perjury.

Looking puzzled, Leon Stanski answered, "Did you and me talk yesterday or the day before?" He hesitated again. "Or is it you and I? I don't think my third-grade teacher knew the difference, so I never learned it."

"Oscar Caliente, Mr. Stanski. Is that a name you ever heard?"

"You mean before today?"

"Before today."

"Like I said, maybe."

"Did you ever meet a man from South America who said he played polo?"

"I've met thousands of people. A lot of them said they did funny things, or things that were funny to me at least. Cricket players, guys who liked to swim the English Channel, people who were champions at chess. Funny stuff."

"Let me ask you this, Mr. Stanski. You do know, don't you, that it's illegal, that it's a crime, for a super PAC to take money from a foreign person or foreign company?"

"Somebody told me that. You gotta understand. I don't read laws. I just get the people who write them elected."

"And that it's a crime for a candidate or her campaign to take money, directly or indirectly, from a foreign source through a super PAC?"

"I've heard that, too. The lawyers told me. Lawyers love to say no."

Decker said, "Judge, can I ask Ms. Hooker to project Government Exhibit 673 on the computer screens?"

Janet Hooker was a technician responsible for displaying exhibits onto the computer screens.

"What," Naomi Goldstein asked, "is 673?"

"It's a photograph."

"Show a copy of it to Ms. Rematti first."

Decker handed the actual picture to Raquel, who glanced at it quickly and noticed only that Leon Stanski appeared in it. It would be futile to object. "No objection," she said.

Naomi Goldstein said, "Exhibit 673 can be displayed."

Every computer screen in the courtroom was instantly filled with a photograph at the center of which was Leon Stanski standing among other people at a crowded event.

Decker asked, "Do you see Government Exhibit 673?"

"Sure do."

"Are you in that picture?"

"Sure am. Boy, could you have come up with a worse picture of me? I look like Mel Brooks playing Moses."

"Are you talking to someone in that picture?"

"Sure looks that way. I talk too much."

"Who is he?"

"Got no idea."

"Did you ever meet a man who said he was a polo player?"

"There you go again." He smiled. "You're kidding, aren't you? No. I'm not even sure what polo is. Is it guys on horses with sticks whacking a ball?"

"Do you see Ms. Baldesteri in that picture?"

"Sure."

"Can you tell by looking at this picture whether you were at a fund-raiser?"

"Must have been. I don't breathe without trying to raise money. If I run into somebody on the street, I'm at a fund-raiser. I may even ask you for a contribution."

"Do you know when this picture was taken?"

"A year or so ago. I had that tie last year. I ruined it at an Italian restaurant. I liked it. The tie, I mean. The restaurant, too. And it bothered the hell out of me when I got pasta sauce all over the tie."

"Who is the man you're talking with?"

"Don't know."

"Is it Oscar Caliente?"

"Could be, might not be."

"Did he have an accent?"

"Don't remember."

"Did you know him by the name Robert Calvaro?"

"Come on, will you? He coulda been James Bond."

"Did he promise to give money to your super PAC?"

"I hope so. But I don't remember."

Raquel was puzzled. She wondered whether Hunter Decker was as smart or skillful as he thought he was. He had made a deliberate decision to put this sprightly, laughable old man on the stand as his second witness in the most widely reported trial of the steadily maturing twenty-first century. Distilled to its essence, all that Leon Stanski's testimony had shown so far was that Angelina Baldesteri was apparently influential enough to act behind the scenes to have a somewhat senile jokester appointed as the chair of a powerful super PAC.

But, as Raquel knew, Leon Stanski's cameo on the stand wasn't over yet. "Your Honor," Hunter Decker said, "I want to ask Mr. Stanski to look at an enhanced version of photo Exhibit 673 on the monitors."

"Any objection, Ms. Rematti?"

Only a week earlier, Raquel had been given a computer disk containing proposed Government exhibits. It displayed thousands of sheets of paper, most of them facsimiles of indecipherable bank checking accounts. There were also hundreds of photos and hours of secretly taped conversations. With a normal client facing as many as twenty years in jail, Raquel would have expected the client to be in her office day and night reviewing the newly produced material and talking through the likely course of the trial.

But not Angelina Baldesteri. She was not a normal client. She had a long-planned trip to Iowa where the first nominating caucus would be held a year later and, on the Saturday and Sunday immediately before the trial's start on Monday, Angelina had a series of lunches and dinners and "town hall" events in New Hampshire.

So, Raquel had found herself alone, sifting very late at night with no real assistance or sense of direction through thousands of pages of largely useless documents in the midst of which a jewel such as a crucial email, memo, or note could be embedded. She tried to listen to some but not all of the secretly recorded tapes that were filled with the everyday meaningless chatter in which anyone, including a United States Senator, engages. It was literally impossible to listen to every word of every tape or look at even a fraction of thousands-upon-thousands of pages of documents.

And the Government had turned over at least three hundred photographs, in many of which Angelina Baldesteri did not even appear. Raquel couldn't recall whether she had seen the photograph that was now Exhibit 673. She said, "No objection to the enhancement."

"Do you or do you not see a hand on the man's shoulder in the enhancement?"

"Looks that way, doesn't it?"

"Let me try the question again, Mr. Stanski. Do you see a hand on the shoulder of the man you were speaking with, Mr. Stanski? Yes or no?"

"I do."

"Whose hand is that?"

"Angelina's. Senator Baldesteri's hand."

"She is standing behind him, correct?"

"Sure, you can see that."

"Had you ever seen the defendant with this man before?"

"Maybe once or twice."

"Where?"

"I can't remember. New York? Washington? Places like that."

"Did you ever hear what they said to each other?"

"Sure, I heard them talking. But specifically what about, beats me. Must have been money, campaign contributions."

"Do you see in the enhancement that Ms. Baldesteri is also speaking to someone standing directly beside her?"

"It looks that way."

"Who is it?"

"It's a Hispanic guy with long black hair knotted into a ponytail. Very good-looking kid."

Uneasily, unexpectedly, as she stared at the frozen image of the man with the ponytail, Raquel was overtaken by a sense that she was looking at Juan Suarez. The face of the man standing next to Angelina was somewhat altered, as if it had undergone skillful plastic surgery. But it was the face, she was virtually certain, of the charming Juan Suarez, *The Blade of the Hamptons*, as he was called by every media outlet in the world during the trial at which he was accused of murdering Brad Richardson in East Hampton.

Decker said, "Listen to me, Mr. Stanski. Who is he?"

"You mean his name?"

"Let's start with that."

"How would I know?"

"Do you know his name?"

"No, not that I can remember."

"Had you ever seen him before this photograph was taken?"

"Probably."

"Did you have any understanding as to why the handsome man with the ponytail was there, talking to Ms. Baldesteri?"

"You've shown me this picture before, Mr. Decker. You showed it to me again yesterday or maybe the day before. If I thought about the ponytail guy at all, I thought he was a bodyguard for the guy I was talking to. But I'm not sure. The ponytail guy is a very strong kid. The kind of guy you see these days who works as a bodyguard. He could be a movie star for all I know. He's that good looking."

"But you are sure that the guy you were talking to was the guy who told you to let Ms. Rematti know Ms. Baldesteri wanted to hire her and to send the five-hundred-thousand-dollar wire?"

"I'm pretty sure of that."

Decker said in a quiet voice as he gathered up the notes on the podium, "No further questions, Your Honor."

The tactic was abrupt. It was skillful. Decker knew it was time to get Leon Stanski out of the witness box. He had proven himself to be unreliable. It was only midmorning, not the time for a bathroom break or even to ask for one.

Naomi Goldstein, without missing a beat, said, "Your witness, Ms. Rematti."

CHAPTER 6

RAQUEL HATED USING sports analogies or references, especially during trials. One expression she particularly disliked was "swinging for the fence." As she often told the eager young students in her trial practice seminars, lawyers who "swing for the fence" not only failed to hit a home run, they missed the ball. Usually, she said, it was the steady player who won. "Trials" were called trials for a reason. They were trials, not a game played for fun.

And yet, as her time for cross-examining Leon Stanski had already and unexpectedly arrived, she had only one thought in her mind: *Swing for the fence.*

"You and I have never met before, Mr. Stanski, is that right?"

"Yes."

"But we've talked before, haven't we?"

"Once."

"And that, as you've testified, was when you let me know that the Senator wanted to hire me?"

"Right."

Raquel, still without notes, was at the podium next to the jury box. "Let me ask you," she said after a pause, "to look at Senator Baldesteri."

He did.

"How long have you known her?"

"More than ten years. Eleven, twelve maybe." Suddenly he sounded sober, concentrated, mentally present.

"How did you meet her?"

"When her husband was still a Senator himself and still in the early stages of his presidential campaign."

"Why did you meet her?"

"President Young, who was then Senator Young, needed a veteran campaign manager for his presidential run."

"And you were under consideration, right?"

"I was."

"And Senator Young's wife interviewed you?"

"She did."

"What was her role at the time?"

"She had his complete confidence. They were partners in every sense of the word right up to the day he was assassinated."

"So is it fair to say that you have known Senator Baldesteri for at least ten years?"

"That's fair."

"And spoken to her frequently?"

"Yes."

"Including the time she was the First Lady?"

"Sure."

"And after President Young was assassinated?"

"Many times. Yes, we met and spoke to each other many times before and after that terrible murder."

"Let me ask you this. In all the time you have spoken to Senator Baldesteri, has she *ever* asked you to do something you thought was questionable?"

In a clear voice, Leon Stanski answered, "Never."

"Has she ever asked you to do anything you viewed as illegal?"

"Not once. Never."

"Has she ever asked you to do anything you did not want to do?"

"No. Not ever."

"Has she ever asked you to obtain money or support from foreign sources?"

"Never."

"And you do not know anything about the man shown with you in the picture?"

"Nothing more than I've already testified about."

"And you don't know anything about the man with whom the Senator appears to be talking in the picture?"

"Nothing at all."

And here, Raquel knew, was the ultimate swing for the fence. "As a seasoned professional, you believe in Senator Baldesteri's absolute integrity, correct?"

"I certainly do."

Raquel stared at Leon Stanski for the pulse of a moment. "No further questions."

CHAPTER 7

HAYES SMITH, AS the nightly news anchor on NBC, was world famous. His apartment on Central Park South overlooked all of the park's hundreds of acres, a spectacular view at all hours of the day and night, in all seasons of the year. He was in his midforties, several years younger than Raquel. He had a full head of brown hair beginning to turn gray at the temples. He was as handsome as a middle-aged Robert Redford.

For the last six months, Raquel had spent almost every night at Hayes' apartment. She entered the building through the service doors. All the staff knew who she was, and all of them kept the secret that she was virtually living with the NBC anchor. On the weekends they stayed either at her somewhat run-down house on the dunes in Montauk or at his freshly re shingled house near the jewel of a pond on Main Street in the Village of East Hampton. Because of stories in *People* magazine, the *New York Post,* and elsewhere, there was no secret that Hayes Smith and Raquel were full-time lovers, a celebrity couple; they both thought, however, that it was important her nightly presence in Hayes' apartment remain private information. It was simply a decision they had tacitly made even though they knew it was almost futile to maintain the charade. She kept her old-world apartment on Riverside Drive, where she had lived for two decades.

When the trial started, Hayes and his producers at NBC decided that in the nightly broadcasts he would say as little as possible about the trial. Each time a story about it came up, as it often did, Hayes would simply announce, "And here are more developments in the trial of former First Lady Angelina Baldesteri." And then for details, Danielle Quinn, an NBC reporter for five years and herself a lawyer, would appear on the courthouse steps to broadcast the day's events. No cameras were ever allowed in federal courtrooms. When the now defunct *Court TV* was in its heyday, all the broadcasts of trials were in state courts, not federal ones.

Hayes and Raquel were an intimate couple. They were unrestrained in what they told each other about their private histories and about their current feelings and experiences. To Raquel only, Hayes had described the night when, at midnight, the police arrived at the family home in rural South Dakota to arrest his father, a small-town lawyer who, without effort or plan, resembled Gregory Peck playing Atticus Finch. Hayes' mother had screamed, "What are you doing to him?" as the State Troopers put handcuffs on his father. One of the troopers bluntly answered, "Your husband sucks little boys' cocks, ma'am." On his first night in the local jail, Hayes' father hanged himself by tying bedsheets together and looping them over an exposed steam pipe in the ceiling. The small-town prosecutors and the state police altered their records forever to show that Hayes' father had a heart attack while he was in a police ambulance after a minor injury sustained in a single-car accident.

Hayes, who had never described the sickening scene of his father's arrest to anyone, told Raquel about it not long after they became lovers. It was at that moment that he fully realized he loved Raquel, for he had imparted to her, and her alone, his most painful, private secret.

Raquel for a time was more reserved. At first, she said little about the cancer that had afflicted her for thirteen months four years earlier. She kept hidden in her now seldom-used apartment the three pictures she took of herself with her iPhone when she was bald from the chemotherapy—she privately called them the "Dead Sea Selfies." There were still some traces of the radiation burns on the sides of her beautiful breasts. Hayes would never have noticed them until she pointed them out, as if to prove to him that she had once struggled with cancer, her own secret that he at first naively appeared not to want to believe.

But by now she felt no restraints. They had agreed when the Baldesteri trial started that she'd tell him everything about each day's events and that he would repeat none of it to anyone, not even to the ambitious Danielle Quinn or her producers and assistants. The trial dominated Raquel's life, just as it dominated the news, eclipsing Putin's invasion in Syria and the migration of hundreds of thousands of Muslims to Europe and the drowning of many of them in rickety boats in the Mediterranean and Aegean Seas.

Leon Stanski's testimony at the trial earlier that day had been harrowing for Raquel. It was the picture marked as Exhibit 673, not his testimony, that profoundly disoriented her. She was certain that the man in the forefront of the picture was the man known as Oscar Caliente in her other celebrated trial after her recovery from cancer. And in the same picture, she was certain she recognized the man she had known as Juan Suarez, her client, the Mexican immigrant accused of murdering Brad Richardson at Richardson's oceanfront estate in East Hampton. During that trial, in fact during the weeks she had prepared for it, she'd violated so many of the cardinal rules of her profession, including her belief that the handsome Juan Suarez, who exuded simplicity and straightforwardness, was innocent and that he was prosecuted solely because he was an "illegal"

Latin American immigrant, a victim of the hidden prejudices of the rich, famous, and odd men and women of the fabled Hamptons.

In fact, Raquel had passed even further into the territory of the forbidden: she had, she knew, fallen in love with Juan Suarez, even though their physical contact was limited to the quick embraces they exchanged each morning as she waited for him to be released from the holding cell in the courthouse before each day's trial session. Only the cynical guards detected that.

"I'm frightened, Hayes," Raquel said at his dining room table at the end of the day when she had "swung for the fence" with Leon Stanski and in fact had hit a home run.

Hayes was surprised. "Tell me about it. What's up?"

"During the Suarez trial a few years ago, the name Oscar Caliente was repeated over and over again. The prosecutors argued that Juan Suarez was really named Anibal Vaz and that Anibal Vaz was in fact a skilled drug-runner for Oscar Caliente."

Hayes said nothing. He simply tilted his head, waiting for more.

And Raquel said, "I only saw pictures and surreptitiously recorded films of Oscar Caliente. The prosecutors, whom I couldn't stand because they were racists, I thought, out to punish an 'illegal' in the Hamptons, claimed that Caliente was the leader of the Sinaloa cartel in New York City who was trying to expand his 'market'—that is what the prosecutors called it—to East Hampton and Southampton. He had already succeeded in completely dominating the drug trade in Manhattan. Caliente, they said, had ordered the murders of dozens of competitors. And Juan Suarez, or Anibal Vaz, or whatever his real name was, had the job of being Caliente's loyal soldier. And Suarez, the prosecutors said, murdered Brad Richardson because Richardson, a secret addict, had somehow upset Caliente. And Caliente wanted Richardson dead for the sport and pastime value of it. And because Caliente is, to put it simply, crazy."

"Don't you remember," Hayes said, "that I first met you during that trial? Suarez was convicted. I interviewed you. And after the conviction, didn't some kids then find in the old Sag Harbor dump the actual machete with Richardson's blood on it? They found the clothes the murderer was wearing, and there was nothing on the machete or the clothes to connect Suarez to the killing. So, *The Blade of the Hamptons* was someone else, and your client's conviction was tossed out. He was deported and he's free. Another victory for Raquel Rematti."

"I wish," she said. "No, Hayes, Juan Suarez was the killer. Just before he was thrown out of the country and *after* his conviction was set aside, I met him in the big federal prison on the Brooklyn waterfront while he was waiting to be deported. I told him he could never be tried again, because of the rule against double jeopardy, for the killing of Richardson. He was more sophisticated than I thought: he already knew the total immunity double jeopardy gave him.

"And then he told me the truth. He, in fact, was the killer. Caliente gave him the assignment. He had Caliente's cooperation in an elaborate cover-up that involved cleaning the machete and the clothes so that Richardson's and another man's blood and DNA would then be smeared on the murder weapon and the clothes. And then Suarez and others drowned the other man, the stalking horse. At night, five miles out from Montauk in the Atlantic. The body was never recovered."

"Is there more?" Hayes asked.

"On the day before he was deported, Suarez also told me that Caliente was very angry with me for bringing his name up at trial, as I did when I was cross-examining some of the prosecution's witnesses. Suarez had repeatedly told me not to do that. He was adamant about that. Suarez was a man in an altered state after I brought out Caliente's name. He was no longer the gentle, appealing soul I'd come to know. I ignored him. After all, I'm the lawyer, I know what has value. My bringing up Caliente put the focus elsewhere, other than on my client. If I did what Suarez wanted, it would be like a patient telling a doctor what instruments to use during surgery."

"Why are you telling me this?"

"During that trial someone tried to kill me. You remember I had an assistant, a young woman named Theresa Bui who had been a student of mine at the Columbia seminars I give?"

"Sure, Raquel, I remember. I know you're still disturbed by it. You're a good Catholic girl, after all: you think you're responsible for her death."

"The rifle shot came at night into the big bedroom at the Montauk house where I always slept, except that night. Theresa was sleeping in that room that night. Whoever did the shooting that killed Theresa was sent by Caliente to kill me."

"How do you know that? There are thousands of crazies with guns and rifles, even in Montauk, who shoot just for the fun of it. At all hours of the day and night. Everywhere. Everywhere. The joys of the Second Amendment."

"Suarez told me, in that last conversation I had with him in the federal prison, that Caliente ordered the shooting."

"What happened to Caliente?"

"The police, the DEA, the FBI—they all tried to find him. He vanished."

Hayes said, "That's good. So why are you afraid? Not every bad thought we have is an existential threat."

"Well, Suarez' last words to me were *be careful.*"

"Has something happened?"

"I saw Caliente again today." She paused. "And I saw Suarez again today."

"You did? Where?"

"They were both in a picture the Government has that was a trial exhibit today."

"In the Baldesteri trial?"

"Yes."

"What kind of picture?"

"It turns out that Angelina knows them. In the picture, Angelina was talking to Suarez. But her hand was on Caliente's shoulder."

"What was she doing with them? Did you ask her?"

"I did. She said she never heard of Oscar Caliente. The man in the picture, she said, is Robert Calvaro, a naturalized U.S. citizen who made a fortune with oil exploration in South America, and now with fracking in this country. And that Suarez, or Vaz, or whoever, was the president of one of Calvaro's companies. Angelina said he is Hugo Salazar. She said Calvaro was a huge contributor to the super PAC that provides sixty percent of the money used for her campaign. He is, she said, a Yale graduate. And Salazar, she said, is from a big, reputable Bolivian family."

"Why isn't she right?"

"I'd recognize Suarez in a dark closet, Hayes. I spent hundreds of hours with him. Caliente's hair color is different, and he has had some plastic surgery, but I saw more than enough secretly taken pictures and film of him that there's not a doubt in my mind that it's Caliente. The same is true, I'm convinced, of Hugo Salazar. Different color hair than when he was Juan Suarez. Even some plastic surgery. But I know."

"What else did you say to Baldesteri?"

"Nothing. Remember, I'm defending her at her criminal trial. I can't ask her whether she knows that Calvaro as Oscar Caliente is a key part of the Sinaloa cartel, and that Salazar is a killer. I can't go down that rabbit hole. I suspect she still sees both of them and that

Calvaro still feeds funds to the PAC that supports her campaign. And it was Calvaro who had that old fox Stanski tell me that Angelina wanted me to represent her. Calvaro, I'm sure, arranged to pay my fee. I could ask her whether she knows who these men really are. But there are some things, many things, in fact, that a lawyer shouldn't know."

"Come on, baby. There's no way she could know."

"Really, Hayes? You don't know the sainted Angelina Baldesteri as well as I do. Nobody does."

Hayes walked to the floor-to-ceiling windows overlooking Central Park. It was night. Lights like laces of pearls shined along the twisting walkways of the park. Hundreds of runners and speedy bicycle riders filled the closed-to-traffic roads even in the dark. Many of the cyclists had tiny headlights that raced through the darkness. Farther north was the immense, irregular oval of the reservoir, its shore defined by dozens of stately lanterns. Near the southern end of the reservoir, a powerful fountain pushed tall towers of water at least sixty feet above the surface. Lights illuminated the rising water, silver columns in the dark.

"I'll make arrangements for private security details to protect you day and night. Whenever Angelina leaves you, the Secret Service goes with her. You become just an ordinary civilian."

"No, Hayes," she said, moving to stand behind him and wrapping her arms around his chest. "It's sweet of you, but I don't want that."

"Why? I love you. I don't want a group of punks out there thinking they can hurt you. Christ, Raquel, they've already tried. Isn't that why Theresa is dead?"

"I can deal with it—fear. I dealt with it for the first time with the cancer I had. The cancer was, I think, a deadlier killer."

"I'm just talking about two big guys with hidden weapons shadowing your movements around town when the Secret Service has left with Baldesteri. They'll be unobtrusive. They'll become part of the atmosphere around you."

"No. My real concern is a host of ethical problems. Do I have to tell the feds that two men they've been searching for, Caliente and Salazar, are within easy reach when I only know that because I'm the trial lawyer for Baldesteri? Or do the feds already know that? Are they playing some game to catch Baldesteri? To catch me? I've been a pain in the ass to them for years. My only job is to represent her, not to be a handmaiden for the FBI or to be concerned about myself. And what happens to Baldesteri, my client, if the feds learn that she's partying with Sinaloa people, even if, to give her the benefit of the doubt, she does not know who they are? It would blow my defense of her out of the water."

Hayes gently unclasped Raquel's hands. He turned and embraced her. Instinctively they walked to his bedroom. They undressed. They lay in his familiar bed. They pressed as close together as possible to calm her. And they slept.

CHAPTER 8

ALTHOUGH SHE HAD served as a New York Senator for seven years, Angelina Baldesteri had never, in fact, lived in any city, town, or village in the State of New York. One year after Jimmy Young, her husband, had been assassinated on a sidewalk on the Avenue of the Americas after an interview on Fox News, a media nemesis of his, she had bought a large, somewhat run-down Tudor house in middle-class Larchmont in southern Westchester County. She had actually slept there four or five nights each year. But she'd quickly moved to establish the Larchmont house as her "permanent residence," registered to vote as a New Yorker, and designated the Larchmont house as her address on all her tax returns. As a Larchmont resident, she, the former First Lady and stoic widow of a widely popular President, was twice overwhelmingly elected to the Senate. Like most Senators, she kept an apartment in Washington; it was a handsome place, not just a convenient hotel-style room, and it was there that she actually lived.

To deflect the media's attention, she had allowed Ellen Samuells—a woman who bore an uncanny resemblance to her—to live in the Larchmont house. There was so much security around the house of a former First Lady that even some of the agents didn't fully grasp the ruse that Angelina Baldesteri was using a

Hollywood-style body double. Those who knew said nothing. It seemed natural to them that the widow of a President killed by an ISIS suicide bomber would need multiple layers of protection, charades, and ruses, including the use of a phantom image. Ellen Samuells was well paid for her playacting by *America Renewed*; it was her only job, and she lived well.

Each night during the trial, it was Ellen Samuells, not Angelina Baldesteri, who slipped into the SUVs that drove on a variety of routes from Raquel Rematti's office to the Larchmont house. Raquel knew that Senator Baldesteri, when she left the office, used the service elevator in the office building to make her way, heavily but discreetly guarded, to a suite in the Waldorf Astoria. Raquel had once met Ellen Samuells. Even Raquel, an acutely observant woman, was struck by the virtual physical identity between Senator Baldesteri and her look-alike. It was not Raquel's business as to what security measures her client and her client's Secret Service managers did or did not use. She was the Senator's lawyer, not her bodyguard or friend. And it was not her job to disclose Government secrets. She never mentioned any of this even to Hayes.

The Waldorf Astoria, although in steady decline like a gracefully aging dowager, was still the hotel-of-choice of Presidents and their families as it had been since at least Franklin Roosevelt's era. It had a variety of presidential suites, designed so that anyone with evil intentions could never be completely certain where the President actually was while staying there. Like a medieval castle, the building also had a bewildering multiplicity of internal hidden hallways, stairwells, and surprisingly located service elevators. And it still had the advantage, facing the business district of Park Avenue, of being one of the very few hotels in the heart of Manhattan.

By the time President Jimmy Young—his real and Mayflower-derived name was Josiah Pierce Young IV—was killed, Angelina

Baldesteri detested him. He was so obsessed by politics, and with the mean-spirited necessity of concealing that he was gay, that in the ten years of their marriage, they had barely spent any time with each other, except at innumerable public events.

So, at the Waldorf Astoria, on all their fund-raising trips to the city and his appearances at the United Nations and elsewhere, Jimmy Young and Angelina Baldesteri had never stayed in the same suite at the Waldorf. The well-trained staff referred to the "His" and "Her" suites, not just to "His" and "Her" towels. On the night before he was spectacularly blown to shreds by the suicide bomber, Jimmy Young had stayed at the Waldorf while Angelina was in Seattle to give a speech to five thousand delegates at a NOW convention.

She and Jimmy had not made love, embraced, held hands, or kissed even demurely in years, except for public embraces and chaste media kisses. In truth, Angelina, although horrified by the way President Young had died, immediately thought his martyrdom would advance her own well-formed ambitions.

In the years of her husband's presidency, she had at least twelve lovers, from A-list movie stars to one of the White House gardeners. Even in the age of the Internet, the mainstream media assigned to the White House, like the far more private, all-male club of journalists in the JFK years, had simply turned a blind eye. Jimmy Young, too, had carefully guarded his secrets. His attraction to men was hinted at, never exposed. No one had ever outed him. He certainly never outed himself.

When the Senator, wearing a New York Mets baseball cap, arrived at the Waldorf on that rain-soaked night after leaving Raquel's office, and as Ellen Samuells was driven to Larchmont along the twisting and bucolic Bronx River Parkway in Westchester County, Angelina was surrounded by an almost phantom Secret Service phalanx. With women agents, she entered one of the Waldorf's 1950s-style ground-floor public bathrooms. Through a narrow door that opened to what looked like a janitor's room, she entered a smelly stairwell that, twelve stories higher, opened onto the floor where one of the several presidential suites was located.

She entered it alone. Standing near one of the ornate but now unusable fireplaces was Robert Calvaro.

"Robert," she said, "how long have you been waiting?"

"Not long," he answered. "It's never a long time, Angie, when I'm waiting for you. I just think about what I know is coming."

Without another word, she unfastened every button and zipper of the blue sweater and dress she'd been wearing all day and kicked off the high heels that had caused her pinching pain for hours, particularly on her fast, strong strides up the twelve flights of stairs to this suite.

Within five minutes she and Robert Calvaro were in the oversize bed that she and President Young had never shared. She loved what they did to each other. Pure bliss.

CHAPTER 9

"Agent Grover," Raquel Rematti asked, "how long have you been with the FBI?" It was her first question on cross-examination.

"Eight years," he answered. Grover looked and sounded like a routine Irish beat cop. But that was a craftily prepared façade. Raquel knew that she had to work methodically and carefully with him. He was skilled at the art of testifying.

"And before that you were a detective with the New York City Police Department?"

"Right."

"Assigned to the narcotics unit?"

"Actually, for the last three years, to a gang investigation unit. Not necessarily narcotics. Any gang activity."

"The Crips and the Bloods?"

"Those were two of them."

"The Young Lords?"

"Another of them."

"MS-13?"

"That, too."

"It was dangerous work, right?"

"Some people thought so."

"Did you?"

"Not really. I was more concerned about smaller, newer gangs. Russian and Ukrainian primarily. They were the most violent. Nothing much scares me."

"Did you make any arrests when you were with the NYPD?"

"Quite a few."

"While you were with the NYPD, did you ever testify at trials?"

"Many times."

"And were there convictions in those trials?"

"Almost all the time, Ms. Rematti."

"How many trials at which you testified ended in convictions?"

"I didn't count."

"And were some of those convictions reversed on appeal?"

"Some."

"How many?"

"Don't know. Not many."

"Were any of those convictions reversed on appeal because of something you falsely testified to?"

"I don't know. I did read a few times that some appeals judges, who never saw me and who certainly were never cops and who had no idea what the streets are really like, were upset by what I might have said at a trial. I don't pay attention to that. I just do my job."

"Did any of those judges write that you falsified evidence?"

"Did they? I don't know. It's easy for a judge in a robe who has never been on the ground to get fantasy ideas."

"You testified you left the NYPD to join the FBI?"

"I did."

"Why did you do it?"

"Why not? It's a better job. You get better resources with the feds. Better pay. More prestige. And nicer offices. Better pension. Stuff like that."

"And you were assigned to a narcotics unit?"

"Right. I've had many assignments along my career path. But a gang is a gang. I know about gangs."

"When did you first hear about the Sinaloa cartel?"

"Not sure. Five years ago, four years ago."

"How did that come about?"

"Not sure. I was on a team that was given responsibility for assessing the location, evolution, direction of various foreign-based cartels. Sinaloa was one of them."

"Where did Sinaloa rank?"

"Rank? Do you mean in terms of its power and reach? Or do you mean like the difference between a lieutenant colonel and a colonel?"

"Was Sinaloa a powerful narcotics group?"

"At first—say, five years ago—not a big factor. There was a lot of competition in the New York area."

"Did that change?"

"It sure did."

"In what way?"

"In just three or four years, Sinaloa, which was for a long time solely a Mexican operation, essentially wiped out its competition in the city. It was almost breathtaking."

"How did that happen?"

Hunter Decker stood. "Objection. That question could lead to dangerous and confidential information."

Raquel withdrew the question.

Naomi Goldstein gave an almost benign, admiring smile. She didn't say a word.

Raquel asked, "You know the name Oscar Caliente, don't you?"

"Certainly do. He's been the head of the Sinaloa cartel in this area for four or five years."

"And you told the jury that this morning when Mr. Decker was questioning you?"

"That's right."

"You called Mr. Caliente a terrorist, right?"

"I shouldn't have used that word. But that's how I see him. He's a man who likes to have the people who work for him kill people he doesn't like. And he often has people who work for him kill other people who work for him if he thinks his orders have not been carried out. He never does it himself. Word is that he throws up when he sees his own blood from a paper cut."

"How do you know that?"

"As we grew more interested in Sinaloa, we took thousands of pictures and film footage of him and the people who kept company with him and who did what he told them to do, including murder. Many murders, in fact."

"Did you ever see him?" Since Grover, quick-tongued and always eager to speak, hesitated, Raquel asked a subtly different question: "Isn't it true you never saw him face-to-face?"

"That's true."

"You don't know whether he has blue eyes, correct?"

"No. I don't have much interest in the color of men's eyes."

Naomi Goldstein stirred slightly, as if preparing herself to reprimand Grover. But Raquel Rematti was accelerating and wanted no distractions.

"You don't know how tall he is, do you?"

"No. In most of the tapes and pictures, the men around him are taller. Even some of the women are."

"You don't know if he wears glasses, do you?"

"In some pictures he does. In others, he doesn't. He probably doesn't need glasses. They're artifices of disguise."

"The man you say is Caliente changes his appearance a lot, isn't that right?"

"Ms. Rematti, that's what I just said, I don't know for sure. I think he does. Lots of gang leaders change the kinds of clothes they wear, the color of their hair. And plastic surgery. They buy six-thousand-dollar wigs."

"Does he have scars on his face?"

"Look, Ms. Rematti, what I know is this. Caliente is the boss of a cartel with an army of killers. Those killers take orders from him and only from him. By now, because of those killers, the only drugs that are sold on a large scale in Manhattan are from the Sinaloa cartel. There is no competition. Caliente has seen to that."

"Mr. Decker showed you several pictures this morning, correct, sir?"

"Sure, he did."

"And in one of those pictures you saw Senator Baldesteri, correct?"

"She was there."

"And standing in front of her, you testified, didn't you, was Oscar Caliente?"

"Yes."

"But you never saw Oscar Caliente, did you, sir?"

"I saw Oscar Caliente hundreds of times."

"But on videotapes, correct, sir?"

"And in still photos, too."

"But never face-to-face, correct?"

"Like I said, never. What's the problem?"

"Why didn't you ever arrest him?"

"We concentrated on trying to flip one or more of his people— one of his inside guys."

"*Flip* means an informant?"

"Sure. Like Sammy the Bull Gravano testifying against John Gotti, just to give you the biggest example. There was never a way to convict Gotti without Gravano."

"Did you know a man named Juan Suarez?"

"We did. We weren't certain of his name. But we knew there was a guy who was a major carrier for Caliente. And that he called himself, and other guys called him, Suarez."

"When was the last time you saw Suarez?"

"Last time? This morning. He was in that picture. He was talking to your client."

"Do you know that man's actual name?"

"Not really. When we videotaped Caliente several years ago and the other guy was there, we just called him Juan Suarez. Suarez spent lots of time in downtown after-hours clubs. In the old Meatpacking District. And in what we used to call Alphabet City—Avenues A, B, and C on the Lower East Side—but now I guess it's called the East Village by the computer industry kids who live there and the real estate people who are tearing down the old slums and putting up nice new buildings."

"Have you ever heard of a man called Hugo Salazar?"

"Not until a few months ago."

"How did you hear it first?"

"When Mr. Decker began preparing for this trial."

"And you heard Mr. Decker call him that when he put Government Exhibit 673 on the computer screen?"

"To me the guy is still, in my mind at least, Juan Suarez. He's the guy. He could call himself William Shakespeare if he wants to."

Raquel looked at Naomi Goldstein who was, as always, alert in her own way. "Your Honor," Raquel said, "could I ask the videographer to post Baldesteri Exhibit 35 on the computer screens?"

"Any objection to that, Mr. Decker?" Goldstein asked.

"Let me first see what it is," Decker said as Raquel handed him a glossy brochure. Decker flipped through it. "No objection."

The exhibit instantly materialized on all the computer screens. Suddenly, the staid courtroom, in which the lights were now slightly dimmed, resembled a large video parlor because of the flicker of images on multiple computers.

"Do you recognize this exhibit, Agent Grover?"

"I recognize it, Ms. Rematti, only in the sense that it was shown to me by Mr. Decker and his team for probably a mini-second a week or two ago."

"Do you know what it is?"

"Only by glancing at the cover. It's like one of those shiny annual reports or view books that companies and colleges put out."

"This exhibit relates to *America Renewed*, doesn't it?"

"That's what it says on the cover."

"When you saw this brochure with Mr. Decker and his team, did you open it?"

"I doubt it, Ms. Rematti."

Calmly Raquel said, "Judge, I'd ask the videographer to turn the brochure to its page three."

Naomi Goldstein gave the slightest wave of her index finger, as if mimicking the turning of a page.

Under the heading "A Word from Our CEO" was an airbrushed photo of a handsome and dapper man. "Agent Grover," Raquel Rematti said, "is that man Oscar Caliente?"

"Does it say he is?"

"Can you read the name printed below the picture?"

"Sure. It reads *Robert Calvaro*."

"You are an experienced detective, aren't you, Agent Grover?"

"I've been in the business for a long time."

"In your trained eyes, does the man depicted as Robert Calvaro look like Oscar Caliente?"

"Lots of people look like Oscar Caliente."

"Really? There are about one hundred people in this courtroom, Agent Grover. Do any of them look like Oscar Caliente?"

Grover was a man with a supercharged internal anger beneath the surface of an impatient Irish beat cop. He didn't even make a pretense of looking around the room. "No," he said. "Not a single one of them."

"Have you ever investigated *America Renewed*?"

Hunter Decker stood. "Objection."

"Sustained."

"Have you ever investigated Robert Calvaro?"

"You mean the guy whose picture in the brochure is next to the words *Robert Calvaro, Our CEO*?"

"That's right," Raquel said. "That man."

Decker, who knew how tenacious Raquel Rematti was, hadn't sat down. "Objection," he repeated.

"Sustained." Naomi Goldstein, ordinarily terse, stared for a few seconds at Raquel. "Ms. Rematti, you know an agent can't testify about ongoing, current investigations, if there are any. Or even if there aren't any."

"Have you investigated Hugo Salazar?"

"Objection."

"Sustained."

"Have you investigated a man named Juan Suarez?"

"Objection."

Naomi Goldstein said, "Ms. Rematti, are you asking about current, active investigations?"

In her long career, Raquel had lost all fear of the consequences of challenging a judge. She simply ignored Goldstein's question. "Have you ever investigated Juan Suarez?"

"Objection."

The judge, too, was tenacious. "Sustained."

"Have you ever attempted, or do you know of any attempt, to subpoena Robert Calvaro to appear at this trial?"

"Objection."

Even Raquel was surprised when Judge Goldstein said, "Overruled. He can answer *that* question."

Impatient, Grover folded his arms. He said, "To tell you the truth, Councilor, we've tried to subpoena him."

"Have you subpoenaed him?" Raquel asked Grover. She never allowed herself to be distracted.

"We can't find him."

"There are more than four hundred FBI agents in this district alone, aren't there, Agent Grover?"

"I don't know. There may be. I wouldn't tell you that even if I knew."

"And not one of them has been able to find Robert Calvaro, is that your testimony?"

"It is. You have to hand a witness a subpoena, Ms. Rematti, you can't email it to him. You still have to do it the old-fashioned way."

"Is he hiding?"

"How would I know? He could be on vacation in New Zealand. Anywhere in the world. He gets around. The leaders of drug rings travel. They have more houses and apartments than Donald Trump."

"There's an address in the brochure for *America Renewed*, isn't that right?"

"There is."

"What is the address?"

"275 Park Avenue South."

"Have you gone there to find Robert Calvaro?"

"I have. Personally, which I don't often do at this point in my career. Nothing called *America Renewed* has ever been at that address." Grover took a sip of water. "Ask your client where the man is. Until three weeks ago, we saw your client with the man in the picture many times. They seemed to be able to find each other whenever they wanted to. Like lovers."

Naomi Goldstein leaned ever so slightly forward to speak into the slender microphone in front of her. "Agent Grover," she said, "your role here is to answer questions. Not to volunteer information, not to make comments. I'm instructing the jury to disregard your last comments. Please control yourself."

Raquel had long ago learned not to open doors in her questioning of a witness. At her law school seminars, she often warned her students: *Be careful not to open doors. They can lead to dangerous, unknown places.* She had already done the job she set out to do. She had sown doubt as to who the men in Government Exhibit 673 were, including the man on whose shoulder Angelina Baldesteri's hand rested. For a defense lawyer, it was always important to generate confusion at every stage when the prosecution was presenting its case. *Make the prosecution's case twisted,* she instructed her Columbia students, *not linear, not easy to follow, not a road map. Where there's confusion, there's a potential for an acquittal. All it takes to win is one juror who says, "No, I can't convict. I'm not convinced beyond a reasonable doubt."*

Raquel said, "No further questions."

CHAPTER 10

IT WAS ALREADY dark when she and Hayes Smith arrived at his shingled, two-hundred-year-old house in East Hampton. It overlooked the crystal-clear pond, surrounded by sloping lawns and well-tended trees, at the end of Main Street. Swans and geese abounded there, and in the winter, it iced over so firmly that skaters glided on its surface. "In the winter, it looks absurdly like a Currier & Ives postcard," Hayes had told her. "It's impossible not to love it." Raquel and Hayes had not been together long enough for her to have seen the pond in winter. *Who knows,* she wondered each time she was there, *whether I'll ever see it again?* She loved Hayes, and believed him when he said he loved her. Yet he had never been married, he had no children, and any Google search of his name made it clear that he was an inveterate, lifelong practitioner of multiple love affairs, many of them with famous women, many at the same time. In an old-style word, a womanizer.

Raquel was astute. Hayes Smith, one of the most recognizable men in America, had an undeniable reputation as a serial, short-term lover. She knew from articles embedded eternally in the Internet that he had once had a two-year, apparently exclusive relationship with a very attractive, well-known movie star. That affair had almost evolved into a marriage that never happened.

As at the end of every week of every trial, Raquel was exhausted but always rallied herself to be bright and alert for a weekend's reprieve whether she was alone or with someone. She had spent time, before Hayes picked her up at her apartment on Riverside Drive, carefully applying her makeup. Her Italian mother, despite the fact that the family lived in a working-class area of the long-decaying, pollution-ridden Lawrence, Massachusetts, was very skillful in applying makeup to her own Sophia Loren–type face, a skill she passed to her attentive daughter. "Don't let those feminists tell you that a pretty face isn't important," her mother told her when Raquel was a teenager. "It is now, always has been, and forever will be." And, much later in her life, when Raquel became more and more of a television presence on CNN, CBS, Fox, and other networks as a talking head for legal stories, she had spent a great deal of time in rooms with genuinely experienced makeup artists. Despite her clear, private recognition of the vanity involved in it, Raquel practiced and perfected the skill of transforming her face in the years since her fearful, body-ravaging struggle with cancer.

Hayes was a news junkie, an addict for current information. Even in the privacy of his immaculate saltbox house in East Hampton, there were television sets in every room, including the two bathrooms. After they brought their small weekend bags into the bedroom, they stretched out on the quilt-covered bed. Hayes immediately turned on the television.

Suddenly and unexpectedly, Angelina Baldesteri was on the screen. She was being interviewed live by Anderson Cooper on CNN. Raquel herself had been interviewed many times by the slender, silvery Cooper.

Raquel groaned. "How many times, Hayes, do you think I've told her not to do TV interviews while the trial is on? Seventy times at least."

Hayes held up his hand, signaling that he wanted to listen. He heard Cooper ask in his whimsical, not completely grammatical, curious-boy style, "Why do you believe that you could ever get Congress, even if it was controlled by your own party, to pass a law requiring all employers to pay all employees a minimum wage of $20 per hour?"

"Although President Spellman doesn't recognize it, we have reached the point in our country's history, Anderson, and in the world economy, where our private employers can afford to pay every worker at a level that will enable them to take care of and educate their children, to send them to college, to plan for retirement. Contrary to what the Republicans say, this is not a giveaway that will enable every American worker to vacation in the Caribbean."

"Republicans argue, don't they," Cooper asked, "that a minimum wage at that level will result in loss of jobs and destroy small businesses?"

"That," Angelina Baldesteri said, "is what the Republicans of 1933 argued about Social Security when FDR introduced it, and the Republicans of the 1960s argued about Medicare and Medicaid. Same old song, new singers. All wrong."

In Hayes' beautiful, fragrant bedroom, Raquel Rematti, dressed only in an unbuttoned bathrobe, sat up in bed, watching the screen and touching her toes. Hayes, naked, lay beside her, his head propped on two pillows. Raquel said, "You know, I've often in the past sent packing clients who don't listen to my advice. She's the worst offender."

"Sweetheart," Hayes said, "this is a special client. You're not as free as you usually are. She is a famous First Lady, a Senator, and a serious candidate for President of the United States. Or at least she was."

"Sure, and she could also become federal Bureau of Prison inmate 007. She makes it difficult for me to do my work."

It was Hayes who held the remote-control device, which, like a magic wand, controlled the screen. "Do you want to watch a movie instead on Netflix?" he asked.

"No," Raquel said. "Gloria Vanderbilt's little boy is bound to ask her about the trial. I need to hear it."

And at that moment, Cooper, in his customary taut black suit and black tie, said, almost tentatively, "And I have to ask you, Senator, about your ongoing trial for fund-raising fraud. How do you feel it's going?"

"Here we go," Raquel whispered.

Angelina Baldesteri smiled calmly, as if she were Nigela Lawson being asked a question about a recipe. "You know, Anderson, the trial is a blessing in disguise. I've said from the beginning that it's like a third-world show trial. A Republican President whose policies are bankrupting the middle class and deepening the miseries of the unemployed and the most unfortunate millions in our society has his Republican Attorney General let loose a Republican prosecutor to persecute me. And what evidence do they use? A liar who was once one of my husband's most trusted people who will now say anything in a pathetic attempt for leniency and a comical octogenarian who, in telling the truth, does nothing but help me. And an FBI agent whose long history includes many, many demonstrated cases in which he's falsified evidence to send innocent people to jail."

"But the trial will take five more weeks, Senator. Aren't there risks for you and your candidacy?"

"The only risk, Anderson, is that I have to sit in a courtroom in Manhattan when I should be in the Senate chamber and traveling the country to lay out for the people my vision for restoring the prosperity and peace and security that the United States enjoyed during the years of Jimmy Young's presidency."

As the screen dissolved into a commercial, Raquel said, "In which world is that woman living?"

Hayes lowered the volume of sound on the television almost to silence. He said, "She is a better politician than her husband was."

"And the worst defendant," Raquel said, reaching for her iPhone. On it she typed a text message to Angelina. The note read, *Call me.*

The Senator's text appeared almost immediately: *Have a great weekend.*

* * *

Raquel and Hayes passed the entire weekend in East Hampton. They went to the library, they walked holding hands down the exquisite Main Street, and they watched two movies at the East Hampton Cinema. They ate at the restaurant at the ancient Huntting Inn where, although they were recognized, they weren't bothered.

Raquel and Hayes never detected the listening devices and minute cameras implanted everywhere in Hayes' sweet, tidy house.

And they never noticed the two men who followed them. Uncannily similar, both were slightly over six feet tall. They were blond, and each had close-cropped hair. Just above his left ear, each had a zigzag mark shaved in his hair almost to the scalp. They were dressed casually in Ralph Lauren–style clothes. East Hampton had a large gay community, and these two large men could easily have been taken as part of it, apparently bonding with the "Z" in their hair as some men would with wedding rings.

They had an assignment. It was to become familiar with Hayes Smith's physical presence, his styles of movement, his gestures. They were to return that information, as well as the sounds on the listening devices and the images on the tapes, to a man they knew only as Mr. Jones, obviously a fake name because "Mr. Jones" was plainly South American as his accent conveyed.

Mr. Jones had shared some information with the men with the blond "Z" markings faintly etched in their hair. At some point someone was going to "reach out and touch" Hayes as a way to "set on fire" the mind, emotions, and fears of Raquel Rematti. Raquel needed to be conditioned to fail, particularly since failure had rarely been part of her experience. She had spent a lifetime evading failure. She had always sought out success. If her life was altered, Mr. Jones had said, she would now fail. The men with the "Z" did not even question the bizarre "Mr. Jones."

It was only later the men marked with the zigzags learned his two names: *Robert Calvaro* and *Oscar Caliente*.

CHAPTER 11

IT WAS ONE in the morning when Hugo Salazar stepped down from the black SUV at the corner of Greenwich Street and Vestry Street in downtown Manhattan. Three large men, also dressed in black clothes, left a nearby SUV when Salazar emerged from his. They separated and formed a loose triangle around him as he walked casually, confidently, along the white cobblestone street toward Le Zinc. They were far enough away from him, and yet close enough that they didn't seem to be with him but could still protect him if anyone posed or seemed to pose a threat.

A dense mist had settled over Lower Manhattan. It was, after all, an island surrounded by immense bodies of water—the Hudson River, New York Harbor, the East River, and, at its northern edge, the narrow estuary known as the Spuyten Duyvil that separated Manhattan from the Bronx. The mist made the brick-shaped cobblestones glisten, creating magical halos around the city streetlights.

Hugo Salazar was a night lover. Night was his element, his ocean of possibilities, the river in which he loved to swim. It was when he felt most safe, most alert, most fun-loving. Although a throng of men and women waited in the chilly mist for entry through the velvet ropes, the club's bodyguards unfastened the clasps as soon as they saw Hugo. His three bodyguards also entered just behind him as the velvet rope was again fastened to its pole. The line of people who stood behind the velvet cord was very long.

Hugo was there for a reason. Lydia Guzman was twenty-five, from the Bronx, and a fun lover. Hugo also knew she was one of the jurors in the trial of Senator Angelina Baldesteri. Even though the prosecutors hadn't wanted her on the jury, they had used up all their automatic challenges before her name gradually rose to the surface from the old-fashioned wooden box that a court clerk spun on its axis when someone in the large jury pool was disqualified. Dozens of potential jurors had been excused for a variety of reasons—financial hardship, travel plans, caring for sick relatives, and in some cases mental, emotional, or personality disorders that were evident to the prosecutors, the judge, and Raquel Rematti. No one wanted a patently screwed-up, utterly unpredictable man or woman on the jury. So Lydia Guzman's name, as the wheel revolved, began its gradual climb through the painstaking selection process.

Since Naomi Goldstein was a meticulous judge who knew all the rules, one of which was that each side had only a limited number of times it could reject a possible juror on instinct for any reason or no reason at all. After those peremptory challenges were used up there had to be a coherent, nondiscriminatory, legitimate reason to reject a juror. Lydia Guzman was eventually seated as one of the actual jurors because there were no nondiscriminatory grounds on which to reject her. Hunter Decker had wanted an anonymous, sequestered jury. Naomi Goldstein refused after Raquel argued that sequestering a jury in a hotel room for at least five weeks, deprived of all contact with the outside world, sent a subtle message that the defendant was dangerous or guilty or both.

For several years, Hugo Salazar had casually seen Lydia in various all-night clubs but had never made an effort to dance with her, "to hook up." He didn't know her name until the trial started. Her exotic looks were unmistakable, as was her fluid dancing style, her ravishing body, and her love of cocaine. As he entered Le Zinc, a club on the ground floor of a renovated century-old warehouse, he wasted no time. She was on the dance floor, illuminated in flashes by strobe lights. It appeared she was dancing with no one and every one. The music was loud, amplified from tall black speakers strategically placed throughout the immense club. There was only one man on the stage who controlled the thunderous dance music, most of it rap and hip-hop, solely through a silver Apple laptop perched on a glittering music stand. There was no need for a live band.

Hugo moved across the crowded dance floor in Lydia's direction. Most of the dancers were unattached women. When he reached Lydia, he simply faced her and joined her as she danced. He took her hand. He held her hand and his aloft as she spun around under their joined hands, almost ballerina-like. Soon they were both sweating: in its own way, that was erotic. It was a sensual bond.

*　*　*

Lydia remembered him. Several years earlier, this handsome man, whom people called *Juan the Goodguy*, had often arrived at two or three a.m. at the teeming downtown after-hours clubs. He was always treated by the managers as royalty and always accompanied by big men and expensively dressed, stylish women who actually handed over the cocaine, heroin, and pills they had ordered from the *Goodguy* while he was on the dance floor. The subtle handoff of the goodies only happened after Salazar gave the signal that he'd been paid in cash. There were never any refunds, as he enjoyed saying. But there were never any mistakes: once the users paid, they got what they paid for. *Juan the Goodguy* was a reliable businessman.

But then, for several years, he had simply vanished. Lydia knew enough about drug dealers to know that they were elusive—they moved from place to place frequently. She had also learned that some vanished because they were arrested. And some, she had heard, were murdered.

Hugo Salazar was a great, sexy dancer. He had lost none of that skill in the years of his total, unexplained absence. He was changed now only because over those few years his thick black hair had grown so much that it was tied into a long ponytail, a change that made him even more attractive, more sexy, more hot.

Within seconds Lydia pressed her large breasts into his chest. In Spanish, barely audible in the total immersion of the throbbing music, she said, "Hey, we've missed you. Where have you been, man?"

Gently pushing her black hair from her left ear, Hugo whispered, also in Spanish, "I've been in Miami and L.A. You're still the most beautiful woman anywhere, my love."

Playfully, Lydia Guzman, spreading her fingers, pushed at his chest. "You're good at what you do, aren't you?"

She danced around him. She wasn't going to let him go.

*   *   *

She was, as Hunter Decker and Raquel Rematti both recognized, the least attentive of the jurors. Lydia didn't recognize that the man with whom she was now dancing was the man who had appeared clearly in Government Exhibit 673 talking to Angelina Baldesteri, as her hand rested on the shoulder of the stylish man standing in front of her. She also didn't know that this gorgeous man had been tried on Long Island several years earlier for the machete murder of Brad Richardson. Nor did she know that Raquel Rematti had represented Hugo Salazar, then known as Juan Suarez, *The Blade of the Hamptons*, whose conviction for murder had been set aside when two boys discovered the actual murder weapon, a machete, and the clothes the killer had worn in the Sag Harbor landfill soon after the trial. None of that contained any traces of the DNA of the convicted man, and Raquel successfully moved to have that conviction vacated before he was deported to Mexico.

Deportation for a man like Juan Suarez was a joke. Easily returning to the United States with yet another assumed identity, Hugo Salazar now had a special assignment: to make certain that Lydia Guzman would never vote to convict Angelina Baldesteri. His way of winning her loyalty and her commitment was by sex, cocaine, and money. Robert Calvaro, the source of the assignment, had learned Lydia Guzman was an easy target. "She's a slut and an addict," he had told Hugo. "You can't lose with her, Hugo. Grab her and don't let anything happen to her."

"Nice of you to give me fun work, Oscar," Hugo Salazar answered. "I'll have her fast."

CHAPTER 12

UNLIKE MANY OF her peers—and there were only four or five others in the entire country, all men in New York, Miami, Chicago, and Los Angeles, who were the best, the go-to criminal defense lawyers—Raquel Rematti never resorted to shouting at a witness. She often started her cross-examinations by making even the most seasoned witness let down his or her guard. But she was a panther pretending at first to enjoy playing coyly with the young antelope before surging for the kill.

Like every other style, hers sometimes failed. Raquel picked up quickly that it would never work with Carol Bronson. She was a lawyer with a huge Washington law firm who had been put on the stand by one of Hunter Decker's associates to explain, as an expert, what a super PAC was. Skilled lawyer as he was, Hunter Decker knew the jurors had heard the two odd words often, but could not be expected to fully grasp their meaning.

"What again is the name of the firm you work for?" Raquel asked as soon as Naomi Goldstein said, "Your witness." It was not going to be possible to discredit the carefully dressed, corporately immaculate, thoroughly prepared Carol Bronson on her accurate and lucid description of a super PAC. So Raquel's job was to make the jurors dislike Carol Bronson, even to hate, and to distrust her. If Raquel couldn't discredit her on the merits of her testimony, she would make her thoroughly unlikable. In Carol Bronson's Republican, corporate, non-Manhattan demeanor, she was different from every member of the jury. There was a secret truism in Raquel's business—if you represented an obvious murderer, you would defend the client by trying to show that the victim "deserved killing," as did any witness who testified against the defendant.

"SloaneJones."

"You testified that is a law firm, correct?"

"It is."

"Mr. Sloane is a former United States Senator, correct?"

"Yes."

"Mr. Jones is a former U.S. Congressman, is that right?"

"He is."

"Both are Republicans?"

"Yes."

"And isn't it true that SloaneJones is a registered lobbying firm, not simply a law firm?"

"That's accurate."

"And you're a registered lobbyist, too?"

"I am."

"And lobbyists get paid for advocating with Senators and Congressmen and Congresswomen, even with Presidents and their staffs, for the benefit of their clients, correct?"

"No, that's not correct. We provide information that lawmakers need to hear."

"You spend much more of your time as a lobbyist than a lawyer?"

Standing, Hunter Decker said, "Objection, beyond the scope of the direct examination. Ms. Bronson was called by the Government as an expert on super PACs. And Your Honor qualified her as that based on her experience, education, and articles to assist the jury in a full understanding of words—super PAC—the jurors have heard and will continue to hear but may not fully understand."

"Overruled," Naomi Goldstein whispered distinctly. "This is Ms. Rematti's cross-examination. She has a right to try to demonstrate the bias of a witness, including an expert." Goldstein added, "If in fact the witness has any bias. That's for the jury to hear and decide. I don't have any views on that."

Raquel repeated, "And you spend more of your time as a lobbyist than as a lawyer, correct?"

"I do. That's what the firm's website states. I lobby for corporations, trade associations, even individuals."

"For the oil and gas trade associations?"

"Among others."

Unusual for her, Raquel raised the volume of her voice. "And the others include the national Right to Life Committee?"

"Yes."

"The National Rifle Association?"

"Yes. We do have a Second Amendment, as the Supreme Court not long ago reminded us."

Although Carol Bronson's tone of voice remained corporate-style and spare, Raquel sensed that she was gaining ground on her as a witness. Bronson was too condescending, even supercilious. This was good, because Raquel had a pathway now for pressing forward. The panther steadily on the chase, relentlessly closing the distance between her and her prey. "And you never lobbied for NOW, or for the ACLU, or the Sierra Club?"

"I was never asked."

"And you are an expert on super PACs, correct?"

"I am."

"You've written articles on super PACs, correct?"

"Certainly. It's on my resume. That resume was posted on the computers as an exhibit."

"You've written many times for the *Wall Street Journal*, correct?"

"Several times."

"For the *American Spectator*?"

"Yes." Carol Bronson paused. "I didn't create super PACs, Ms. Rematti. The Supreme Court allowed them on freedom of speech grounds."

"You've been interviewed on the Breitbart site, correct?"

"Yes."

"And you are often a guest on Fox News, correct?"

"I am."

"You are a friend of Stephen Bannon, aren't you?"

"I know him."

"And Ann Coulter?"

"I know her."

Raquel shifted ground, asking, "Where do you vote?"

Hunter Decker stood. "Objection."

"Overruled."

Raquel repeated the question with a slight variation. "You're registered to vote in New York, aren't you?" When cross-examining a hostile witness, the premium was on the art of surprise, of making a witness confused and wary.

"I am."

"Have you ever voted for Senator Baldesteri?"

"Isn't that my business?" Bronson asked.

Goldstein intervened: "Just answer the question."

"Never."

"Did you ever vote for President Young, the Senator's husband?"

"No."

And now another shift of ground, as Raquel asked, "A person or corporation can give unlimited amounts of money to a super PAC, correct?"

"That's correct."

"But not to an individual candidate, correct?"

"Yes."

"And super PACs can, in turn, give the same money to a politician's campaign or issues or positions?"

"So long as it's properly accounted for and publicly disclosed."

"So the PAC money can be used to fly a candidate with his or her entourage from Bangor, Maine, to San Diego, all expenses paid, if the candidate's views are consistent with the PAC's?"

"Perfectly legal."

"And the PAC's funds can be used to buy meals and drinks and lodgings?"

"I testified that was so to the extent the expense is tied to an issue endorsed by the super PAC. Do you want me to repeat it for you?"

Raquel relished Carol Bronson's fully obvious hostility. "Who decides when and on whom a super PAC's lavish spending will be bestowed?"

"Each PAC has a steering committee."

"Selected by the PAC's major donors?"

"I said that before."

"Selected by the PAC's major donors, Ms. Bronson, correct?"

"Again, yes."

"And most PACs have Chief Executive Officers?"

"Every one that I'm familiar with does. At last count there were two thousand super PACs created in the last several years. The major ones I've been in contact with have a CEO—a Chief Executive Officer."

"And he's the face of the organization, right?"

"Often. But many of the CEOs are women, Ms. Rematti."

"Thank you, Ms. Bronson, for the correction. Why do super PACs need a public face?"

"That's because the names of the donors and the amounts of their donations don't have to be disclosed. If you, Ms. Rematti, were in an anti-Muslim march and shouted anti-Muslim slogans, you wouldn't be forced to disclose your name. Donors have the same privilege of anonymity as you do, no matter what their views are. So the Chief Executive Officer is the only real name and face of the PAC."

Raquel, quiet and persistent, had brought this quintessentially corporate woman where she wanted her. Bronson was irritated, as if she felt her time were being wasted. She was a busy woman.

"You've sat in that witness box for four hours, Ms. Bronson, is that about right?"

"I don't know. This is a beautiful courtroom, as we can all see. However, the impressive new clock over the door isn't working. And I'm not wearing a watch."

"And you prepared a ten-page expert report on super PACs?"

"I did."

"And it was distributed to the jury?"

"It was. You saw that happen."

"When did you write it?"

"When?"

"That's the question. When did you write it?"

"Three years ago. I revise it frequently."

"Are you being paid by the Government for that expert report in connection with this trial?"

"Of course. You teach courses at law schools and bar associations, as I understand it, and you're paid, or so I assume."

"What is your hourly rate when you testify about super PACs for the Government?"

"Fifteen hundred dollars."

"And that's for each hour, correct?"

"It is."

"How much have you been paid by the United States so far for this ten-page outline and your time here today?"

"Fifty thousand dollars."

"Do you expect to be paid more?"

"I do. I have a contract that requires a final installment of $25,000. And I get paid, Ms. Rematti, whether your client is convicted, or acquitted, or there is a mistrial. My expert role and fees don't depend on victory."

"Let me ask you this: Have you ever met President Spellman?"

"From time to time."

"Did you ever discuss Senator Baldesteri with him?"

"In what context?" Bronson asked.

"Any context?"

"Yes," Bronson said.

"Were any of those conversations connected to this trial?"

"No, of course not."

"What have you ever heard the President say about the Senator?"

"Do you," Bronson asked, "really want to know that?"

Raquel said again, "Tell the jury what you heard President Spellman say about Angelina Baldesteri."

"That she's never been a grieving widow. That she's power hungry. That her candidacy is a joke. That she's dangerous for the country."

"Did you ever hear him say that her candidacy had to be stopped at any cost?"

"Never."

"And let me ask you this: Did you ever discuss Senator Baldesteri with Attorney General Harrington?"

"Objection," Hunter Decker said.

In her sepulchral voice, Naomi Goldstein said, "Overruled."

"It was the Attorney General who hired me for this case."

"What did he say about Senator Baldesteri?"

"I can't specifically remember."

"Can you generally remember?"

"Yes. That she probably had the President, her husband, blown up in order to open the door to the presidency for herself. He was joking, of course."

"How often have you met the Attorney General?"

"Only that one time."

"And you came to know him so well that you know when he's joking, is that your testimony?"

Carol Bronson said, "I have a sense of humor, Ms. Rematti. I can pick out people who have a sense of humor. It's a skill I've developed."

"And another skill you've developed, Ms. Bronson, is to use your expertise to bolster the people who hire and pay you?"

"I resent that."

"You know the expression *He who pays the piper gets to call the tune*?"

One or two of the jurors laughed, audibly.

"Never. I never heard that."

Raquel stared at her, scorn in her gaze. "Thank you for your time, Ms. Bronson."

Carol Bronson didn't respond.

CHAPTER 13

HUGO SALAZAR'S APARTMENT on East 62nd Street and Third Avenue was, Lydia Guzman instantly saw, a miracle of modern decorating. To her left, in the quiet lighting from above the burnished oven, the kitchen gleamed. Directly in front of her was a wall of windows beyond which hundreds of thousands of city lights in other apartment buildings and office buildings glittered and glimmered. Lydia was uncertain in which direction of Midtown Manhattan the windows faced. But for her, it was a breathtaking view. She was now in a world she had always desired, far above the Emerald City of Midtown Manhattan.

Hugo Salazar was not just a handsome man, he was polite and respectful. At that first night of dancing, he asked, over the music, for her name, email address, and cell phone number, all of which he already had, although Lydia didn't know that. He made a pretense of entering all of that information into his iPhone.

Three days later he called her and asked her to dinner. She was so anxious to see him that when the U.S. Marshals returned her cell phone at the end of a trial day, she immediately returned his call from the monumental steps of the old federal courthouse on Foley Square. Hugo asked, in Spanish, whether she could meet him at seven at Michael's, a very expensive restaurant on West 55th Street in Manhattan. She decided she didn't have time to return to her apartment in the Bronx to change into the kinds of clothes she would want to wear on this date—a dress, moderately high heels, a tailored coat—but instead slowly made her way by the No. 6 Lexington Avenue subway to Midtown and wandered among the stores such as Saks Fifth Avenue, Bergdorf Goodman, and the modernistic Apple store in the underground of the GM Building in which she liked to gaze at objects she could never buy.

At that dinner at Michael's, where Robert de Niro and his wife were eating quietly at a corner table, Hugo asked her nothing about the trial. He gave no hint he knew she was on the jury, and she volunteered nothing about it because, in reality, she didn't care about it. What she did care about was how beguiling he was, how gracefully he dealt with the tuxedoed host, and how smoothly he slipped the plastic bag into her hand during the meal, a bag that she quickly took with her to the privacy of the women's room, where she spread the magic powder on the gleaming counter, used the edge of a crisp dollar bill to create three straight lines of powder, then rolled the same dollar bill into the shape of a straw and, holding back her fabulous black hair, quickly inhaled. Not a trace of the white powder remained on the counter but, to be certain, she used the tip of her moistened index finger to touch the area where the coke had been spread, and then licked her fingertip. With all the powder inside her, she passed over into the world of calm and potent ecstasy.

Hugo had kissed her passionately after the fourth of the elegant dinners they had over the next several nights. From the first moment at the first dinner, she had wanted to kiss him and let him know he could readily have everything her body could give him. Each time they had dinner he knew it would have been a simple step, when he took it, to bring her back to his apartment. Instead, each time, he had one of his security men drive her to the Bronx after he gave her five or six of those plastic bags with white powder.

Within five minutes of first walking through the door of his apartment, Lydia Guzman had simply taken off all her clothes, leading him to an opulent room that was obviously his bedroom. There was a platform bed. As he undressed, Hugo also lit the fragrant candles spread around the room. All over the room the air was soon suffused with a soft glow.

Hugo was a prodigious lover. He began by kneeling between her legs and softening and stimulating her with his tongue for at least ten minutes. He touched against each soft surface. He entered her only when she pulled gently on his shoulders, saying, "I want you in me." He seemed to hold his erection for hours, and she shuddered and came time after time. How, she wondered, was she going to keep him?

During their first night in the apartment, Hugo whispered, "Lydia, *amor*, I don't even know what you do for a living."

"What does it matter?" she whispered, playfully.

"It doesn't," he said.

"I'm a hair stylist. I work in a salon on the Grand Concourse."

"Why, *amor*, are you always free for dinner? For being with me?"

"I come and go to the salon as I please, whenever I get called. I either say yes or I say no."

"It's great," Hugo said. "All that freedom."

"Right now I'm wasting my days in some courthouse listening to bullshit."

"You mean you're on a jury?"

"Yes. I'm in the room, but my head is off the reservation."

"Drug trial? Lots of those in Manhattan."

"*That* I'd enjoy. Might learn something useful."

"So what kind of trial?"

"Some Senator. A woman. Baldestrana? Baldi? I don't know. Some Italian name."

"Lydia, that woman is one of the Senators from New York. And her husband was once the President of the United States."

"Who gives a fuck? It's also costing me money. I get sixty bucks a day for jury service. That's not even close to what I get for cutting and coloring hair for an afternoon."

Hugo asked, "Can I tell you something?"

"About the trial?"

"Yeah."

"The dried-up old bitch who's the judge says every time she opens her mouth that nobody is supposed to talk about the trial, read the newspapers, look at Google, or even go on Facebook."

"That shit, forcing you off Facebook, must drive you crazy."

"For sure. Besides, I really don't care. I wish I could wear my earbuds during the trial and listen to music."

"There's something," Hugo finally said, "I could figure out for you to do."

"I tried everything I could to get off that jury."

"This is different. I want you to stay on it." He lapsed into silence, stroking her breasts as she, luxuriant, lay beside him. "I'll give you $100,000 in cash if you stay on the jury. And say she's innocent. Pure and simple. No matter if everybody else on the jury tells you, or screams at you, that she's guilty as shit, you say she's innocent, not guilty. No matter how many times they have you vote, you check the box that says *not guilty*."

"Come on, man, what crazy talk is that shit?"

"Nothing crazy about it."

"How come?" Lydia asked.

"You *all* have to agree she's guilty. If one of you, just *one*, says not guilty, she walks."

"Why do you care?" Lydia asked.

"I don't. The people I work for care."

"Does she know about this?"

"You mean the Senator?"

"That's what I mean."

"Sweetheart, don't ask too many questions."

"Well, I do have another question. What if other people think she's *not* guilty so it turns out you didn't need me? Do I still get the money?"

"Sure you do. You're my *mama*. I keep my promises. When we have dinner two nights from now, bring a big pocketbook, and I'll put fifty of the $100,000 in it. Then we come back here and fuck. Like sealing the deal."

"What about the other fifty?"

"Hey, *amor*, I work for smart people. The other fifty is insurance. They deliver, through me, when you deliver. All you need to deliver is that *no* vote."

"You have any more coke for me?"

"All you want."

"Do you have anything else for me right now?"

"Anything you want."

CHAPTER 14

HUNTER DECKER WAS a meticulously dressed lawyer. His suits were expensive, unlike those of the Assistant U.S. Attorneys who worked for him. This was because Hunter was to the manor born, the heir to the fortune that his family had amassed during more than one hundred and fifty years of constructing massive farm equipment that was used around the world, including the vast farmlands of the Soviet Union when there had been a Soviet Union.

In a windowless beige conference room in the austere brick building that housed the U.S. Attorney's Office for the Southern District of New York, Decker listened quietly as two Special Agents of the FBI, Joe Giordano and Neil Curnin, told him something that he simply didn't believe. Raquel Rematti, they said, was involved with a group of people who were making arrangements to pay $100,000 and give unlimited quantities of cocaine to a juror in the trial of Angelina Baldesteri so that the juror would never vote for conviction. Every high school civics student in America knew, or should know, that a person could only be convicted if *every* juror agreed that the defendant was guilty beyond a reasonable doubt. "Even a stupid Puerto Rican cokehead knows that or can learn it," Giordano said.

Hunter Decker's skepticism of Special Agents Giordano and Curnin was deep-seated. In two trials over the last three years, they had given testimony that, Hunter believed after the defense cross-examination, was not true. Since he had no solid proof of that, he had done nothing. Both defendants were convicted because of the weight of the other evidence against them. Giordano's and Curnin's testimony, even if not true, made no difference to the outcome of the trials. Privately, Decker was unsettled by his suspicions of the recklessness of these two rogue men, yet he had no credible evidence that they were liars or benefited tangibly by what they did. Decker actively disliked them without revealing it. He enjoyed challenging them, and doing so from a position of *noblesse oblige*.

"These," Decker said, "are serious claims. Raquel Rematti is a legend. She's been watched hundreds of times by people like you for anything that would take her out of the game. The CIA, Homeland Security, the IRS, the NSA, local cops, the Secret Service—every spook in America waiting to *get* her. Even the FBI." He stared at them. "And now you two are sitting there like sixth-grade parochial school boys with something that sounds like make-believe about a well-regarded priest. Or, to put it so you'll really get it, pure bullshit."

On the opposite side of Decker's desk, Giordano and Curnin stared at him. They hated him, but his old wealth and his position made him untouchable. "Our job," Giordano said, "is to find out information for guys like you. What you do with it is your business. Take it or leave it. Up to you."

"You gentlemen have lied to me before."

His voice almost sibilant, Giordano said, "What the fuck you talkin' about? You've said this to us before. I'm kind of sick of it by now, you know. Do something about it if you believe it. You can get our asses transferred whenever you want. You just can't fire us, and you know that."

"What you've told me about Rematti isn't information. Words become information when facts support them. I may not like Rematti—she represents the wrong people and does it too well and, worse yet, she likes it—but I'm not doing a thing to bring her down unless and until you give me facts."

"The juror," Curnin said, "is a junkie. Lydia Guzman. She's also a talker. Suddenly she has enough coke that she's not just a buyer but a dealer, although small scale so far. She told one of her girlfriends—someone the DEA has had under surveillance for months because of the girlfriend's connection with a new ambitious dealer who is too stupid to know that Oscar Caliente's people will soon get around to putting him into the East River without an inflatable tube, he's a drowning dead rat—that she has a new boyfriend. Hugo Salazar. Hugo is the guy Angelina Baldesteri is talking to in Exhibit 673."

"You don't need to remind me who Salazar is," Decker said. "I'm listening."

"It turns out that the juror's girlfriend is smart," Curnin said. "Since she knows the DEA is on to her, she's feeding info to us, thinking she'll get a deal or protection for cooperation. Particularly if she can deliver something as big as this. She told the DEA that Lydia Guzman has said that Hugo is giving *mucho dinero* and *la coke* if Lydia does something special for Angelina Baldesteri. Now what else in the world can Lydia Guzman do for Senator Angelina Baldesteri except never ever vote for a conviction? She's sure as hell not going to color her hair for her."

Hunter Decker leaned back in his swivel chair. "And who used the magic words *Raquel Rematti* in talking about cash and coke and a junkie juror?"

Giordano spoke out. "No one. But you don't think a Senator is handing money, or arranging to hand money, through a trusted loyalist, to a member of the Sinaloa cartel like Salazar to give to a junkie to get a *get-out-of-jail-free card*? Think it through. Who among all the people Baldesteri knows would know Salazar well enough to pull this off? Only Rematti, Salazar's onetime lawyer. And Salazar, when he was Rematti's client named at the time Juan Suarez, was also the object of her affection. It all fits."

Decker stared at them and finally said, "Maybe in your minds it all fits together. But you haven't yet made the sale to me, fellas. You need a wiretap or pictures or something else for me to feel, see, or touch before I'm about to tell a judge or anybody else that a lawyer with Rematti's stature is carrying bags of cash and coke or is part of a plan to buy an acquittal."

"What do you mean," Giordano asked, "by 'stature'? Rematti has been a pain in the ass to us for years. She's kept dirty politicians, stock fraudsters, Mafioso, revolutionaries, Arabs, subversives, all kinds of scum, on the streets and out of jail for a long time."

"And then," Curnin added, "she's had the balls to make a celebrity out of herself because of this dirty work. Television shows, teaching at frickin' law schools. Now getting a TV star for a live-in boyfriend. Christ, she even played a movie role in a Pacino movie. And what was the name of the character she played? *Raquel Rematti*."

Decker leaned forward, saying, "You know what? That's her job, gentlemen. It's not your job to chase a vendetta the FBI has against her. You need to do a hell of a lot more work than you've done before I can act on any of this. But I'm interested. I can't go to Goldstein with any of this. And I can't get any other judge or magistrate to issue a wiretap or search warrant for Rematti on the basis of a single thing you've told me. That's my job—to be responsible."

"Are you protecting Rematti?" Giordano asked. "Is there something special between you and her? She's one good-looking woman."

Decker said, "I'm not going to throw you out of this room for saying that. If you two actually do real work and come to me with real evidence, I'll bring down Jesus Christ, Raquel Rematti, or Pope Francis, or Donald Trump. I can't tell you how to do your jobs. I can tell you to do your jobs before you take up any more of my time."

CHAPTER 15

FURIOUS, ANGELINA BALDESTERI wrote on a yellow legal pad for Raquel Rematti, "Get this bitch. She's a liar. Ask her if she ever fucked Spellman. The President." With her pen she twice underlined the words *Spellman, President, Fucked.*

As usual, Raquel knew very little before a witness took the stand for the Government about what the witness would say on direct examination. There were never any pretrial depositions in federal criminal cases where she could herself examine a witness for a preview of the testimony. Some witnesses were never even brought in front of the grand jury before a trial and as a result there was no existing written record of what they had said; they were a dangerous *tabula rasa*. And when the Government prosecutors, as sometimes happened, were forced by a particular judge to provide a last-minute list of their potential witnesses and mention next to each name "probable information," that information had been honed to the very fine skill of cryptic descriptions. In the case of Georgina Draper, the meaningless description was for "relevant transactions."

As usual, when the prosecutor's direct examination was over—and Hunter Decker was a quick, deft examiner who almost never meandered—Naomi Goldstein yet again directed the terse words "cross-examination" to Raquel. As Raquel had learned, it was point-less to ask for even a short bathroom break.

"Ms. Draper," Raquel started, "let me ask you a simple question: You remember, don't you, saying that in the seven months you worked in Senator Baldesteri's office you saw the man some have called Robert Calvaro hand several big manila envelopes to the Senator?"

"I certainly did."

"But you never saw what was in them?"

"No."

"The Senator never told you, isn't that right?"

"That's right."

"Robert Calvaro never told you, correct?"

"Correct."

"You never spoke to Robert Calvaro?"

"Never. My job was to be the polite liaison with her constituents. He wasn't a constituent. As far as I knew, his job was to help build a war chest for her presidential campaign."

"How often did you see Robert Calvaro with the Senator?"

"Seven or eight times."

"How did you even know the man's name was Robert Calvaro?"

"That's what the Senator called him. So everyone did."

"You were never introduced to him by the Senator?"

"No."

"Did he always carry an envelope?"

"Not always. He sometimes had a leather valise."

"What happened when this man visited?"

"He went straight into her office. He never had to wait."

"The Senator's chambers are large, right?"

"Very. There are separate offices in the suite for her aides, interns, press secretary. And, of course, the Senator had her own room. Huge, an inner sanctum. All Senators do."

"Did you have an office?"

"No. There was a big central area with desks. Her interns—and she had many of them; she seems to like having people around most of the time—sat at those desks. I had one. I was the oldest."

"Is it fair to say that when this man visited, whether he had an envelope or a valise, there were always numerous people around?"

"That's fair to say."

"Did you ever hear her call him Robert?"

"Yes, I heard her use the name Robert."

"Did you ever hear her use the name Oscar?"

"Never."

"Did she ever call him Mr. Caliente?"

"No."

"What happened when he arrived?"

"As I said, they always went directly into her office and she closed the door. And that was unusual."

"Why so?"

"Even when other Senators visited, she left that door open. She's generally open to view, receptive, nothing hidden, transparent, as she always liked to repeat. Except where Robert was concerned."

"How long would he stay in there?"

"It varied. Five minutes sometimes. Other times, an hour or more."

"When he left, did he ever carry anything?"

"Usually the envelopes. But they were folded, empty, unlike when he arrived. They were full when he arrived."

"At one point, Ms. Draper, you worked on the campaign staff for President Spellman, isn't that right, when he was running for President?"

There was no change in Draper's expression. And there was no change in Raquel Rematti's.

"I did. Years ago, it was his first, unsuccessful campaign. I've been in Washington a long time. I've never been married, I have no political views, I'm comfortable with all kinds of politicians. I'm a professional. It doesn't matter to me whether I work in a Democrat's office or a Republican's."

"How much did President Spellman pay you?"

Standing, Hunter Decker said, "Objection."

For the first time in the trial, Naomi Goldstein looked puzzled. "Do you mean, Ms. Rematti, now or years ago?"

"At any time," Raquel answered.

There was the slightest semblance of surprise, or even disdain, in Judge Goldstein's expression. "Objection sustained."

"When," Raquel asked, "did you leave Senator Baldesteri's staff?"

"Six months ago, seven perhaps. Do you want to know why?"

"Unfortunately, Ms. Draper, I get to ask the questions," Raquel said. "I ask, you answer."

Naomi Goldstein, in an exasperated whisper, said into her microphone, "No, Ms. Rematti, I get to make the rules. The witness can continue with her answer."

"Judge, I did not ask *why*. I asked *when*."

Goldstein said, "The witness can continue her answer."

"FBI agents," Draper continued, "came to my apartment early one morning and asked if they could take me for coffee at a nearby Starbucks. I said *yes*. They asked me many questions there. About the Senator. About her office suite. About her visitors. About her fund-raising. About super PACs. About Robert Calvaro. And about someone they called *Oscar Caliente*."

"What did you say?"

"I said I knew nothing about fund-raising for the Senator, except that it was obvious to me it was her main preoccupation. And I told them I never heard the name Oscar Caliente."

"You weren't in a position, literally or figuratively, were you, Ms. Draper, to know what the Senator's main preoccupation was, isn't that right?"

"No." She paused, a trace of hatred in her expression. "When we were at Starbucks, the agents showed me a spreadsheet with dollars in each column. It was a computer printout. It had the title *Donations to Presidential Fund*. They asked whether I had seen it before."

For the first time, Naomi Goldstein did what many judges did. She asked her own questions. "Had you seen that spreadsheet before, Ms. Draper?" Goldstein interrupted.

Draper looked at the judge. "One very much like it."

"Maybe I wasn't clear in the question, Ms. Draper," the judge whispered, her voice clearly audible because of her microphone's projection of sound and the utter absence of any other sound in the courtroom. "Had you seen that particular spreadsheet before?"

"One very similar to it. But not the same one. It contained different columns, different numbers, but covered the same time periods. The dollar amounts were larger. Both for what came in and what went out."

Judge Goldstein, looking at Raquel through big, circular glasses, said, "You can resume, Ms. Rematti."

"Ms. Draper, a few minutes ago you told these jurors that your job in the Senator's suite was to speak politely to any of her constituents who called the Senator, isn't that right?"

"Yes. That was my job."

"Yet now you are saying you looked at the Senator's financial information, correct?"

"I did. Even for a woman of a certain age like me, I'm pretty adept with computers. I had the first Apple computer Steve Jobs put out on the market in the early 1980s. I've bought two or three generations of Apple computers since then. Computers are a passion of mine. I'm just too old for anyone to hire me for that skill."

"Did the Senator ever give you permission to look at her financial information?"

"No."

"How did you get access to it?"

"One day the Senator was on a speaking tour—or a series of listening tours, as she liked to call them—in Iowa. Her suite was pretty much empty. She takes many staffers with her when she travels. She left me behind."

"And you did what you had no permission to do?"

"I don't know that I needed permission, Ms. Rematti. I worked in her suite, after all. I had the run of the house. Her inner office wasn't locked. I went to her iMac and I found the information. Two summaries that were in the computer. It was easy to see that one of the summaries was filed with the Federal Election Commission. And that the other, even though it covered the same period, was not."

"And why did that mean anything to you? You're not an expert on campaign reporting requirements, are you? Nor are you an accountant, isn't that so? Is that part of your resume, Ms. Draper?"

"No, it isn't. But I knew the forms when I worked for President Spellman during his first campaign for President, the one that failed. He was honest. Anything he filed with the FEC was accurate."

"And how do you know that?"

"Experience and instinct, Ms. Rematti. Your client does not have the qualities Mr. Spellman has. When I looked at Senator Baldesteri's computers, it was clear as day that she had two sets of books, one for the FEC and the public and another, more detailed, richer, and secret one for herself and people like Mr. Calvaro and Mr. Gordon Hughes. Like a candy store owner with a phony set of books for sales tax examiners. In other words, another set of shadow books, but also secret real ones, for private use."

"What did you do when you, with no authority to do so, saw this? Did you print the spreadsheets out?"

"No. I quit, I left her staff. Never went back."

Raquel asked, "These reports never existed, isn't that right?"

"Oh, they sure did, Ms. Rematti."

"But you never had them, right?"

"I don't. I didn't take them. I could have put them on thumb drives, but I didn't. They felt dirty to me, like a toilet as you're cleaning it." She waited. "But the FBI does have them. The agents showed them to me at Starbucks. They told me they took copies of her computer drives with a search warrant when they started investigating your client."

"Did you tell President Spellman or his people about this conversation with the FBI or the reports after this Starbucks conversation happened, if it happened?"

"It happened, Ms. Rematti. And, yes, I told the President's Chief of Staff." She waited again. "And I showed the Chief the pictures I took at Starbucks with my cell phone of the agents and the printouts. I asked their permission to take the pictures. The agents said, 'Sure.' I wanted to protect myself, Ms. Rematti. Your client, the Senator, is ruthless. She loves to demean and hurt people. Maybe more than that, even. As much as she can, whenever she can, and wherever she can."

"Who were the agents?"

"They gave me business cards. One card was for Giordano. The other was for Curnin."

CHAPTER 16

TEN MINUTES AFTER Georgina Draper stepped down from the witness stand, Angelina and Raquel were alone in the women's bathroom on the floor where the trial was taking place. It was a public restroom. Any woman—reporter, observer, the future Government witnesses who were banished to the hallway while waiting their turn to testify—could be there so long as the Secret Service agents stationed at the bathroom's entrance let them pass. The room had three stalls. Angelina opened each of the stalls with heavy oak doors from another era, examining them. They were empty. The old bathroom, with chipped black-and-white tiles on the floor and an immovable translucent window, was in effect soundproof; it was a relic of a time when public buildings were like the Parthenon.

The Senator, an arm fully extended so that Raquel couldn't enter the stall whose toilet she so badly needed after three uninterrupted hours in the courtroom, blocked her lawyer's way.

"Do you realize," Angelina asked loudly, "how much you just fucked up?" Her expression was rigid and furious. "How much you just fucked *me* up?"

In her long and varied career, Raquel had represented the *capos* of the Lucchese and Genovese crime families, Latin drug lords, a member of the Harvard Board of Overseers accused of securities fraud, Willie Nelson when he faced apparently insurmountable tax evasion troubles, which Raquel had remarkably resolved, and even the bizarre but beguiling Oliver North at the start of her career when he was at the heart of the Iran–Contra trial in the long-ago era of the last years of the Reagan administration.

No client had ever spoken to her in the way Angelina Baldesteri now spoke.

Raquel said, "What the Christ are you talking about?"

"You don't listen to me. That prim little bitch Draper is a whore. She fucked President Spellman more times than you fucked pretty boy Hayes Smith."

"And how am I supposed to know about her and Spellman?"

"I wrote it on a piece of paper for you when you stood up to cross-examine her. I even underlined the words: *She fucks Spellman.* You ignored it. You ignored me. You had a perfect chance to destroy her. You didn't do it. Instead, *you* fucked *me.*"

Raquel, who was nearly six feet tall and had regained much of the inherent strength her breast cancer and horrific treatments had drained from her, easily pushed away the Senator's arm.

"Let me tell you a few things, Senator, just to make sure you get *it. First off,* nobody but nobody blocks my way when I want to go somewhere. Not a man, not a woman, not anybody. If you do it again, you'll get your arm broken.

"*Second,* I'm a lawyer. And that involves ethics. One of the things I need is what's called a *good faith* basis for asking a question. I can't ask her as a throwaway, Hail-Mary question if she killed JFK. Just because you scribble on a piece of paper the word *fuck* and the word *Spellman* does *not* give me a good faith basis for asking a question about whether she fucks Spellman. How, in any event, would I know if Spellman fucks anybody?"

Angelina, defiant and angry, now stood against one of the old marbled sinks, its original white texture bearing dozens of intricate fault lines from years of use. Angrily quiet, she glared at Raquel.

"*Third*," Raquel said, "we're bound at the hip for this trial. Even if you hated me as much as you seem to, or thought I was as incompetent as Goldie Hawn in a physics lab, Goldstein would never let me out of this and let you get another lawyer. It's gone too far. We are in too deep. If she bought any of your bullshit grievances, and she won't, her attitude would be *too little, too late*.

"*Fourth*, Senator, where were you when I needed you? I got the list of Government witnesses four weeks ago. Her name was on it but with no word as to who she was, where she worked, what she did, what she might testify to. I'm not a mind reader or a seer. I'm not clairvoyant. I had no idea who she was. You were too busy on one of your campaign 'listening' tours, whatever that means, to Iowa to even glance at the list. You said not one word that would give anyone any reason to know that she was one of Spellman's lovers if, in fact, she was."

Baldesteri finally said, "Maybe I haven't made as much of an impression on you as I should have. Maybe it's *you* who just doesn't get it. I have to win this trial and this election."

"All I can deal with is the trial. Your election, whether you get to be the first female president and lead us all to the Promised Land, is about as interesting to me as a rat's ass."

"That's totally irresponsible—"

"Save it for the television shows, Senator. And, by the way, don't ever mention the name *Hayes Smith* to me or anyone else . . ." She stared at Baldesteri. "You know, I never asked you, and you never volunteered to tell me, about Robert Calvaro and Hugo Salazar. Maybe, just maybe, you don't know who they really are. I do. Caliente and Suarez."

"Who? I never heard those names before this trial. So, lady, what do you know?"

"They're killers. They'll kill you if they decide to. It's a sport and a pastime for them. Let me give you a word of unsolicited advice. Whatever you're doing, whatever deals you may have with them, you are playing games with the most dangerous men in the world. What was it that Shakespeare said? *The gods kill us for their sport.*"

Just then the heavy twin doors to the bathroom opened and then closed, and Kimberly Newsom, the Fox newscaster who had attended every day of the trial, walked in, obviously not expecting to see Senator Angelina Baldesteri and Raquel Rematti there, and obviously, too, not having heard a word of their conversation.

Like consummate stage actresses, Raquel entered her stall and locked the door and, without skipping a beat, the Senator opened her purse and began applying lipstick at the hazy and time-tinged mirror above the sink.

Kimberly Newsom said, with the tone of a college-age sorority sister, "I didn't mean to intrude. I had no idea you were in here."

Angelina gave a welcoming, campaign-style smile to Kimberly as Kimberly looked into the same big, cracked mirror. The Senator said, "Just girl talk. Isn't that right, Raquel?"

Just before flushing the powerful toilet, Raquel said from the closed stall, "That's right, sweetie. Pure girl talk."

CHAPTER 17

THE BLACK MERCEDES SUV moved, almost noiselessly, through the sheets of rain on the glistening roadways inside JFK. Powerful halogen lamps on tall poles lit everything as if in a perpetual screen image, the silver rain descending through the artificial glare. It was late, two in the morning. In the almost deserted airport, the experienced driver sped with no hesitation to the KLM terminal in the international airlines row. In the back seat, Raquel Rematti, weary from a difficult trial day, held the left hand of Hayes Smith. Also weary, Hayes raised her hand to his lips as the empty KLM terminal drew closer. The only sound in the powerful Mercedes was the steady, rhythmic *rub-rub* of the windshield wipers.

Quietly Raquel expressed her concerns, as she had several times over the last two days after Hayes told her that his NBC producers had directed him to fly to the refugee camps in Lesbos where thousands of Syrian, Iraqi, and other migrants had gathered and were confined in detention camps so that he could make his twice-yearly broadcasts from the "field" rather than from the air-conditioned studio on the 18th floor of Rockefeller Center. "You're going to a dangerous place, Hayes. I'm afraid for you."

"This is part of the way I make my living, baby. Remember, I'm a journalist, not just a pretty boy cosseted in a studio five nights a week. These assignments give me credibility." An urbane man, he was laughing at the absurdity of his own words. "Besides, this is part of the reason I make the big bucks. They even had me bring the phony flak jacket they bought from the Beretta shop on Madison Avenue. It has pockets for my ammunition. Of course, I don't have ammunition and couldn't fire a BB gun."

Raquel, when seized by a thought, was never deterred. "There are hundreds of confused, trigger-happy Greek soldiers on Lesbos with no idea how to handle thousands of restless, fearful, angry Muslim migrants. You could get caught up in anything. Why couldn't they send you to Paris, Brussels, or Berlin instead to cover the hunt for the ISIS guys who shot up the cafes, bars, rock and soccer stadiums, and drove big trucks into vacationers in Europe?"

"That's old news, countless cycles ago. Besides, mine is not to reason why," he said, quoting Tennyson's "Charge of the Light Brigade" like the good Yalie he was, "mine is but to do and to die. If it makes you feel any better, the network has hired about ten guards, all former Marines, who used to work for Blackwater. They'll be inches away from me."

Raquel said, "Blackwater? Jesus, now that's the part that worries me most."

They both wanly smiled. As the SUV's door opened at the KLM terminal, they kissed. "Have a safe trip," she whispered.

"You be well," he said. "And go on kicking ass in that trial."

Those were the last words they ever spoke to each other. And the kiss was the last time they ever touched each other.

*   *   *

Raquel asked the NBC driver to take her to her apartment on Riverside Drive. She hadn't been there in more than three weeks.

Her relationship with Hayes had deepened, not suddenly or unexpectedly, but naturally over those last weeks. She had realized as she waved at him while he passed through the terminal's oversize revolving doors that she didn't want to be without him during any part of the next days in which he'd be gone. When was the last time, she wondered to herself as the Mercedes made its swift and practically solitary drive from the far regions of eastern Queens to Riverside Drive on the Hudson River, that the thought of not seeing the same man each day filled her with a sense that was close to deprivation, to a sensation of void?

Raquel had been married while in law school to a man who later became a famous movie producer. The marriage lasted fewer than two years; without rancor, she had simply avoided being in the same space or room with him and now, years later, remembered him only when at the start or close of a new movie his name appeared on the credits. She held no resentment, no anger, simply no real memory of him. Life and the passage of time change people: he was now bald and much heavier, almost unrecognizable to her on those few times she had glimpsed pictures of him in glossy magazines.

And, before Hayes came into her life and as her own fame grew, she had known other men, some famous, some not, all interesting in their own ways, who said they loved her. Nothing had lasted for more than a year, most for fewer than six months. They were all men whom she enjoyed but in whom she gradually—or sometimes suddenly—lost interest. With the advent of iPhones and computers, she found it easier just to "ghost" them, simply not answering when they continued to reach out to her until they stopped and disappeared. There was, she believed, no point in misleading them by even sending one-word responses.

Not one of them until Hayes was a man whom she wanted to see and be with every night. And, despite his deserved or undeserved reputation as a womanizer, he, too, wanted her with him all the time.

As the Mercedes pulled up under the green awning of her old-world West Side apartment building, she said, "Thanks so much for the drive, Nick. I'm sorry I took you out of your way."

"No problem, Ms. Rematti. This is what I do for a living. You and Hayes are beautiful people together, by the way, if you don't mind me saying so."

She smiled gratefully at him. Nick had been Hayes' driver for eight years. Instinctively, she wanted to believe Nick had never said that before to another woman, despite all of the opportunities Nick must have had to do that with all the other women who had traveled with Hayes and Nick as his loyal driver.

Through the revolving doors to her own building emerged Jose, the talkative and engaging Puerto Rican night porter, carrying a big open umbrella. It was three in the morning. He held the umbrella aloft over her as she stepped out of the car.

There was not another person on the sidewalk or on sinuous Riverside Drive. And there was no one visible in Riverside Park, that long, narrow, sublimely landscaped urban space dividing Riverside Drive from the majesty of the Hudson River.

In Spanish, Jose said, "God, Ms. Rematti, you work too late. You ask me, you need more free time. More fun."

Speaking in Spanish, she joked, "When this trial is over, I'll let you take me to a dance club, is that a deal?" It was impossible not to like him. He was a homely, vibrant little man.

"Best I ever heard of," he answered, laughing. He pressed the elevator button for her in the ornate lobby.

CHAPTER 18

As SOON AS she entered her apartment on the seventh floor, even before she turned on the light switch adjacent to the door, she knew something was altered, radically, about her home. In the living room, there was no overturned furniture, yet the sofa and chairs were all slightly out of the exact places they had long occupied. The curtains facing Riverside Park and the Hudson River were drawn closed, something she never did because she loved at all times the outside light that suffused her home, whether daylight or the night-time lights from the outdoor street lamps on Riverside Drive.

Raquel's body tingled with fear as a profoundly uncomfortable and rare wash of cold water coursed through her blood. She thought of fleeing the apartment and taking the elevator to the lobby to find Jose. Instead, Raquel, trembling, ran through all six rooms of her home, turning on light switches and shouting, pointlessly as she knew it was, "Where the fuck are you?"

There was no sound, no answer.

Some of the rooms were in greater disarray than the living room. The sheets, blankets, and pillows of her old bed—the only remaining relic of her long-ago marriage—were scattered over the floor.

She rushed to the kitchen and opened the freezer door. Groping among the stored ice cubes, she discovered what she intuitively knew. The twenty thousand dollars she always kept there, that secret reservoir of cash she stored in plastic baggies for emergencies and for reassurance, was missing. This wasn't a surprise to her. She had long known it was an obvious, almost useless hiding place that any common thief with enough time would find. She actually laughed out loud when her cold right hand quickly determined that the big internal ice reservoir contained only ice cubes.

Raquel was far more worried about the fate of the Ruger pistol she had bought not long after Theresa Bui was shot in Montauk. On her knees, she opened the kitchen cabinet doors below her gleaming sink. She leaned forward, her torso twisting without strain, and, palms upward and groping, found what she had hidden taped into the corrugated underside of the sink. The Ruger. Once she had stripped away the adhesive masking tape, she felt that surge of safety's reassurance pulse through every muscle of her body. Her sense of relief, of grabbing a rope attaching her to safety, only increased when within a foot of the unloaded pistol she reached out for the six magazines, also taped to the sink's underside, containing bullets that made the Ruger such a powerful weapon. Before Theresa was murdered, Raquel had never touched any kind of weapon. Indeed, the sight of assault weapons carried by soldiers in camouflage at airports after 9/11 made her uneasy and never reassured her.

And now, in the sickening disarray of her own home, she made a deliberate decision to carry it and several of the bullet-packed magazines everywhere. Her permit was a nationwide conceal-and-carry license that a friend in the Secret Service arranged for her after Theresa's death. The pistol and several of its bullet-filled magazines would fit easily into the large over-the-shoulder briefcase she always carried while on trial. It would only be in the courthouse that the pistol and magazines would have to be turned over to the U.S.

Marshals—many of whom she had known for years—who scanned everyone entering the building. Not one of the seasoned U.S. Marshals at the court's security entrance ever seemed fazed or surprised that she carried a pistol and ammunition. Indeed, they felt a kind of camaraderie with her, especially because of the rarity of a universal, carry-everywhere license. That impressed them.

In her violated apartment, at four in the morning, exhausted but fully alert, she began the long, but to her, essential process of putting her desecrated home back in order—a place where she would never feel safe again.

CHAPTER 19

HUNTER DECKER LOCKED the door marked *Juror Conference Room: Private*. Almost deferentially, he said, "Sit down, Raquel. Make yourself as comfortable as you can. These rooms were never made for ease and that sense of coziness, you know. I think the idea was to force jurors to work quickly and get their jobs done. If you make them feel as though they're in their living rooms, they want to stay."

"If you think this is bad," Raquel answered, "try a case across the street in state court. The juror rooms there are medieval."

Raquel was tired from the rigorous day in the courtroom, dismayed that Decker had fully reached his stride with a dozen witnesses, all of them financial forensics experts, who testified in rapid succession about many millions of undisclosed, unreported waves of cash and checks that had made their way into Angelina Baldesteri's multiple campaign accounts and safe deposit boxes without being reported to anyone.

Most of all, Raquel couldn't overcome the visceral dislike that continued to grow in her for the Senator. That day's testimony, like much of the other testimony and documents in the case, made it increasingly clear that Baldesteri had lied to Raquel every step of the way. For weeks they had sat fewer than two feet from each other at the defense table. There was never a time when any one of the hundreds of often sleazy, often vicious, often charming men and women Raquel represented through the years made her feel this queasy and repelled.

Now Raquel and Decker were the only people in the locked room. They had been together with many others at working sessions before the trial but they had never been alone with each other.

Raquel's mood was somber and irritable. Without veiling her annoyance at the day's accumulation of events, she said, "You didn't call me in here, did you, Hunter, to tell me how great your day was?"

"I'd never do that, Raquel. I'm not a baseball fan, but you win some innings and lose some. Today I won the inning. You've won other innings."

"I'll bet," she said, suddenly almost with charm, "you're a squash player. You never went to a baseball game in your life."

"Is it that obvious? Yes, I've played squash since age eight."

"I didn't know what a game of squash was until I went to college at seventeen. And then I thought it was a rare vegetable you tossed around like a Frisbee."

Were they flirting with each other? With a deliberate effort, Raquel, suddenly businesslike, said, "What do you want?"

"Not a deal. I want your client, as I've always told you, in jail and out of office. Nothing's changed on that. It's the only deal."

"Good. Simplicity itself. No deal. She said that months ago, as I told you." She waited. "So, now that we've cleared the air on that again, I need to get back to my office."

"I had no intention of interfering with your time."

"I'm tired, Hunter. Tell me what you really want to tell me."

"It is, as they say, complicated."

Raquel ever so slightly raised her face, expecting more information while saying nothing.

"We think your life is in danger."

She continued to stare at him. Her face was impassive.

He said, "That man in the picture which is one of the exhibits, the man talking so engagingly with the Senator who has her arm over the shoulder of Robert Calvaro, is Juan Suarez, or Anibal Vaz, or whoever. The man you represented so successfully a few years ago. *The Blade of the Hamptons*, as the *Daily News* and the *Post* and every other paper and TV network in the world called him."

Raquel didn't respond.

Hunter continued, "Now he's back. Some plastic surgery, different hair. He made the mistake not long ago of tossing espresso cups into wastebaskets on the street. We picked up the cups. The DNA match is perfect. He has a new name. Or perhaps it was his original name: Hugo Salazar."

Raquel in many ways had the ethics of an old-fashioned lawyer: when she was given secrets and information by clients, she kept them. It was a client, Juan Suarez, who had told her that Oscar Caliente wanted her dead because, during the trial of *The Blade of the Hamptons*, she had revealed Caliente's identity and his role of ruthlessly seizing all of the drug trafficking in all five boroughs of New York City and had been then given the same task of dominating the cartel for all the drug-traffic in the rich and drug-hungry Hamptons. She also knew, from Juan Suarez, that Oscar Caliente had given the order to a sharpshooter to kill her at her seaside run-down house in Montauk; it was that bullet, meant for Raquel, that had killed Theresa Bui.

And Raquel knew that Oscar Caliente, a driven, single-minded lunatic who never wavered from orders he gave, hadn't lifted the edict that she must die. She kept that a secret, too, because Juan Suarez, in the last conversation they had in the federal prison overlooking the Brooklyn waterfront on the day before he was deported, told her that. It was a *fatwa*, an order that would never be revoked. The sharpshooter in the dunes who, through sheer mistake, had killed Theresa, had never been found. He still was in the world. Or someone just like him or her was.

"How do you know that?" Raquel asked Hunter.

"Wiretaps."

"Who is speaking on the tapes?"

"I can't tell you that, you know that. We think we know who they are."

"Let me listen to the tapes."

"I wish we could. But we can't."

"Why don't you arrest them? If you have wiretaps, you know who they are."

"The taps by themselves don't give us enough information to arrest them." He stopped. He had the quiet sophistication of a New England prep school headmaster. "Now if you were a federal judge, a federal agent, or a federal lawyer, we could detain them on the basis of the inconclusive talk on the wiretaps. There is such a thing as the freedom of speech. These people are talking about *taking you out*, which could mean an invitation to dinner. But we're not naïve. We do know who the people are. They're talking about killing you. No, they haven't used that word and there is nothing about specific plans, nothing about *where*, *when*, or *how*."

"Then why are you telling me this? To knock me off my stride?"

"We can offer you a deal to save your life. They may be stupid, but they seem to have it in their sick little heads that Caliente thinks that if you are taken out, Goldstein will declare a mistrial, there won't be a retrial, and Baldesteri can put this all behind her and that will open the path for her to become President. Caliente apparently has it in his mind that with her as President, some of the pressure on him will be alleviated."

"That's all magical thinking," Raquel said.

"Maybe," Decker answered. "But I think—*we* think—a deal for you makes sense."

"A deal? *For me?* Why would I need a deal?"

"We know from several sources that Lydia Guzman is being bribed not to convict."

"What does that have to do with me?" Raquel asked.

"The sources say you know it and are facilitating it. Meaning, of course, the bribery."

"That's a lie," Raquel said, her clenched fist striking the plastic table. "You could even be making it up. Prosecutors, with impunity, can make up lies out of thin air."

"I'd never do that."

"Then your *informants*, whoever the idiots may be, are lying to you."

"I don't think so."

"And bribery of a juror? Get real."

"Do you want our help?"

"I don't want it."

He said, "As you wish."

"Any other bullshit you want to tell me, Mr. Decker?"

Again, she waited. She was always a listener. Hunter said, "Hugo Salazar is still as seductive as ever. After all, he got *you* under his spell even when he was in jail. Now that he's free, he has wined and dined and bedded the juror. He has also arranged to give her—Lydia Guzman—cash and all the cocaine she needs to feed her addiction."

"What a surprise. Dogs keep company with dogs."

"But there's more, Raquel. Some of our investigators believe you are the conduit for the money."

"You must be on some illegal substance yourself, Mr. Decker. Anyone would be out of his gourd even thinking I'm a bagman or would help a bagman. Do you believe for one second that I'd risk throwing away a thirty-year career on anything, especially as stupid as paying off a juror?"

"Do you want to hear the terms of the deal we have for you?"

"No."

Hunter Decker ignored her answer. "You give us cooperation by telling us what Baldesteri has told you. You of all people know how cooperation works. If your cooperation is complete, truthful, and of use to us, we will let you plead guilty to one count of obstruction of justice, not bribery, a far more serious offense, and we'll recommend a sentence of probation for you. Of course, you'll be disbarred."

"I wish I had a tape recording of this garbage," she said, utterly exasperated and angry.

"You're making a mistake, Ms. Rematti."

"It wouldn't be the first time," she said. "Nor will it be the last."

"And you made another mistake," Hunter Decker said.

"Which of many?"

"You *loved* Juan Suarez."

"You basically said that garbage just a second ago. It's horseshit, Mr. Decker."

"Hugo Salazar, *The Blade of the Hamptons*, was in prison for a long time during your Richardson trial. There's no privacy in prison, Raquel. There are guards, surveillance equipment, rumors, talk. Prisoners love to talk."

"Let me follow this. Juan Suarez was scapegoated as a killer of one of the richest men in the world precisely because he was an outsider, an illegal alien. I defended him. Free of charge, by the way. Once his conviction was tossed out, he was deported. Miracle of miracles, he may have found his way back to the United States. I never imagined I'd see him or anyone like him again until you put up a picture on a big screen at this trial. In that picture a Latin man with a ponytail is talking or appears to be talking to my client. I'm not sure who the man is who is talking to the Senator. I'm not sure, in other words, that it is the man I saved. And because of that picture of a man whom I don't really recognize, you not only think I *love* him but I'm a bagman for an airhead cocaine addict like Lydia Guzman because *you* didn't have brains enough to keep her off the jury."

"My, look at you," Decker said. "Look at how excessively upset you are."

Raquel pushed her chair back and stood. "Can it be that you are as stupid as your dumbass investigators are?"

Hunter Decker, as a seventeen-year-old incoming prep school kid at Choate, had been taught that men never reacted to insults or taunts except by responding in a patient way, as if to help the other person to learn the virtues of self-control. "You shouldn't be so provocative, Ms. Rematti."

"Let me tell you what I mean, because there is a charming candy-ass element in your personality. For good and sufficient reason, at least in his fluid mind, some not-so-nice man wants Angelina to be President. Think hard about this. If something happens to me, Naomi will call a mistrial. It doesn't mean Baldesteri is acquitted. If somebody shoots me, there will also be a retrial."

Still standing, she said, "You think all the risk is on me. It's on you. If there's a mistrial for any reason, such as my having a heart attack or sleeping with the judge, *you* will have to handle the next trial. Unfortunately, for many reasons, *you* and you alone hold all the cards. But if, in fact, there are not-so-nice men out there, men who didn't learn their manners at Choate or Groton, then they will figure out that without *you* there will never be a realistic chance of winning a retrial, or even of having one."

"Are you threatening me? I am the United States Attorney, don't forget that."

Raquel said, "You've had a charmed life, Mr. Decker, by anyone's standards. The men you say who want to take me out are the ultimate egalitarians. They kill people with charmed or derelict lives—they are equal-opportunity murderers."

As he watched Raquel move to the closed door, Hunter Decker calmly said, "I think I failed to mention the pictures we have of you and Salazar and Lydia Guzman. All together. At a party. Just a week ago."

"Shove the pictures up your ass or arrest me."

CHAPTER 20

HAYES SMITH WAS a man who never displayed a great deal of emotion, except recently for his loving attachment to Raquel Rematti. But as the helicopter crossed the blue Mediterranean—why had Homer centuries ago called it the "wine dark sea"?—and approached the ancient island of Lesbos, he was astounded. He had never had to develop the experienced, seasoned journalist's skill of accurately estimating the numbers of people in a crowd, whether it was a demonstration, a football game, a presidential inauguration, or an immense gathering of men and women standing at a concert of the Grateful Dead.

From two thousand feet above ground, as the helicopter pivoted in dazzling sunlight and sky in search of one of the three landing zones on the sterile island, Hayes saw a scene he had only previously witnessed in broadcasts and pictures of refugee camps—thousands upon thousands of densely packed people occupying every inch of miles of land. It was almost biblical, he thought, like the ancient Jews gathered on the shore of the Nile, waiting for Moses to part the waters.

Yet there was nothing biblical about the world Hayes encountered when he stepped out of the air-conditioned helicopter, its rotors still swirling above him and driving down an intense, steady stream of air as hot as a furnace. As soon as he moved out of the conical range of the rotor's downward rush of wind, the world changed. The first difference was the overwhelming stench emanating from thousands of people who had been gathered densely together for months. They lived among steadily accumulating, never-cleaned human debris—emptied cans, tampons, soiled diapers, abandoned and decaying clothes. And, above all, human waste—shit, urine, menstrual blood, vomit. The few portable latrines had long ago been filled to overflowing and were now useless; many of them were knocked over, oozing their contents.

It was obvious, too, that most of the thousands of Syrians, Iraqis, Afghans, and others slept on soiled blankets, sheets, and rugs. During the day, innumerable men, women, and children simply stood, squatted, lay down, moved as much as they could—essentially the inactivity of masses of people, stricken by sunlight and dust, with no end date in sight and nothing to do. Smoky fires burned in empty oil barrels.

Like all the other helicopters arriving at Lesbos, Hayes' helicopter had touched ground in a cordoned-off landing zone. Armed Greek soldiers stood at intervals of five feet in the heat along the ropes and yellow tape that defined the landing zones. Hayes waited, in awe and fear, as his team of producers, camera crews, writers, and the ubiquitous caterers stepped out of the helicopter. Loosely assembled around Hayes were his guards, all military veterans who had once worked for the defunct Blackwater mercenary organization. One was a woman; she had the hard-bitten expression of an Ozark waitress, but she was big, lissome, powerful. The guards were large men in civilian clothes; most had blond, buzzed crewcuts. Some of the crew cuts had zigzag areas cut down to the scalp two inches above the men's left ears. Hayes had no idea what the "Z" markings symbolized. All of the guards, including the woman, carried heavy black pistols.

Waves of migrants moved toward the helicopter, just as they did toward every helicopter that landed in the cordoned-off zone. Since food and other supplies all came in helicopters, Hayes' helicopter could have carried relief supplies rather than reporters. The Greek soldiers lining the perimeter became visibly more tense and attentive. No one from the masses of refugees breached the perimeter, which consisted of chain-link fences mounted by razor wire. Word seemed to pass quickly among the refugees that Hayes' helicopter carried only reporters. The refugees had long ago lost interest in reporters: they came, they filmed, and they soon left, and they never brought food or water. They never made a difference. They might as well have been demented tourists.

* * *

Just three hours later, in the unbelievably hot midafternoon, Hayes' crew was filming him as he stood near the perimeter's chain-link razor-wire fences. Just to his left, with their backs turned to him, were several of the Greek soldiers facing the crowd. The soldiers all wore surgical masks, obviously in an effort to filter out at least some of the stench of human waste and unwashed bodies that intensified in the escalating heat of the afternoon. Hayes had gagged many times, but believed that by now he could get through the taping without wearing a mask or choking on the stench.

Dressed in the khakis and the phony safari-style gear NBC had purchased for him at the Beretta store on Madison Avenue, Hayes faced the cameras. Behind him in the television frame were not only the Greek soldiers but a view of the thousands of dour imprisoned men and women, many with their fingers gripping the small rectangular chinks in the fence.

For an hour, Hayes, his writers, and his producers had worked out the substance of what he would broadcast. They wrote at first on traditional, small, wire-edged reporters' notebooks. Then they compared notes before deciding on the essence of what Hayes would say. Once that hour-long work conference ended, an old-fashioned set of three blackboards came out of one of the equipment bags. On the blackboards his crew wrote out not a script but a series of key points to display, out of sight of the cameras, to keep Hayes' broadcast on track. He was a smart man, spontaneous, able to talk seamlessly, but in a place like this and a time like this, he didn't want to speak completely extemporaneously. He needed what were in effect large cue cards.

During the time Hayes and his crew were working, they didn't notice the ominous escalation of the noise of voices, even chants, in the masses of migrants and refugees. But the Greek guards had noticed, slightly raising the slant of their black assault rifles.

So, too, the ten private guards accompanying Hayes and the members of his crew became more concentrated and vigilant, gradually drawing closer to him. The guards were all grim. Hayes had taken his broadcast position at a slight elevation, with his back to the masses. The chants from the refugees continued to rise rapidly, almost the sound of crowds at a wild soccer match.

Even though he sensed the dangerous shift in sound and mood, Hayes calmly continued to follow the careful, telegraphic cues on the row of blackboards. Later, members of his crew, as well as other journalists and broadcasters around the world, commented on how he "kept his cool" as the din of voices rose dramatically and violently together with the mounting sound of sporadic gunfire. Even when five or six oil barrels in the camp exploded like unexpected fireworks, he continued the broadcast, turning almost casually to the places where the barrels flew to pieces in enflamed fragments.

Hayes did go to his knees when the tense Greek soldiers, reinforced by dozens of others he had not seen before, began a steady fusillade of shooting over the crowd. Hayes, standing and still being filmed, said, "The Greeks are obviously trying to control the sudden unrest by firing, apparently randomly, into the air above the crowds."

At that moment, a young Greek soldier staggered backward, dropping his rifle, and falling. All of his dying movements from the moment of impact were recorded in the scene behind Hayes. The bullet that killed him came from some place, some utterly unidentifiable place, in the masses of people in the internment camp. Almost immediately, dozens of other Greek soldiers at the perimeter went either to their knees in military firing position or to their chests and stomachs, also in firing position.

Although he had never been in a war zone—had never heard shots fired or bombs exploding—Hayes spoke calmly into the two cameras that continued to record him. He was nervous but not visibly so. The cameramen showed no apparent fear: they had been filming battles in the midst of weapons fire since the Balkan Wars in the 1990s. In contrast, Hayes' writers and producers, most of them in their twenties and thirties, were on the ground, gripping the dry earth; this was all new to them, and it was terrifying. One of them, a young man, was crying, a wail.

Hayes' security guards formed circles around him. Each of them was on one knee, balancing weapons in combat-style positions, scanning everything around them. They all had TEC-DC9 automatic pistols. They were the weapons of choice for these people; the exotic guns were overpowering, utterly reliable, and rare. Closest to Hayes was the only woman guard.

In an instant—an instant captured vividly by the cameras—a black hole in Hayes' right temple opened as he stopped speaking in mid-sentence. Blood spurted upward out of his head like an obscene surge of water from a pierced bag. He collapsed to his side, making no sound. Two of the crew-cut guards turned him over. One pressed on his chest. The other put his mouth to Hayes' mouth, blowing his breath into Hayes' open mouth before sucking his own breath back and wiping away with the back of his hand the drool and blood he had just extracted from Hayes' mouth. The guard was well trained for this. Just above his left ear, vaguely visible as one of the cameras drew closer and closer, was his "Z" mark. After a minute, his effort stopped.

One of the men could be heard saying, "Forget it, the fucker's wasted."

Hayes was dead. Every second of the killing was on film. The cameramen never flinched. They turned off their cameras only after dwelling for ten further seconds on one of the most familiar faces in the world.

CHAPTER 21

IT WAS SIX in the morning when the iPhone on the nightstand next to Hayes' bed vibrated, a throbbing loud enough almost to shake the bed's iron frame. After the two hours of effort she spent putting her apartment into a semblance of its usual order, she decided she would be far more comfortable in the familiar environs of Hayes' apartment on Central Park South even in his absence on Lesbos. She had arrived in a taxi well before dawn; it was still black night. She hoped she could rest because, for some unexplained reason, Naomi Goldstein had announced at the end of the Wednesday session that the trial was adjourned for Thursday and would resume on Friday. Raquel didn't care what the reason was. As a federal judge, Naomi Goldstein had complete control of her schedule and by extension of the schedule of everyone else in the courtroom. It often struck Raquel as the irrational, arbitrary power of ancient royalty or of modern-day dictators.

Aroused from her sleep, Raquel groped for her cell phone and immediately saw on the screen not a person's name or telephone number but the letters *CBS*. This meant to her that the network, which had her under a loosely defined contract to provide commentary on cases during the morning shows, must have learned that she had the day off from the Senator Angelina Baldesteri trial and wanted her in the studio to give live commentary on some other high-profile, ongoing case. Although focused on her own trial, she knew, for example, that in Oregon, a jury the day before had announced the acquittal of a white supremacist accused of killing an FBI agent. In an hour she could be dressed, driven to CBS's studio, given a briefing by a producer while she was in the makeup room, and then ushered into the studio for a live interview. Raquel made no secret to herself that she loved to be called suddenly and frequently for these cameo appearances. They brightened her day.

Yet, on this morning, she was too exhausted and too unsettled by the ransacking of her home to want to make any appearance on television. She pressed the *Decline* frame on the iPhone screen, not even wanting to talk with one of the pleasant booker-producers. CBS had a reservoir of at least five other celebrity lawyers to call on.

Fewer than ten seconds later, as she was struggling with the vexing issue of whether to go to the bathroom or just roll over and let sleep overtake her if it could, the cell phone vibrated again. What she saw on the caller box were the letters *CNN*. This time she touched the *Accept* frame on the screen because CNN usually scheduled her for late afternoon or early evening appearances.

"Is this Raquel Rematti?" It was a male voice that she didn't recognize. Ordinarily the bookers' and producers' voices were as familiar to her as those of friends; most of the bookers were young women.

"It is," she said. Her voice was soft. "Who is this?"

"Norman Van Zandt."

She recognized the name. They had briefly been introduced three months before when she was a guest commentator on Anderson Cooper's show and Van Zandt was a young and newly hired reporter from a station in Chicago. He was a big, self-confident man, a rising star in national broadcasting.

"I'm sorry for your loss," Van Zandt said.

What loss? Raquel wondered. Exhausted and bewildered, she thought only that she had at that time six other cases on appeal awaiting decisions and that she hadn't been aware that she had lost one of the appeals.

"Loss," she repeated groggily. "What loss?" In her sleep-impaired state of mind, the words *Sorry for your loss* were a trite expression of phoniness, one that could encompass the death of a pet gerbil or a venomous one-hundred-year-old grandmother.

"Hayes," he answered, after hesitating. "Hayes Smith."

She sat up in the bed, crossing her legs under her. "I don't know what you're talking about." But Raquel innately knew, in every tingling cell of her body, that Hayes was dead. He was the "loss."

In the several months Van Zandt had spent at CNN, he had picked up a reputation as a person who was cold, hardworking, and ambitious. Yet his voice now was surprisingly quiet and respectful. "I'm so sorry, Ms. Rematti. I just assumed you already knew that Hayes Smith was killed an hour or two ago on Lesbos. I never would have wanted to be the first to tell you."

She took several shallow breaths, as though she were about to drown and gasping for air. "What happened?"

"Mr. Smith was recording a segment near a huge refugee encampment on the island. I was there, on Lesbos, last week. It was scary. The Greek Army has no idea what to do. The island is almost overwhelmed. New refugees land every day."

"But what happened to Hayes?"

"I'm not sure, Ms. Rematti, that I should be the one to tell you."

"Tell me."

"The video has gone viral, as they say. It shows that, just as he was taping a broadcast, gunfire rang out. You can all of a sudden hear it on the tape as he's speaking into the camera. The shots first came

from the refugee camp, and it's not clear who the targets were. The
Greek soldiers started scattering warning shots in the air above
the crowds. All of this is on the tape, Ms. Rematti. The screen position where Hayes stood was wide and panoramic. You can see the
Greeks begin to lose control behind him. Some old oil barrels in
the camp explode. One of the Greek soldiers is killed, possibly even
by friendly fire. The whole act of his dying is on the film behind
Hayes. Chaos.

"The cameramen in Hayes' crew are combat veterans. They kept
filming steadily. Hayes gets on his knees, still facing the cameras. In
the meantime, all hell is breaking loose, but Hayes, incredibly
calmly, keeps broadcasting."

"What else?"

"Honestly, Ms. Rematti, I'm really uncomfortable to be the one
to tell you all this." He hesitated, sounding genuinely anxious,
almost like a small boy withholding a big secret. "It's all over the
news. It's on YouTube, Instagram, Facebook, all those instant social
media devices. Maybe you can see it for yourself."

"What happened?" she insisted.

"A bullet hit him in the temple. The cameramen kept filming.
Two big American guys tried CPR. There was no way to save him."
He paused again. "I'm so sorry."

"He had ten former Blackwater guards with him. Where were
they?"

"That's news to me. I've watched the whole awful tape many
times. The two big blond guys who did the CPR looked like they
might once have been Navy SEALS or Army Special Forces people.
They knew what they were doing. They certainly were not members
of any kind of broadcast crew I ever saw."

"I appreciate your telling me all this." It was difficult for Raquel
to control her tears. "How does the tape end?"

"That's a bridge too far for me, Ms. Rematti. The camera crew, those unflinching guys, kept filming for at least another ten, fifteen seconds."

"What were they filming?"

"Not the chaos or battle or the refugee camp or the confused, stumble-down Greek soldiers."

"So they were filming Hayes' body as he bled to death?"

"They were."

"You people are in an awful business."

Quietly, in an effort to soothe her, he said, "I know."

"It's not your fault," she said. "But please, Norman, just say I had no comment."

"Agreed, agreed," he answered.

The call ended. She fell backward onto the bed, the place where they had so often in the past made love and laughed, watched television, and read books. Nothing in the world could have stopped her wailing cry.

* * *

More sleep, Raquel knew, was impossible despite her exhaustion and crying.

On a nightstand next to his bed, Hayes had one of those relics from what seemed like an antique era, a bulky answering machine connected by a wire to an old-fashioned landline. She noticed that the answering machine's small red dot was blinking. It was the only time in all the months she had lived there that a message had been left on the answering machine. She pressed the play button.

And there, in all of its richness and understated wryness, was Hayes' voice, preserved during the last three hours of his life. "Hey, baby, your cell must be dead or locked up with the guards at the courthouse. Hope you get this message. We just landed in Athens. The powers that be at the network must want instantaneous service since there's a helicopter for my writers and producers and crew and guards waiting for us. We don't even get to go into the terminal, much less visit the Parthenon. It's straight to the copter. Lesbos is not far from here. Orders are that we start broadcasting as soon as we can. Which is great, really. A quick in and a quick out." He laughed. "That means I get back on your beautiful ass very soon. Enough for now. These old tapes run out quickly. As Edward R. Murrow used to say, 'Good night and good luck.'"

She rewound the tape and replayed it three times, worried each time that she would hit the nearby delete button.

She popped the old fashioned microcassette tape out of the bulky answering machine, wondering if she would even be able to find an old device on which to play the tape in the future. But, as word on the street had it, you could find anything in New York.

The tape was, she realized, the only memento she would ever have of him and that loving phase of her life, now over forever.

CHAPTER 22

EVERYONE IN THE world knew Hayes Smith, or so it seemed to Raquel, and everyone also seemed to know that she and Hayes had been with each other as lovers for months. Her office phone was flooded with messages from reporters. The inbox of her iPhone was far beyond its capacity. But instead of returning calls—she returned none—her main obsession was to gather up the things, mainly clothes and shoes and books—that had gradually migrated from her apartment to his. One of the porters in Hayes' building had a small van in the underground garage. Quickly and for one thousand in cash to pay him and another off-duty porter as their shift ended, she gathered up her belongings—dresses, slacks, and jackets on hangers, books, and her shoes and other loose objects, all traces of herself—in black plastic bags, and within three hours had them all transported to her apartment on Riverside Drive. Just as she at last stood at the door to Hayes' light-filled apartment, knowing that it would be the last time she saw it, Raquel said, aloud to herself, "Why did you leave me, Hayes? I loved you so much."

No one heard her.

Reporters waiting for her thronged both the sidewalk in front of the lobby to Hayes' building on Central Park South and the sidewalk in front of her building's lobby on Riverside Drive. She ignored all of them. What in the world, other than complete inanities, could she possibly say to them? Her private life was for her and her alone.

Once she settled in her home after the porters delivered all of her clothes and shoes, she opened her iPhone's inbox. There were text messages, she knew, that she would have to return.

At least ten emails were from "Senatorangelina@usgov.gov." The insistent emails and texts from Baldesteri were all peremptory and essentially the same: "We must meet today, call me."

Not a word of sympathy, regret, compassion.

Finally, Raquel emailed: "Will be at my office at five."

*　*　*

In the reception area of Raquel's office were the four or five young men and women who followed Senator Baldesteri wherever she went. Each of them carried laptop computers and other electronic devices. To Raquel, they all gave the impression of characters from the *Star Trek* movies: people dressed in the same style, all wedded to the same devices. Some even wore outdated heavy black-framed glasses.

As Raquel hurried through her own reception area, a timid female voice spoke out: "We're so sorry, Ms. Rematti."

Raquel smiled in gratitude.

When she opened the door to her big inner office, Raquel saw Angelina turn sharply toward her. The Senator had been standing impatiently at the office window, gazing at the traffic flowing uptown and downtown on Park Avenue, divided by the straight median strip of flowers and ornamental trees that ran in well-tended rows from 44th Street to 96th Street.

"I hope," the Senator said as soon as Raquel firmly closed the door behind her, "that this does not mean you'll ask for a mistrial."

"The thought never crossed my mind," Raquel answered, "until just this second."

"Would the judge do it on her own?"

"Not in a million years. That's not the way the system works. Judges react, particularly during trials. A lawyer needs to ask for something. Judges respond to initiatives."

"Would Decker ask for a mistrial?"

"Not a chance." Raquel stared coldly at her. "Where, Angelina, are these thoughts coming from?"

"Where? Everybody knows Hayes Smith. And everybody knows you were his—what can I call this—his *partner*."

"Only people who read the gossip pages of the *Post* and the *Daily News*. I don't think those are on her everyday reading list."

The Senator said, "A mistrial would be a disaster, as I've said before."

"Listen to me, Angelina. I said there would be no mistrial. He wasn't my husband. He wasn't the President of the United States. He was a journalist. He was killed in the line of duty. I can't even be sure that old Naomi Goldstein knows who he was. And she certainly is not likely to know I was in love with him. Anyhow, judges don't call mistrials because a lawyer's lover dies. In fact, I'll be amazed if she lets me take an afternoon off for his funeral service."

"I have to get this trial finished. If she called a mistrial, I could end up on trial in the middle of my campaign."

Still standing, Raquel folded her arms. "So that's what you're thinking? That's it? That's your universe? You are a nasty piece of work, Angelina."

"What did you just say?"

"You're a nasty piece of work." She stopped speaking as she felt her muscles shake with the onslaught of rage. "Do I need to repeat it?"

"No, but maybe you can explain it."

"Sure. You know a man I loved was killed. You haven't even expressed a sympathetic word."

"A man I loved, too, was killed, Ms. Rematti. And that man happened to be the President of the United States. And my husband."

"And you were the noble, stoic widow. The cool Jackie Kennedy of the twenty-first century, weren't you?"

"What's your problem, Ms. Rematti? Are you losing your nerve?"

"No, I'm losing my patience. I don't trust you."

"And what do you mean by that?"

"You've never told me that you know who Robert Calvaro really is or why he has such a connection to you that you find so deep."

"Robert Calvaro is Robert Calvaro."

"Or that you know who Hugo Salazar is."

"What is this? Hugo Salazar is Hugo Salazar. He works for Robert Calvaro. Anyhow, we've had this conversation."

"They aren't who you think they are. You are not telling me the truth about what you know. You're playing a dangerous game, Senator. Do men like this appeal to you?"

"What can that possibly mean? Let's not get unhinged."

"Stop playing games with me, Senator. Calvaro and Salazar aren't apparitions who just appeared out of nowhere, South American oilmen with the power to direct unimaginable, untraceable money into super PACs that happen to believe you are the most desirable lady in all the land. They're men who want you to be President because then you control the attention, or more precisely, the actions of the DEA, the FBI, the Border Patrols, the IRS. The quid, the pro, and the quo. And you know they would have no problem fabricating a background more credible than Pope Francis."

"You know what? I don't think you really know who I am. You've been deranged by the last twenty-four hours. Or maybe the trial is too much for you; maybe you're out of your depth. But you listen to me: I'm a United States Senator. I was the First Lady of the United States. I lost a husband to a terrorist bomber. That husband was the most popular President since Reagan. You are not my equal, not by any conceivable stretch of the imagination."

"I know that I'm a hired plumber here to fix a leak in your mansion."

"I'm not here to share grief counseling about lost husbands and lovers with you. Or about plumbing. This is not a sisterhood that we have. You are my hired servant. I'm here because I want to know how strong you are, how firm, how much of a ball-buster. It's my life and my reputation that are at stake here. My future. My legacy. I need to save myself. You need to save me. You, in fact, need to do anything and everything to protect me. So, to be blunt, you—the legendary Raquel Rematti—don't matter. I do."

Raquel asked, "Who is Lydia Guzman?"

Despite all the icy fury she felt, Angelina was taken aback by the question. "What? A pole dancer? A Miami pop singer?"

"She's a juror."

"Great. I do well with Latina voters."

"Let me tell you something. Hunter Decker and the FBI believe Lydia Guzman is being paid a bribe to vote for your acquittal."

"Really. Best news I've heard in some time."

Raquel's voice was controlled, sibilant and angry. "I need answers. I think you have the answers, but don't want to tell the truth. Is she being bribed?"

"*Omertà*," Angelina coldly said. "It was you who taught me about *omertà*."

And, gathering her scarf and handbag, the Senator left Raquel's office, to which she never returned.

CHAPTER 23

EVEN THOUGH RAQUEL Rematti was bold, assertive when necessary, and rarely fazed by anyone, she was impressed by Lydia Guzman. A genuinely exotic woman, Lydia was escorted by three beefy and bland U.S. Marshals into Naomi Goldstein's grand private chambers. It struck Raquel that Lydia, a hair stylist, had probably never been in a room like this in her life, yet she strolled in with the same relaxed attitude she probably used when she entered the salon where she worked in the Bronx.

Certainly, as Raquel intuitively knew, Lydia Guzman had never been suddenly plucked from a crowd of people—the other jurors—and brought into a closed room and asked to sit down among people like the paper-dry old federal judge, Hunter Decker, Raquel, Angelina Baldesteri, three anonymous young law clerks, and several men in nondescript, inexpensive suits standing along the wall.

And yet Lydia showed no sign of confusion or concern. If anything, Raquel thought, Lydia's face conveyed a "what-the-fuck-are-you-bothering-me-for" demeanor that Raquel, raised in that tough, working-class neighborhood in grimy Lawrence, Massachusetts, quietly and defiantly admired.

Once the room was completely silent, Naomi Goldstein, not wearing her judge's robe, said, "Good morning, Ms. Guzman. Thanks for seeing us."

Lydia simply raised her chin, waiting. No reciprocated greeting, no "Good morning," no "Yes, Your Honor," no words at all.

"Ms. Guzman, my only real work here is to ensure that the defendant, Ms. Baldesteri, has a fair trial. I have no views about guilt or innocence, or anything else. No stake in the outcome. Do you understand?"

"What's not to understand?" As if exasperated, Lydia repeated the same words in Spanish.

The bewildered court reporter glanced at the judge. "I didn't get those last words, Your Honor. I don't understand Spanish, if that's what it was."

Goldstein waved her heavily veined hand at the court reporter, saying to him, "No need to ask for a translation, Mr. Shaw. Ms. Guzman simply repeated what she had just said in English, isn't that right, Ms. Guzman?"

"I guess."

"Use English from now on, Ms. Guzman," Goldstein said. "You don't need an interpreter, do you?"

"An interpreter? Don't disrespect me. I still don't know why I'm here. Tell me. And in English."

"At the beginning and end of each day's testimony," Goldstein said, herself unfazed by this unintimidated woman, "I remind everyone on the jury to keep an open mind only on the evidence they hear and see in the trial and not to be subject to any outside influences, such as newspaper, television, iPhones, Twitter. None of those."

Lydia said, "How many times have I heard you say that? Fifty?"

"And I know you understand. However, it's been brought to my attention that, from time to time, you've come into contact with a man whose face has appeared in at least one of the trial exhibits. In one of the pictures, the man is speaking to Ms. Baldesteri."

"I've seen lots of pictures at this trial. And I know lots of men. I go out dancing almost every night."

"At this point I'm not concerned with casual contact with other dancers, Ms. Guzman. Some of the men you see along the wall are FBI agents. They have pictures of you entering and leaving this particular man's apartment."

"Wow, you know, sweet Jesus, I thought this was a free country. These goons must have lots of pictures of me entering and leaving men's apartments. Are you joking? What kind of job do these guys have, following me around and taking pictures? It's like sick, you know. Snooping. Sick stuff. What do you call it—stalking? And *you* knew about this?"

"Have any of these men you've seen given you any money?"

"Say that again?"

"You heard me, Ms. Guzman."

Lydia was plainly angry, utterly undaunted by this old federal judge. "Men don't give me money. Ever. Unless I color their hair at the salon. I work for any money I get."

"Has any woman given you money during this trial?"

"Women pay me, like men do, when I work at the salon." She glared at the judge. "How much of this *mierde* do I have to listen to?"

Goldstein was impassive. "Let me show you a picture, Ms. Guzman," Goldstein said, handing a glossy photograph to one of her young law clerks, who stood up and put it in front of Lydia. She didn't even glance at it.

Goldstein folded her hands. If she were angry or impatient, she didn't show it. "I have to ask you to look at that picture, Ms. Guzman. That's why I had it put there."

Lydia glanced down. "So," she said, almost instantaneously pushing the picture away from her.

"What is the name of the man in the picture with you?"

"Hugo. Hugo Salazar."

"Where did you meet him?"

"Dancing."

"Had you ever seen him before?"

"No."

"Didn't you see him in a photograph marked as an exhibit at the trial?"

"Like I said before, there's been lots of pictures in this trial. I don't memorize them."

Goldstein stared at her through her age-occluded eyes. After a long wait, she said, "I just have one more issue I want to address to you."

"Go ahead."

"Do you still believe, as you told us during jury selection, that you can keep an open mind and determine the facts solely on the basis of the evidence in court?"

"Listen," Lydia said, "I take this serious. It's important. I never even heard the name Baldesteri before. I'm not even sure what a Senator is or does. I'm told her husband was President. If I ever thought about him, I guess I would have thought he would have a wife, and would've thought they had the same last name. I'm from Puerto Rico. I'm a citizen. Like you. I always knew that a citizen might also have to be doing this, be on a jury."

There was absolute silence in the room.

"Very well, Ms. Guzman. You may leave. Thank you for your time. You can resume your seat on the jury."

Lydia didn't move. "You know what? Now *you* wait a second. I'm not finished yet. I still want to know why it's me and not anyone else who was brought in here. Is it because I'm a Latin woman?"

"Of course not," the judge calmly said. "There are pictures of this man in the trial. And the pictures of the same man with you. I had an obligation to ask you about this. It's my job. You have your job, I have mine."

An expression of scorn on her face, Lydia stood. She went out alone. None of the U.S. Marshals who had escorted her left the room until after Lydia, almost slamming the door, was gone.

* * *

Naomi Goldstein slowly gazed around the room. "Do you have anything you want to say, Mr. Decker? You asked for this conference."

"No." He glanced disapprovingly at Giordano and Curnin and the other FBI agents.

"Ms. Rematti, is there anything you have to say?"

"Absolutely not."

"Have you ever met this lady outside of the courtroom during the trial?"

"What?" Raquel asked, surprised and indignant. "To be frank, Judge, I resent the question."

Goldstein had other glossy photographs spread out in front of her. The morning glare through the windows shining on the surfaces of the photographs made it impossible for anyone else in the room to see what they depicted. "Let's get back to work," Goldstein said.

Although Raquel was angry, she concealed it with her customary expression of calmness. She led the way out of the room, followed by Hunter Decker, the U.S. Marshals, and the several FBI agents, including Giordano and Curnin. Raquel knew they were agents. At that point, she didn't know their names. The Senator was the last to leave.

* * *

One of the photographs in front of Judge Naomi Goldstein showed Raquel, Hugo Salazar, and Lydia Guzman standing together. In the background, men and women were dancing at an after-hours club. Raquel, Hugo, and Lydia were not dancing. They were talking, not touching. No words were recorded. The picture was digitally dated a week earlier.

CHAPTER 24

HAYES SMITH'S BODY was flown back to New York two days after he was shot. Doctors performed an exhaustive, muscle-by-muscle, organ by-organ analysis. Just a day after the autopsy was complete, Willis Jordan—the Executive Producer of *NBC Nightly News* and, at least technically, Hayes' boss—left a text message on Raquel's iPhone during the day. The message read: *Please call me when ur trial day is over. WJ*

As soon as the trial day was over and Raquel recovered her iPhone from the security station at the courthouse's door, she took a taxi to her Riverside Drive apartment. She scrolled through her iPhone for Willis Jordan's contact information. She pressed his name, and the magical instrument soon connected her directly to him. He was an intelligent and ambitious black man born into poverty in southern Georgia. A Harvard graduate, Willis spoke with that complete assurance endowed on him during four years on Harvard Yard, with just an endearing trace of a lilting rural Georgia accent. Hayes had genuinely liked and respected him. So, too, did Raquel.

Willis spoke first. "Raquel, I should have called you before this. Hayes talked about you all the time. He loved you, young lady. I'm so sorry."

"Thank you, Willis. He had tremendous respect and admiration for you."

"He was a pleasure to be with. None of that prima donna stuff you see so often in people in this business."

"I know." Raquel suddenly felt her throat swell and thicken, a sure sign of grief. Once again, she dwelled on the inescapable reality that she was alone now in the world because Hayes was dead. It was the reality of death: she would never see or touch him again.

Willis said, "I do have something I need to tell you, Raquel. It's difficult, and we don't know what to make of it."

"Go ahead." Her swelling throat made her ordinarily clear voice sound like a rasping whisper.

"We sent him to Lesbos with a security detail. I didn't pick any of them. We have a department here—all military veterans—that selects freelance security people to protect reporters when they are out of the country and in dangerous areas. On this trip there were at least ten who always kept Hayes in sight."

"Just before he left, he told me that. He said they were all veterans who had once worked for Blackwater, that company with mercenaries. I told him, jokingly, that was the part that most worried me."

"Well, I don't know anything specific about what jobs they once had. But I do know one thing. They all were enthusiasts for a weapon—and I don't know anything about guns—called TEC-DC9 automatic pistols. They're apparently very rare."

Raquel simply waited, asking no questions, saying nothing.

Willis was blunt. "The autopsy shows that the single bullet that killed Hayes was from a TEC-DC9."

"There were Greek soldiers there. Do they use TEC-DC9s?"

"I asked that. No."

"Didn't people in the refugee camp have guns?"

"They do. The likelihood that any of them had a TEC-DC9 is low, low indeed. In any event," Jordan added, "the kill shot was from close range."

"Are you," Raquel slowly asked, "saying that someone in his security detail shot Hayes?"

"I've asked that, of course. These were all supposedly battle-tested, thoroughly vetted pros. The FBI is in the process of talking to all of them."

"Who has their guns?"

"The FBI. All of the weapons have been examined. They were all used. Which is not surprising. There was a tremendous amount of gunfire. You heard it and saw it on the tapes."

"No, actually, I haven't looked at any of it. I never will."

"I surely understand that."

Raquel's typical strength was reasserting itself. "Let me cut through this, Willis. Are you saying that one of Hayes' guards killed him?"

"No, I'm not saying that. No one is sure. Or at least no one is saying so. While there's a lot of film footage, not all of the guards are in it."

"What about the ones who used their guns?"

"Two of them are in the footage. They were close to Hayes, kind of like defensive linemen, and they are all facing away from him, shooting at the Greeks or at the refugees or into the air."

"And was one of them next to Hayes?"

"Yes. He's not in any of the footage. Actually, it was a she—she says she was at the perimeter of the group. Apparently, their training is to form protective rings rather than all gather together."

"What does she say?"

"Her weapon only fired one shot. She says she aimed and fired at the ground just in front of one of the refugees who had jumped over the razor-wire cyclone fence around the camp. According to her, the man jumped right back as soon as her bullet kicked up dirt."

Raquel was staring out at the darkness of Riverside Park as she spoke. In the deepening dark there were strands of street lamps, and on the sinuous walkways there were men and women holding hands, men holding other men's hands, fathers, mothers and nannies pushing strollers, boys balanced on skateboards, innumerable runners, and bicyclists. Everything was as it normally would be on a mild spring night.

Yet Raquel, who loved to gaze out at all that vitality of living while the majestic Hudson flowed in the background, stepped away from the open window.

"If you learn anything more, Willis, you'll let me know, promise?"

"Sure thing, Raquel. Is there anything we can do for you now? I don't have to remind you we're a big organization. You are a single warrior."

"I can take care of myself, Willis. Thanks for calling. You didn't have to."

"Come on, what else could I do? We're always here for you. Tell me you know that." It was a sincere, beguiling, confidence-inspiring drawl. It alleviated her fear while she heard it.

"I know that, Willis."

"One last thing for now, Raquel. Hayes was a worldwide celebrity."

"Honestly, Willis. He hated those words."

"I know he did. He wore his fame like a loose garment, not a chain-mail armor."

"This sounds odd, because he might have been able to use a chain-mail outfit in Lesbos, but he was grace personified. So, no chain-mail outfit for him."

"There is one other thing, Raquel."

"What?"

"Teddy Franks wants to arrange for NBC to do a huge, tasteful memorial for Hayes at Riverside Church up in Harlem, near the Columbia campus."

Teddy Franks was the President of all the NBC News and entertainment divisions. It might be that Rupert Murdoch was more powerful in the television news world than Teddy Franks, but not by much.

Raquel said, "That can't happen."

"Why not?"

"Did you know that Hayes had two estranged brothers still living on the prairie in South Dakota where they grew up? Hayes was the youngest. One of them is a small-town pharmacist. The other doesn't work. He's an opioid addict. Hayes sent both of them money every month."

"What's the problem? We'll bring them here."

"They never wanted to meet me. Must have been something about my last name. Too Italian for them, I guess. They're the only two people mentioned in his will. Even though he hadn't seen them for ten years, they have all the power. Beneficiaries, executors, trustees, even the decision-makers on memorial services and burials. They want him buried, with no muss and no fuss, next to their daddy on the Dakota badlands. They have an old lawyer—their daddy's former law partner—who's made all the arrangements to fly Hayes' body right away to South Dakota. That's what's happening even as we speak, Willis."

"What about you?"

"Me? I'm a cypher. I don't have what we lawyers call 'standing to do or say anything.'"

"No," Willis said. "You're a goddess. But I'm sorry, so sorry to hear all this. It must hurt."

"You know, Willis, it does. That's our secret."

"Raquel," Willis said, "you be careful."

"Always," she answered.

* * *

She walked to her dining room table, where she had left her shoulder-carried briefcase. She took out the Ruger; a bullet-filled magazine was locked firmly in place.

The last person who told me to be careful, she thought, *was Juan Suarez.*

CHAPTER 25

"THE MONEY ARRIVED in cash, Ms. Rematti."

Raquel continued, "How often, Mr. Ramos?"

Jacinto Ramos, in a Brooks Brothers suit and a red-and-white regimental tie, looked more like a bank teller in a small town than the manager of a Chase branch on Park Avenue. "At least once a week. Sometimes more often."

"Over how long a period?"

"Starting more than sixteen months ago."

"And when did that end?"

"When the Senator was indicted."

"And you testified when Mr. Decker examined you that there was, as I think you said, something nontraditional about the deposits, is that correct?"

"There was."

"What was that?"

"They were all in cash. And they were all between $9,000 and $9,998 in a variety of denominations."

"And by that you mean bills? Ten-dollar bills, twenty-dollar bills, one-hundred-dollar bills?"

"Yes, cash."

"And you knew that it was done that way to fabricate a reason not to have to fill out and file with the IRS a Currency Transaction Report, correct?"

"I knew that. I knew that if I didn't—if the bank didn't—file a CTR, then the person who delivered the money had to do that."

"And the arrangement you had was that no one filed a CTR?"

"Right."

"And you were the person to whom the cash was delivered?"

"Always."

"You weren't a teller at the window, were you?"

"I wasn't."

"You were the regional branch manager of a branch with fifty-three people who reported to you?"

"I was."

"Did you accept cash deposits for any other account?"

"No. Only for the CTEB account."

"The Committee to Elect Baldesteri, is that right?"

"That was the name on the account opening statement."

"You had no idea what those words really represented, did you?"

"No."

"Who brought the cash to you?"

"Almost invariably, as I told Mr. Decker, a man named Salazar."

"So, whenever this man entered your branch, he went to your office and handed cash to you?"

"Yes. My office was at the back of the main service floor. Everyone knew this man Salazar had the right to walk into my office any time he wanted to. The bank has what are called 'Personal Wealth Clients.' He was certainly one of them."

"Did you ever speak to him?"

"Just pleasantries."

"Pleasantries? Such as *How are you? Good morning? Good afternoon?*"

"Just that. I knew why he was there, he knew why I was there. We had no need to talk."

"And you deposited the cash into the CTEB account?"

"I did. I made out the deposit slips for the CTEB account. Salazar didn't want to put his handwriting on anything or touch any paper. He discreetly slipped on plastic gloves as soon as he walked into my office. He only touched the bills if he had the gloves on."

"And you prepared Currency Transaction Reports each time?"

"I did."

"But you never submitted them to the IRS, correct, sir?"

"No, I created them for the bank's records only so that the bank's internal auditors could see them."

"But they were never for the full amount Mr. Salazar handed you, isn't that right?"

"They weren't."

"That's because your original deal with Mr. Calvaro was the seven percent solution, isn't that what you told the jury?"

"Correct. I kept seven percent of every deposit."

"And you thought this nutty arrangement would work?"

"I did at the time."

"But it didn't work, correct?"

"As it turned out, no, it didn't."

"But you did get a real benefit from it, didn't you?"

"Did I? I had to turn over all the cash and penalties to the Justice Department. I lost my job."

"You were given immunity from prosecution, weren't you, for testifying here against Senator Baldesteri, isn't that right?"

"Is that a benefit?"

"Listen to me, sir. You committed, according to what you've said here, money laundering, bank fraud, tax evasion, theft, but you'll never have a criminal record, correct?"

"That's right."

"And you'll never go to jail, correct?"

"No."

"And that's not a benefit to you?"

"It is, Ms. Rematti. In a way."

"You had a lawyer who worked out that benefit for you, right?"

"Yes."

"Who was that lawyer?"

"George Harper."

"And Mr. Harper until a year ago was the Attorney General of the United States?"

"He was."

"Under President Spellman?"

"That's right."

"How did it happen that Mr. Harper became your lawyer?"

Ramos glanced warily at the prosecution table. "Mr. Decker recommended him."

"When?"

"After I was arrested."

"Was it after you decided to cooperate with the Government?"

"Yes."

"Did you know it is unethical for a prosecutor to recommend a lawyer?"

Hunter Decker's voice was sharper than usual: "Objection."

Always surprising, Naomi Goldstein said, "Overruled. Go ahead, Mr. Ramos—you can answer Ms. Rematti's question if you know the answer."

"I thought so," Ramos said. "But I didn't feel I could disregard Mr. Decker."

"Did Mr. Decker tell you that his referring you to a lawyer was an ethical problem for Mr. Decker himself?"

"No."

"You didn't pay Mr. Harper for the work he did to get this benefit for you, did you?"

"No. He never asked to be paid."

"And you don't know who paid him, do you?"

"I've always assumed it was the bank."

Pointing at Angelina Baldesteri, Raquel asked, "Mr. Ramos, do you see the woman at the table where I was seated when Mr. Decker was examining you?"

"I do."

"Who is she?"

"Senator Baldesteri."

"You never spoke to her, did you?"

"Never."

"You were never in the same room with her until now, were you?"

"Never."

"She never saw you, correct?"

"Never. Not until now."

"As far as you know, the CTEB account could have been for anything, right?"

"I only know the name Committee to Elect Baldesteri because that was the name Mr. Calvaro at the beginning told me to arrange to put on the account's outgoing checks and on any wiring instructions when money was sent out of the account. This is when he mentioned that Mr. Salazar would always be the courier."

"Senator Baldesteri had no authority to have money wired out of that account, did she?"

"No."

"Or to write checks out of it?"

"No."

"Or to come to the bank and withdraw money?"

"No."

Raquel had an expression of genuine contempt on her face.

"Does it trouble you, Mr. Ramos, that you're a thief, a liar, a cheat, and that you are here to ruin another person's life?"

Naomi Goldstein raised her voice, but just slightly. "Don't answer that question, sir. Ms. Rematti, withdraw that question."

Calmly, Raquel said, "Withdrawn."

She had done what she wanted to do. The jury had heard her words. She sat down.

CHAPTER 26

IT WAS A remarkably mild late May afternoon. Although Raquel's meetings with Angelina Baldesteri were still taking place at the end of each trial day, they now ended quickly, after only a few desultory words. Raquel couldn't recall a time when she had developed more of a dislike for a client. Baldesteri shared the dislike even though she had confidence in Raquel's ability. The Senator said, "You scored points today," before she left, trailing behind her the Secret Service detail. Raquel was relieved to see her go, as if a troublesome mosquito had conveniently flown out an open window.

As during most of her trials, Raquel, who often ran on the curving drives of Riverside Park, had done almost no exercise other than carrying her own heavy litigation bag and the shoulder-carried valise in which she deposited her makeup, a notebook and pen, as well as now the Ruger and the extra bullet magazines.

She decided to walk at least part of the way to her apartment. She slipped off her signature high-heeled shoes and put on her new suede slip-ons.

Before she left the office, Raquel methodically turned off all the office lights and closed the computers, which could be restarted only with the code symbol: *SmithHayes007*.

Her last act before she locked the expensive glass door to her office suite was to look into the shoulder bag to check again that the Ruger was there. It was, as were its extra magazines. The sight of them was always a source of relief.

*   *   *

She loved Madison Avenue and, without planning, she found herself walking briskly uptown. A mild flow of cleansing wind flowed over her. She wasn't drawn to the stores on Madison, although from 57th Street to 96th Street the avenue was lined with world-famous small shops, all burnished and elegant, like Parisian boutiques. What attracted her was the magic of the natural geography on the avenue's gradual upward rise toward Carnegie Hill and the trees allowing the sky's incandescent light to fill the air. And, of course, there were always the crowds of walkers, all well dressed, many European, but over the last few years many Asian as well. Conversations she briefly heard were in French, Italian, German, Mandarin, Korean, and others she didn't recognize.

Tonight there was a freedom that the fast walk gave her, which she recognized as joy. Although a devoted Roman Catholic, a frequent Sunday Mass-goer who derived peace from the incense-scented and quiet interiors of churches and the comforting predictability of the Mass, she paused briefly at the steps of the modest but beautiful Saint James Episcopal Church, with its exterior of weather-pocked, dark-red, and hewn sandstone, at 71st and Madison. There were homeless people, as usual, on the steps. She put ten dollars each in the empty paper coffee cups at their feet. One spoke in a distinctive, cultured voice: "God bless you." The other two were silent, unresponsive.

Raquel stopped at the corner, one block away, at 72nd Street, a crosstown street, where traffic rushed by in both directions. To her left, as she waited for the light to change, she could see the thick early green foliage of Central Park. The last time she had glanced at the park weeks earlier from the windows of Hayes' apartment with its panoramic view of the entire park, the trees bore only buds that still looked wintry.

Years in New York—and the unexpected, always upsetting sight of too many collisions between people and cars in which the cars always won—had made Raquel a docile watcher of street signals. It may have been, she thought, her only remaining obedient Catholic schoolgirl habit. So only when the light changed at the broad intersection of 72nd and Madison did she step off the sidewalk. Before the change of signals, at least a dozen self-absorbed men and women were already walking through the intersection, utterly focused and transfixed on texting on their cell phones in the midst of hurtling yellow cabs.

As she approached the middle of the intersection, she heard a man's polite voice over her shoulder. "My God," he said, "you're not only generous to the poor but obedient to the street rules."

She turned slightly to glance at him. He was comely: neatly dressed, tall, but with short blond hair like a Midwestern schoolboy except that just above his left ear were two small zigzag shapes deeply cut into his hair and distinctly visible. They were a symbol of something. And that something eluded Raquel. Not really intending it, she laughed, saying, "Didn't anyone ever tell you street pickups are almost impossible in Manhattan?"

"Really? I did get your attention. But your email address and cell number would be even better."

She was almost flattered as she made her way to the northern sidewalk. He was at least ten years younger than she. The man continued to walk behind her. He couldn't see her smile.

As soon as she stepped up on the sidewalk, another attractive man in a suit and the short-shorn haircut with the small zigzag etching in his hair was waiting for her; everyone around him was walking, most in a hurry. The man behind her stopped. Suddenly she was between them, halted as well. The new man said, "We need to talk with you, Ms. Rematti."

"And who are you? And who is your handsome friend?"

"We're FBI agents."

"I'm Mother Teresa."

And she began to walk, pushing her way between the two men. They didn't resist. They let her pass, following her, one on each side. "Do I need to call 911?" she asked.

The man who first spoke said, "Your cell is in your shoulder bag. Take out the cell and call the police if you want. The phone is next to your Ruger. If we see it, we'll have to arrest you."

"That's bullshit. I have a carry permit." *How is it,* she wanted to ask but didn't, *that you know what I have in my bag?*

"We can arrest anyone we want. Do you want to spend the night in a cell?"

Raquel, losing her patience, said, "Show me your IDs."

They each took out plastic badges that were attached to the belts under their suit jackets. The movements revealed their weapons in holsters. "Do you have permits for those?" she asked.

"Ms. Rematti," the man who had waited for her said, "don't make this more difficult for yourself."

"Where did you get those IDs?" she asked. "Staples?"

"You're not helping yourself," the man who had followed her across the intersection said.

"Did I inadvertently jaywalk? I try to be careful."

"Come on, let's just walk up to 79th Street. We'll talk. You can listen or not."

"There are laws against stalking," she said.

And the other man said, "And there are laws against bribing witnesses. And obstructing justice."

As she began to walk uptown, Raquel said, "Were you the guys who broke into my apartment? There are laws against that, too."

She knew that, despite all her well-learned self-discipline and self-instilled absence of fear, she was starting to tremble. And she knew, too, that these men recognized that. Clearly, they knew the many subtle arts of intimidation. There was a tremor in her voice.

One of them—the man who followed her through the intersection—handed her a glossy, oversize picture. Almost against her will, she glanced at it as she walked. It showed her talking, in what looked like a downtown club because there were people dancing in the background under strobe lights, to Lydia Guzman and Hugo Salazar.

"And," she asked, "what photo shop did this work for you? Same place as the phony badges? The only time I've seen this woman is in court."

"And you know the man. He's Juan Suarez, or Anibal Vaz, or Tony Blair." The man paused. "Or *The Blade of the Hamptons*. And whoever he is, he is a slave to Oscar Caliente. But you know that, don't you? And you know Oscar Caliente is now Robert Calvaro, king of the super PACs and drug lord extraordinaire? Not to mention your client's current lover."

Raquel stopped in front of the brick elementary school on Madison Avenue and 82nd Street. PS 6 occupied the entire block in this area of tasteful small shops and elegant, century-old brownstones. Lush trees covered the strip of land between the wrought-iron fence and the wall of the school.

She stared defiantly at both men. She dropped the photograph to the sidewalk. "Let me have your business cards," she said. "Every make-believe FBI agent has a business card. When I have you arrested, the cards will come in handy."

They each took cards from their wallets. "Listen to me carefully, Ms. Rematti," said the man who had been waiting for her when she crossed 72nd Street. "You're the target of a grand jury investigation. Arranging to carry cash and cocaine to a juror is a big-time crime. It's not a good idea for you to continue your infatuation with Hugo Salazar. Or is he still Juan Suarez to you? You need to be careful. Protect yourself. We can help. Any time you want to talk to us about the Senator, just call us. Take care of yourself. And, in the process, you can take care of other people who are close to you."

Hard-edged, defiant, Raquel stared at them. And one of them said, quietly, "Did you ever, Ms. Rematti, wonder whether Hayes Smith died because he knew you?"

The words riveted her: *Hayes Smith died because he knew me.*

"Do me a favor," she said tensely, angrily, as she put aside the thought the harsh words provoked. "That phony picture you gave me fell on the sidewalk. It's yours. It's against the law to litter. Maybe you should pick it up and put it in the trash can at the corner."

As they stood side by side and facing her, she reached into her valise. Her cell phone was in an internal side pocket next to the Ruger. Alerted by her deft movement, both men, suddenly tense, instinctively shifted their hands toward their holsters.

Raquel waved her cell phone in front of her, displaying the screen to them. "Calm down, gentlemen. It's just a cell phone. You're not afraid of cell phones, are you?"

They looked angry and confused. In that instant of uncertainty, she pressed the picture icon and in three rapid successions took their pictures. She also snapped three pictures of the glossy photograph as it lay faceup on the sidewalk.

"Have a nice day," she said.

* * *

Disregarding the traffic and pedestrian rules, she hurried across Madison Avenue at mid-block, leaving the two men behind her. She glanced down the upward-sloping avenue to check for traffic. To the south at 79th Street, the lights had just changed and a horde of taxis, cars, buses, and vans was unleashed by the changing light, racing in her direction. Hurrying, she had time enough to reach the western sidewalk.

Raquel was fairly certain the men wouldn't follow her: they had delivered their message and that, she was sure, was their mission today. It was the process of incremental fear, the messenger whose job it is to whisper: *The cat's on the roof. Pretty soon the cat will fall off the roof. No more cat.*

She was even more certain that FBI agents, if that was who they were, would never follow her into the small, quaint bookstore. She walked into the Crawford Doyle shop directly across from PS 6. The books arrayed in the Parisian-style windows looked as delicious as pastries. The unvarnished wooden floorboards creaked below her feet as she walked among the shelves of new books and paperbacks. When she had first moved to the city, she'd rented for a year a fourth-floor walk-up studio apartment around the corner from the store. It was then known as Womrath's and run by one of the happiest, most engaging men she'd ever known, a Truman Capote look-alike who was simply and openly a sweet man. Jerry—she never learned his last name—was also the first person she personally knew who had died of AIDS during the long epidemic. Although the store's name had changed, the store had not; it was as intimate and pleasantly scented of wood and paper as it had been; and it had retained the flavor, ambience, and charm that Jerry had endowed.

After three minutes, she looked out the window. The men were gone. It was then that she first looked at their business cards. *Curnin* and *Giordano*.

CHAPTER 27

RAQUEL REMATTI HAD the rare ability to sleep soundly no matter what had taken place in the waking hours of any day. Insomnia rarely plagued her. Her capacity to plunge into restful sleep was one she learned as a child in the tenement in Lawrence where her mother and father, frustrated by poverty and dirty factory labor, lunged into violent arguments almost every night, as plastic dishes and plastic cups flew like hail through the three rooms of the apartment. Booze, voices, noise, and pain. As a child, she learned the secure refuge was sleep.

But sleeping was impossible now. Hayes was dead. Willis Jordan had made his frank but ultimately enigmatic call. And the two men who had confronted her on Madison Avenue had deeply unsettled her.

Raquel had avoided overuse of her iPhone for emailing, texting, or anything else. It had been, however, one of Hayes' main means of communicating, and over the last few months, she'd become adept at the use of the sleek device. Hayes had used texts to send her love notes, sex notes, and reminders so constantly it was as though he was with her at all times, as if always whispering in her ear. He often sent jokes. Now it was two a.m., and for the first time, she wondered where Hayes Smith's iPhone was. She had no doubt that it had been in one of the phony oversize ammunition pockets of the silly Beretta flak jacket he was wearing when he was shot. Who now had that phone? And its secrets? She wasn't certain she wanted it even if she could get it. There might be messages in it that she would prefer not to see, a concealed reservoir of secrets she would not want to read. She wasn't concerned about secrets of hers that his cell phone might reveal. She had the lingering sense, because she was a complete realist, that she might not have been, despite all Hayes promised her, the only woman in his life. She would never really know. She didn't want to know.

Except for two or three texts to Hayes when they were apart, Raquel had never sent a text to anyone at two a.m. But she had Hunter Decker's cell numbers. She had never once called him and certainly never sent him a text message. Life had taught her that it was important to be careful about talking or writing in the middle of the night, when the mind tended to be unmoored, vulnerable, prone to fear, and dwelling on unhinged thoughts.

Carefully she opened the text screen. She wrote: *Can you meet me at 8 this morning in the 8th floor cafeteria? Want to talk.* She pressed the *Send* symbol. The cafeteria was on the eighth floor of the twenty-three-story courthouse. It reopened at eight every morning. At that time, it would be empty except for the early-arriving surly cooks, food service people, and cashiers.

Exactly one minute after she sent the message, she was surprised when her cell phone vibrated and illuminated itself with an incoming message.

It was from Hunter Decker. *C u then and there. H.D.*

CHAPTER 28

HUNTER DECKER, APPEARING refreshed and relaxed as he always did, that image of *noblesse oblige* that his lineage had embedded in his genes in the womb, was waiting for her at one of the big cafeteria-style tables next to the north-facing windows. Carrying a tray with a container of black coffee, a hard-boiled egg on a cardboard saucer, and a glazed donut, Raquel walked briskly toward him. He had only a small cup of water in front of him.

Always the well-trained prep school boy, he stood as Raquel slid her tray onto the table. "Good morning, Raquel," he said.

"Thanks for seeing me," she answered.

The early sunlight flooded through the tall windows. Another hot and clear day was starting. Below them, spreading out like an urban fan, were the old, low buildings of Chinatown. Orange, red, ochre roofs glowed. There were several pagoda-style buildings. Farther to the north, the Manhattan skyscrapers began their gradual ascent above 14th Street toward the glittering heights of midtown. The radio tower atop the Empire State Building gleamed like the world's largest sword.

"I don't suppose you're seeing me because your client wants to plead guilty?" he asked with an ironic laughter.

"No, Hunter, you and I have had that conversation, and I've told you pigs will fly before that happens."

Hunter took a delicate sip of water. "Raquel," he said, "I don't often get text messages at two in the morning. What do you want to tell me?"

"Why were you awake?"

"Why? We don't know each other that well, do we? I have a six-month-old girl. I was feeding her. My wife doesn't breastfeed. The baby has an insatiable appetite."

"Got it. And here I was thinking you were awake plotting my downfall."

"I don't plot downfalls of people. They tend to fall all on their own accord."

"This is about me, Hunter. I don't believe you want me to fall of my own accord. I think you, or people you work for, want to take me out. This is not about *falling*. This is about getting taken *out*."

Hunter spoke quietly. "I have nothing but admiration for you, Raquel. I recall years ago, when I was in my third year at Harvard, Alan Dershowitz gave a seminar on cross-examination techniques. The only video he showed was you peeling the skin off a detective in a murder trial in a state court in California. Figuratively, of course. Very instructive."

"That was a long time ago. I may have lost a step or two."

"Not that I can see."

She took a small bite of her glazed donut while sipping her hot coffee. "As you can see, I'm not worried about weight."

"You don't need to be." He sipped his water again. "But *this time* you wanted to see me."

"I did. I'm persistent. I know we spoke about this before. You said you were concerned about me. I didn't trust you. I still don't. And even more so now. You're being taken for a ride."

"Why?"

"Two guys stopped me on Madison Avenue yesterday. FBI, or so they claimed."

"Go on, if you want to."

"They said I was the target of a grand jury."

"As I said before, I can't comment on any of that. Not on grand juries, not on wiretaps, not on witnesses. And certainly not about who might be a target of a grand jury. I can't tell you who I send, or don't send, anywhere. I'm bound by law to secrecy. Sorry, I still can't help. I'd have to turn in my license to practice if I did. You know that."

"Sure I do." She gazed intently into his chilly blue eyes. "But, since I'm only human, I'm baffled. The two men gave me their cards. And said if I wanted to talk, I could. If they're anything, they're water carriers for you. I don't talk to water boys. I talk to their managers. And in this case, that's *you*. You sent them, or people a layer or two above you."

Raquel removed the two business cards the men had given her and placed them on the pink plastic table in front of Decker. "Do you know these men?" she asked.

Decker briefly fingered the edges of each card. They were the embossed business cards of Special Agents Curnin and Giordano. "I can't answer that," he said.

"Let me show you something else, Hunter," she said, removing her cell phone from the inner pocket of the linen summer jacket she wore.

She held the phone aloft with its screen facing him. She said, "These were the two men who gave me their cards yesterday."

Hunter's expression suddenly became thoughtful. "How did you get these pictures?"

"I took them. Cell phones are a miracle. They were standing side by side. I think they were having a good laugh together because they enjoyed thinking they were frightening a woman. What really struck me—and you can see them in the pictures—are the identical zigzag etchings on their short hair just above the ears."

"Didn't they try to take your cell away? Agents—except the publicity-hungry ones who like to give press conferences—don't relish being recognized. Anonymity: that's why they all wear the same suits."

"You know, Hunter, my gut tells me they weren't FBI or any other kind of legitimate agent. Their suits were too nice, although, like all agents, they traveled in pairs. And you're right: agents like anonymity, so they don't have tribal markings in their hair."

Hunter pushed the business cards toward her. He sat silently for at least a minute as he stared out the window at the grandeur of the steadily sun-filling city. Chinatown's roofs had turned an even warmer ochre color. Raquel, too, was quiet.

Hunter at last said, "I shouldn't tell you this." The tone of voice was almost confessional, tinged by reluctance. "The business cards are real. There are agents named Curnin and Giordano. But they are not the men in the photographs."

"I appreciate that honesty."

"Can I ask you to forward those pictures to my cell phone? Curnin and Giordano, in fact, are interested in you in ways you wouldn't like. Whoever those two men are, they're impersonating federal agents. That's illegal. And they're interested in you, too."

"Why are Curnin and Giordano investigating me?"

"Raquel, we've had this conversation. I've told you more than I should. I want to be fair to you. There are troubles here for you that are beyond anything you've ever experienced or imagined. Your client is more dangerous than any mobster, terrorist, or stock scammer you've ever represented."

"There is something I have to tell you because I want to help you, too, Hunter. We're in a deceitful, dubious profession. Listen to me carefully: someone is playing with you. When they had me hemmed in on the sidewalk at PS 6, those blond goons showed me a picture they claimed was of Hugo Salazar, Lydia Guzman, and me talking at an after-hours dance club downtown a week or so ago."

Quietly Hunter said, "I know. I've seen that picture. It isn't pretty for you. I don't have to tell you it's potentially incriminatory of you."

"Hunter, listen to me. The picture isn't pretty because there's a fatal problem with it. And it's a problem for you, not me."

Staring at her, Hunter didn't speak.

"I'm going to give you a little immodest personal history first," Raquel said. "I'm a famous person. People think the famous are invited everywhere. Not so. For years I've found myself spending many nights alone. I don't like that. It's a kind of Marilyn Monroe syndrome. Men were afraid to ask her for dates.

"What I do like is dancing: Salsa, tango, West Coast Swing. Often late at night I do what many women my age do when they are alone and it's late. I head downtown at two in the morning just to go dancing, to have some human contact, with men or even women who simply want to dance. And I never have trouble passing through the velvet ropes and the bouncers of the downtown after-hours clubs. They call us *cougars*, unattached women in their forties and fifties. We're always welcome."

Hunter sipped the last of his water. "So now I know you're not only famous, as I've known for a long time, but a *cougar* who loves to dance. If you're a cougar, should I be afraid of you?"

"Let me tell you another secret that, if you take it to heart, might help you see that somebody is setting you up."

"Raquel, you've tried to send me warnings before. You have to understand. Nothing has ever frightened me. For no reason, I was born into privilege. And wealth. I've led an absurdly clean life. Honor after honor. I'm now the youngest United States Attorney in America. I'm a cardinal at a young age in the church of the American justice system. So, Raquel, who is it with the power to set me up? To hurt me? Isn't there a line in Shakespeare's *Tempest*? *I and my ministers are alike invulnerable.*"

Raquel said, "Let me make it simple, even to American nobility. That picture of Lydia Guzman, Hugo Salazar, and me is a fake."

"How so? There's Hugo Salazar, Lydia Guzman, and you. In a picture. Together. Taken just a week ago."

Raquel said, "And on the velvet curtain in the background, in neon lights, is the name of the club. *Batista y Batista.* The club was once on Mercer Street, in the Village, near the Angelika Theater and Houston Street. That neighborhood is open all night—the tempo never subsides until dawn. You're a good suburban husband and father. You probably have no idea where these places were or are, or how they look when the sun is coming up after a long night."

"Whoever would have thought Raquel Rematti knew the tempo of Lower Manhattan nightlife?"

"Listen to me carefully, Hunter. *Batista y Batista* closed down five years ago. It's been locked ever since. No one has taken any pictures of me or anyone else there at a party in five years."

He stared at Raquel, waiting for her to continue. She did: "And one other thing. When Curnin and Giordano or these idiots I assume are working for you left the Crawford Doyle neighborhood, I walked across the avenue and rummaged like a bag lady through the wastebasket they were stupid enough to throw the phony picture in, and I have it. They're obviously not street-smart New Yorkers or they wouldn't have left it so I could retrieve it. And no one but me will be able to find what is now my copy. I couldn't stand George W., but he once said something interesting: *I'll do things at a time and place of my own choosing.* And, Hunter, I can quote Shakespeare, too: King Lear said, *There are things that I shall do, I know not what they are, but they shall be the terrors of earth.* I'll crucify you, Cardinal, if you ever try to use that picture against me. I have something you don't have. Unlimited access to the press. That's one benefit of fame. You may be royalty, but nobody knows your name."

Balancing her cafeteria tray, she stood up and walked to the brightly colored, segregated trash bins, slid the debris into the narrow holes of the garbage containers, and neatly stacked the tray on the top of one of the containers.

*   *   *

As soon as he saw her leaving the cafeteria, Hunter Decker tapped the speed dial of his cell phone. And he spoke, "Do you idiots want to tell me what you've been up to?"

CHAPTER 29

As THEY WAITED tensely at the defense table for Naomi Goldstein to emerge into the courtroom, Raquel whispered, "You have one last chance not to do this. If you get up on that stand, you're in free fall. Maybe you'll alight in the Land of Oz like the Good Witch of the West and with an emerald wand and ruby-red slippers. Or maybe you'll crash and burn. Once it starts, I can't stop it."

Angelina, not bothering to whisper, said, "What are you afraid of? How many times do I have to tell you that my mind is settled, I'm clear, I make the decisions. You know the questions, I know the answers. No one, but no one, is going to accuse me of cutting and running."

"I'm through," Raquel said, "giving you lectures that you have a Fifth Amendment right not to testify."

"I knew that in the second grade. I'm not a fool. The Fifth Amendment is the kiss of death for politicians."

"And for most defendants, testifying is the kiss of death as well. Once you take the first step, you can't pick and choose the questions you want to answer and those you don't."

Impatiently, Angelina said, "You're repeating yourself. You've told me that before."

Raquel pulled away ever so slightly. "You're doing this against my advice."

"That," Angelina said, "is my decision. Final, end of story. And who are you worried about? *Me* or *you*?"

"Don't ask me stupid, insulting questions. I'm worried about the cross-examination. I have no way of controlling what Decker will ask you on cross. I can't just say *Game over* if things get dicey."

What Raquel really wanted to say was that she knew Angelina Baldesteri was a consummate liar. And Raquel had the same obligations that, in theory, every lawyer had: not to permit willingly a client under oath to lie, and that if Raquel knew the Senator was lying, to let the judge know that.

The commanding baritone of Cyrus Johnson, the courtroom bailiff, resonated through the cavernous room as the door to Naomi Goldstein's chambers opened and the woman began to climb the three steps to her bench.

"All rise," Johnson commanded like a Marine drill sergeant, which was precisely what he had once been. "The court is in session. *United States versus Baldesteri.*"

Even though the resplendent, newly renovated courtroom was filled with light on this bright morning, Naomi Goldstein clicked on her reading lamp. "Mr. Johnson, I understand all the jurors are here. Would you please have them brought in?"

The now-familiar men and women filed obediently, like tired schoolchildren, into their assigned seats. They never spoke to each other. Their clothes were the usual motley assortment of the casual attire of people on vacation waiting at the airport, except for the chic styling of Lydia Guzman.

Formal as always, Naomi Goldstein announced, "Good morning, ladies and gentlemen. I hope you enjoyed your evenings."

There was no response, just a rustle of slight movement.

Goldstein then adjusted the slender neck of her microphone and spoke to Raquel Rematti and Angelina Baldesteri. "I now want to ask the defendant some questions. Ms. Baldesteri, will you stand, please?"

The two slender women stood. Raquel was slightly taller than the Senator. Behind them every seat in the large gallery was filled. The Secret Service agents, normally unobtrusive, stood, too, but they faced the men and women in the gallery rather than looking forward toward the lawyers and the judge as they usually did. Raquel had learned over the months of their presence as part of the background scenery of her life that Secret Service agents concentrated on people's hands, not on their faces, since it was a hand that represented the most obvious possibility of danger. The intent of eyes was difficult to read. Far more easily predictable were the movements of hands.

"Ms. Baldesteri," Naomi Goldstein began, "please understand that I am about to ask you formal but important questions I ask every defendant at this stage of a criminal trial. I want the jury and everyone else to understand that as well. You're not under oath. Nothing I will ask you, nor will anything you say, have any bearing on guilt or innocence. It's simply the case that the rules that govern my role as a judge require me to pose some questions and satisfy myself that you understand the juncture we've now reached. I have no opinion about anything. I'm not the trier-of-fact. The jurors are. Nothing I am about to ask or say should suggest to anyone that I have any views or impressions. I don't."

In her remarkably calm, typically poised voice, Angelina answered, "I understand."

The jurors had until now heard her voice, at least in this courtroom, only on surreptitiously recorded tapes, not live. Some of them, possibly all of them, had for years heard her voice on television shows, radio interviews, speeches, documentaries—any number of the myriad ways that, in the era of computers, live-streaming, and digital technology, the voices of famous people had become as familiar as the voices of family members, coworkers, and lovers.

"You understand that the Government has rested its case against you, don't you, ma'am?"

"I do."

"You understand that it was, and remains, the Government's sole responsibility to prove a defendant's guilt beyond a reasonable doubt?"

"I do."

"You understand that you are entitled at all times to the presumption of innocence?"

"Yes, I do."

"You understand that you are not required to prove anything?"

"I know."

"You understand that you and Ms. Rematti are not required to present a single witness?"

"Yes."

"Or put forward a single document or any other type of evidence?"

"Yes."

"And that you are entirely free not to testify?"

"Yes."

"And that if you do not testify, I will instruct the jury that it is not allowed to draw any inference against you for that?"

"Yes."

"And that you have that right because the Fifth Amendment to our Constitution gives you, just as it gives everyone, the right to remain silent?"

"Yes."

"You understand that if you do testify, however, you will be under oath to tell the truth, the whole truth, and nothing but the truth?"

"I do."

"And you understand that if you do testify, the prosecution will have the right to cross-examine you?"

"Yes."

"And that the prosecution can ask you any question, if I deem the question relevant, that it may choose to ask to discredit you?"

"Yes."

"And that if you and Ms. Rematti put on any evidence, whether you testify or not, the Government has an absolute right to put on rebuttal evidence, including witnesses, documents, recordings and the like, that it elected not to use before this point and which it's foreclosed from using now unless you put on a defense?"

"Certainly."

"And that if you elect, as is your right, to put on no evidence now, we will move to the lawyers' summations and my jury instructions and that the jury will then retire to deliberate?"

"Yes."

"And that I will instruct the jury that any decision it might ever reach to convict you must be unanimous? That you cannot be convicted unless every juror believes that the Government has proven its case beyond any reasonable doubt?"

"I understand."

"And that I will instruct the jury that each of them must use his or her own independent judgment and not be swayed to abandon that judgment even if every other juror reaches a different conclusion? In other words, that what happens in that jury room is not a political balloting?"

"I understand."

Goldstein paused. For the first time she glanced at Raquel. "Ms. Rematti, is there anything else you suggest I ask your client?"

"Ask whether the Senator has considered these issues before."

Goldstein glanced from Raquel to the Senator.

"This is not the first time you've considered these issues, is that right, Ms. Baldesteri?"

"That's correct."

Goldstein directed her gaze at Hunter Decker. "Do you have any suggestions?"

"No."

"Very well, then," Goldstein whispered, leaning backward. "Ms. Rematti, what is your client's intention?"

Without hesitating and without sitting, Raquel said distinctly, "The defense calls Senator Angelina Baldesteri to the stand."

CHAPTER 30

THE SENATOR WALKED to the witness stand as if she were striding forward to a stage to accept a nomination. She did everything but give a victory wave to a convention. As she stood next to the witness chair, she waited for Naomi Goldstein to run through her familiar, almost religious ritual. "Do you swear or affirm to tell the truth, the whole truth, and nothing but the truth, so help you God?"

"I do."

As Angelina settled into the witness seat, Raquel remembered that one of the messages she had conveyed to her client was *Be humble*. Raquel now thought, *Well, that's another suggestion out the window.*

From that unbridgeable gulf of thirty feet that always separated Raquel from a witness, and as Angelina stared expectantly at her lawyer, Raquel finally asked, "Ms. Baldesteri, you're employed, are you not?"

"I am."

"As what?"

"I'm a United States Senator from the State of New York."

"How long have you held that job?"

"Seven years."

"Had you held a job before that?"

"I did. I once some time ago taught economics at the University of Texas."

"I take it you have college and graduate degrees?"

"I have a bachelor's degree in economics from a college in Massachusetts. Wellesley, a small college for women."

"And graduate school?"

"Yes. Yale University in Connecticut. A doctorate degree."

"Also in economics?"

"Yes."

"Ms. Baldesteri, are you married?"

"Not for several years. My husband died."

"How long ago did your husband die?"

"Nine years ago."

"Your husband was the President of the United States, correct?"

"He was."

"And he was murdered?"

"He was."

"How long were you married to President Young?"

"Seven years."

"Did you have children?"

"No, none."

"Stepchildren?"

"No, I was the President's only wife."

"Ms. Baldesteri, did you ever hold an elective office before you became a Senator?"

"No. All I ever wanted before meeting Jimmy Young was to be a teacher."

"Let's step back for a second. Please tell the jury where you were born."

"Jefferson Parish, Louisiana. I was raised there. I left when I went to college in Massachusetts."

The rhythm of testimony: it was always important, Raquel told her students, no matter how well known your client was, to create an intimate back-and-forth when he or she started to testify. Anyone, Raquel said, could be and had to be humanized, had to be made tangible and real and, if possible, sympathetic to jurors. Even when the client was once the First Lady of the United States. Or even a dedicated, murderous member of a Ukrainian gang.

"Did your father work while you were growing up?"

"He was an oysterman. He fished for oysters."

"How long did your father work as an oyster fisherman in Louisiana?"

"Until he was seventy-five. And then he had to stop because of the oil blowout years ago in the Gulf of Mexico. The Louisiana coast became a no-man's land."

"Was he working as an oysterman when you were the First Lady of the United States?"

"He was. The yield was gradually coming back by then. He wanted to go back to work."

"How old is your father?"

Hunter Decker at last stood. "Objection."

Naomi Goldstein didn't glance at him. "Overruled."

Baldesteri said, "Eighty-three."

"Is he here today? Is he in this room?" Raquel asked.

"Objection."

"Overruled."

"He is."

"And your mother?"

"She passed. Years ago. My daddy raised me."

"Let me ask you this, Senator: You know why you're here, correct?"

"I do."

"And that's because you are accused of crimes, correct?"

"Yes."

"And the list of these crimes is something called an indictment, isn't that right?"

"It is."

"And you heard that indictment read to the jurors by Judge Goldstein at the start of the trial?"

"I did. It was painful to hear, Ms. Rematti. I had read it all before, but I knew the judge was doing what the law required her to do."

"And you heard Mr. Decker and his team five weeks ago give opening statements about what they intended to do to prove that you did those things?"

"Yes, I did, Ms. Rematti. Every word. This is my life, this is my reputation, this is my integrity, this is my liberty. So I listened to every word."

"And you heard me speak in my opening statement to the men and women on the jury?"

"I did."

"You never saw any of these jurors before, is that right?"

Attentive and calm, Angelina Baldesteri said, "I may have. I ran for the Senate twice. I met as many men and women and children as I could all through the State of New York who wanted to see me and ask me questions, and I answered them. So, in a way, all of these people are familiar to me."

Raquel knew the Senator was hard to control, but she also acknowledged she had to give Angelina Baldesteri a range of freedom to be herself. Raquel was a realist, not an egoist, a seasoned evaluator of the endless varieties of men and women, including people like Angelina, who had been her clients. Raquel had to be flexible, a skillful reactor to the nuances of other people. And, in Angelina Baldesteri, she had to concede something else. The Senator had a skill, a dimension, a talent, an instinct, that had led millions of people to vote for her. Raquel had once said to one of her paralegals, a slender man with spiky orange hair, "No one would ever vote for me for dog-catcher. But I do have a skill even though I can't add two plus three. And that skill? I could have represented Einstein without ever knowing his general theory of relativity. Baldesteri has her own skills. I have to give those skills some range."

Now Raquel smiled gently at the Senator. "But, it's fair to say, isn't it, Ms. Baldesteri, that you have no recollection of ever meeting or speaking directly to any of these men and women in the jury box?"

"That's right."

"And when each of them told Judge Goldstein weeks ago that none of them had ever spoken to you directly, or seen you face-to-face, you never doubted that, correct?"

"No. And you know what, Ms. Rematti, I only wanted men and women who would put aside any thought they ever had about me, if they ever had any thought about me. Just to put it aside. To think only about what they heard, saw, touched, experienced in this courtroom."

"You agreed with Judge Goldstein?"

"I certainly did and do, Ms. Rematti. I'm an innocent woman. I never did anything Mr. Decker has said I did, and never knew any of the things he said I knew."

Raquel heard an abrupt snort of derision from the prosecution table. Hunter Decker cast a cold eye in the direction of one of the women lawyers to his left.

Raquel Rematti, the master of exploitation of the unexpected, said without visibly reacting to the snort of contempt even though she was certain it would have a negative impact on the jurors, "Senator, do you know Gordon Hughes?"

"I do."

"How long have you known him?"

"Almost eleven years."

"How did you meet him?"

"My husband, Jimmy, when he was a Senator from Wyoming, needed a seasoned insider to manage his campaign."

"You heard Hughes testify to the jury?"

"I listened to him *talk* to the jury."

"Did he ever work for you?"

"He did. He was the manager of one of my campaigns. He also managed one of my husband's campaigns. I helped my husband hire him for that."

"Let's focus on his work for you, Senator. Your last campaign for the Senate was a year or so ago, is that right?"

"Yes."

"And obviously," Raquel said, smiling, "you won?"

"I did."

"And Gordon Hughes managed that campaign?"

"That was the one."

"Generally, what did he do as the campaign manager?"

"Scheduling my appearances was part of it. Supervising the campaign staff. There were at least twenty-five people on the staff on a full-time basis. Hughes is a native, I think, of Iowa. He wasn't particularly familiar with New York State. There were people on the staff who were native New Yorkers from all parts of the state— Buffalo, St. Lawrence, Rochester, Syracuse. I wanted a concentration of offices and volunteers in areas of the state that were poor, underserved, and neglected. Hughes, with the assistance of a diverse staff, was able to bring me to places where Democrats had not done at all well before. We knew we would win New York City and the suburbs. I didn't want to be the Senator from New York City. I wanted to be the Senator of New York State, from the St. Lawrence Waterway to Long Island Sound."

"What happened to Hughes after the campaign was over?"

"I'm not sure. People like Gordon Hughes can be kind of sketchy. They have a skill, some of them are famous, some are in demand, some fall into neglect. They go from place to place. Some just do other things. For example, Senator Sanders' campaign manager ran a baseball card trading shop in Vermont just before he took over Bernie's entire campaign."

"When Hughes ran your Senate campaign, did he have any role in raising or managing money?"

"Not really. We had a treasurer. We had a website and we were so fortunate that funds—and I'm talking about $35, $30, even $10 contributions—just came in from thousands and thousands of people who could afford those amounts and who were committed to the same issues I was. And, taken together, they became large amounts. And there were also funds left over from my first campaign. So, no, Hughes didn't really have anything to do with talking to big donors or raising money. The funds were there."

"And then there came a time when you hired him again?"

"Several months ago, he was put on the payroll of a committee that friends and supporters of mine had formed. These were people who intensely thought I might want to think about running for President in the next presidential cycle. Although I wasn't so certain of that myself, I didn't want to close the door completely."

"What was the committee's name?"

"At the time I reached out to Hughes, the committee had some haphazard name such as Angelina's Committee. Not Angie's List. I knew people wanted me to consider running. As I've just said, I wasn't sure. But people I liked and admired were pulling themselves together, money for campaign funds was gathering, and I believed I needed to do something."

"And what did you do?"

"Among other things, I hired Gordon Hughes."

"Why Hughes?"

"The question at that early stage was *why not*? He had worked on my campaigns. He told me he had learned a great deal about PACs and super PACS, which barely existed when Jimmy ran for President and which really weren't much of a factor in my Senate races because I was fortunate enough to raise enough funds from small donors through the website. And another thing: I had heard he had failed at a casino business. That he was in debt and not earning a living. He had a young wife and five children."

"How much of that influenced your decision?"

"Not that significantly. But I was aware of it. I had trusted him and felt a sense of loyalty to him. Trust and loyalty, Ms. Rematti. Those are virtues I learned early on, from my daddy and others in the Louisiana bayous."

"And let me ask you this, Senator: Do you trust Gordon Hughes today?"

"Gordon Hughes is a liar. He's utterly untrustworthy."

"And loyalty?"

"Gordon Hughes' loyalty is only to himself. His wife left him. His children don't hear from him even though he has every right to stay in touch with them."

"You heard Gordon Hughes mention the name *Dr. Joseph Chuang*. Do you know any such person?"

"Not the one Gordon Hughes referred to, if in fact, there is such a person."

"Had you ever heard that name?"

"As a Senator from New York, I represent *all* New Yorkers, including Chinese Americans. I know our Chinese citizens sometimes like to Americanize their first names to names like *Joseph*. I know there is a dentist with a storefront office on Canal Street, in Chinatown, *Dr. Joseph Chuang*. He was kind enough to organize some small *get-to-know-your-Senator* meetings for me."

"Do you know a Dr. Joseph Chuang who works for the Chinese government-owned Sino Oil Company?"

"No."

"You heard Hughes testify that Dr. Joseph Chuang of Sino Oil brought him $2 million in cash in San Francisco?"

"I heard that at this trial."

"And never before?"

"Never. The Joseph Chuang I know, the dentist, eats in a small Chinese restaurant on Canal Street in Chinatown where the highest-priced dishes cost nine dollars. I've had food there, too. For a Southern girl I've had to eat all kinds of food that at sixteen I never imagined even existed."

"And you heard Hughes mention that he took hours to count the $2 million in cash he says *his* Dr. Chuang gave him, correct?"

"I heard that. His Dr. Chuang must also have given him a pocket calculator or an abacus. I don't know how anyone counts $2 million in dollar bills in his head."

"Have you ever heard the name Oscar Caliente?"

"Not until that name was mentioned here by Mr. Decker."

"The name Caliente means nothing to you?"

"Nothing. Again, I had not heard it until this trial. I don't even know that a man named Oscar Caliente exists. I assume somewhere in the world there are men with that name, but I never heard it before."

"Had you ever, Senator, heard of the Sinaloa cartel?"

"Certainly. As a Senator, I try to stay informed of everything that might hurt the nation's and this state's well-being. I knew it was a drug cartel. But no one ever mentioned the name *Oscar Caliente* to me in connection with Sinaloa or anything else."

"And Mr. Hughes didn't?"

"No."

"Did you ever tell Hughes to give you $75,000 in cash?"

"No."

"Listen to me carefully, Senator: Did you ever tell Gordon Hughes at any time to give you cash?"

"I heard him tell the jurors that happened, and often. He was lying. Gordon Hughes never bought me a cup of coffee." Like Hughes, she looked at the jurors when she answered questions. "Let me be clear. I hired Gordon Hughes early on for the reasons I mentioned. He had a skill, I thought, in organizing people. He was familiar, or so he told me, with the leaders and local opinion-makers in many states throughout the country. He told me he knew experts on super PACs, although he wasn't, he said, an expert himself. My initial reluctance about running for President was, I think, a feeling that I'd done that with Jimmy and it wasn't fun. But then I gradually began to look on it as a duty I had.

"So, knowing that Hughes had only a limited set of skills, I hired a staff of fund-raisers, treasurers, law firms in most states, and experts in something that was new and exotic to me: PACs and then things called super PACs as they became known after a Supreme Court decision, *Citizens United*. When Jimmy ran for President, I'm not even sure we heard those expressions."

Hunter Decker—as Raquel noticed from the periphery of her view while she concentrated on the judge, the jury, and her client—was visibly struggling with the urge to stand and say, "Move to strike." But he continued to sit still.

Raquel knew she had to draw Angelina Baldesteri to the *now*. She asked, "Did you ever have an intimate relationship with Gordon Hughes?"

"No, I didn't"

"Did he ever tell you that foreign money was being used in your campaign?"

"No. And no one else ever said that either. And no foreign money has ever come into my campaign as far as I know. I have never even

used the phone or a face-to-face meeting to ask anyone—anyone—
not Mark Zuckerberg, not Melinda and Bill Gates, not Mike
Bloomberg, not Alex Rodriguez, not Vladimir Putin, not anyone—
for money for my campaign."

"Do you know Robert Calvaro?"

"I do."

"Who is he?"

"He is, he has told me, a native of South America who was born
into a wealthy family and came as a teenager to an exclusive New
England prep school, went to Yale, became a United States citizen,
and returned to Argentina. He and other people I trust have told
me Mr. Calvaro made a fortune in the oil business. He came back
to the U.S. and set up what is called a hedge fund. Ten years ago.
The hedge fund, he said, has only U.S. investors and trades only in
U.S. assets."

"How long ago did you meet Mr. Calvaro?"

With an almost puzzled expression, Angelina continued to look
at the jurors. "A year ago? Nine months ago?"

"Why did you meet him?"

"To the best of my recollection, I was introduced to Robert
Calvaro by one of the lawyers I had hired to make sure that nothing
that I did, or that was done in my name or on my behalf, violated
any of the rules about super PACs or campaign financing."

"And you met Mr. Calvaro?"

"I did."

"Where?"

"He had long been a member of the New York Athletic Club. We
had lunch there."

"What did you talk to him about?"

"He said he was the lead partner in something called the Fund for
America, which was the name of his hedge fund. He described that

the billions of dollars of his own money and his investors' money he controlled through his hedge fund he wanted to concentrate, and did, in fact, concentrate, on projects that I as a Senator advocated."

"Such as?"

"Solar power. Reversing climate change. Desalinating ocean water. Wind turbines. Other progressive businesses. Microloans for small underfunded businesses in disadvantaged communities. Real-world methods of developing religious conciliation."

"Did you say anything?"

"Not a great deal. My priorities were clear to him."

"What else did Mr. Calvaro say?"

"He said he had taken the liberty of formally establishing a super PAC called, I think he said, *America Renewed*, and that he intended to use that super PAC to the maximum extent he could to lend support to the issues important to him that any candidate, presumably a Democrat, who, if elected President, could advance. In other words, the priorities he and I had."

"And you said?"

"That I appreciated his views, his vision, but that I felt very useful as a Senator. I was not at all sure I wanted to be a presidential candidate. He should, I said, talk to other people as well."

"And?"

"Mr. Calvaro said he had and would. But that the only name that kept being raised was mine."

"Did he speak with an accent?"

Calmly, Angelina said, "I don't want to offend anyone. I heard all the jurors speak during jury selection. It was a rainbow of voices. New York voices. I know at times I have that slight Southern accent I absorbed when I was growing up in Jefferson Parish in Louisiana." She smiled. "I can hear it even now, as I speak.

"But I came north as a young woman to go to college in New England. Many of the young men I met had those privileged prep school accents, and Robert Calvaro had gone to St. Paul's in New Hampshire, I think, the most old-fashioned of the New England prep schools. And then he went to Yale. His voice had that kind of elite New England accent." She paused again. "But obviously his first language was Spanish."

"And you knew that because you knew he was born in Argentina?"

"No. I knew that because toward the end of our lunch, which was a very comfortable one—he was a gentleman; I have to confess I have a weak spot for gentlemen; my husband Jimmy was a gentleman—I began speaking to him in Spanish. I learned the rudiments of Spanish in college and when I decided, after my husband died, to live in New York, I learned to speak Spanish well. So we spoke in Spanish for a while."

"What did he say at that point?"

"Surprisingly, he asked me if I wanted to play squash. The New York Athletic Club has the best squash courts in America."

"Do you know how to play?"

"I do, but not well. He had learned at prep school and Yale. I told him it would be for me like getting into the ring with Mike Tyson at his prime. He asked me if it would be okay for him to contact me again. We were just being playful in that part of the conversation."

"Did you leave with an impression of Robert Calvaro?"

"I enjoyed his company. But I enjoy almost everybody's company, or at least I try to."

"Was Mr. Calvaro a United States citizen?"

"He brought that up. He said he was a naturalized United States citizen. He even enjoyed displaying pictures on his cell phone of the day when he was sworn in in this courthouse, as it has turned out, as a citizen along with one hundred thirty-six other people. He said it was the proudest day of his life."

Raquel suppressed the reaction that this was yet another lie from Angelina Baldesteri. She couldn't think of anyone the Senator liked or enjoyed. She never once showed any interest in the personal or emotional lives of the four to five young aides who constantly trailed her.

"What," Raquel asked, "happened next?"

"As far as Mr. Calvaro was concerned?"

"That's right."

"I am a careful person, Ms. Rematti. I used—and my lawyers told me it was perfectly legal and prudent—leftover campaign funds to hire three independent private investigators to check Mr. Calvaro out, thoroughly."

"Did you get answers?"

"I did. They all gave me reports. Everything Mr. Calvaro told me was true."

The mesmerized courtroom was suddenly disrupted. "Objection," Hunter Decker said, "absolute hearsay."

"Overruled."

Decker made a gambit to have Naomi Goldstein reconsider. "Total hearsay," he said.

"Sit down, Mr. Decker. You heard my ruling."

Unfazed, Raquel continued. "You saw Government Exhibit 673, Ms. Baldesteri?"

"Yes. You mean that picture?"

"Your hand is on Mr. Calvaro's shoulder in that photo, correct?"

"It is."

"And what was happening?"

"We talked a little. It was after I announced my candidacy. Mr. Calvaro had kept his promises. Not everybody who wants access to me does that—by which I mean, makes promises and then follows through on them. In Mr. Calvaro's case, the super PAC *America Renewed* put funds into those segments and internal committees of my campaign that focused on issues such as education for the poor, underpaid labor, scientific research on stem cells, peace initiatives in Syria and Kurdistan."

"Did any of that money go to you?"

"No, absolutely not. The *America Renewed* super PAC paid airlines for flights, paid staff salaries of people who worked twenty-four seven and three hundred sixty-five days a year for my committee, but those payments were used to advance issues, not me." She stopped, and then resumed. "You know, Ms. Rematti, there are people who, to put it quite simply, hate me. Some of these haters hold very high offices. Many of them are richer than Midas. There are media outlets that watch, and distort, everything I do and say. So, I surround myself with careful staff members—accountants, lawyers, advisors—who watch and vet every dime."

Decker stood. "Move to strike all of that, Your Honor. Totally self-serving and utterly irrelevant."

Naomi Goldstein adjusted the reading lamp near her face. There was a moment of real hesitation and then she said, to Raquel's surprise, "Sustained. The jury will ignore every word of that answer that begins when the witness speaks of how she is hated."

Adjusting rapidly, Raquel said, "Your campaign hired independent accountants?"

"Yes."

"Did Mr. Calvaro tell you whom to hire?"

"Absolutely not."

"Did he tell you what airlines to use?"

"Never."

"Did Mr. Calvaro tell your campaign what hotels to use?"

"No."

"What advertising to purchase?"

"No."

"Which consultants and employees to hire?"

"No."

Slowly Raquel shifted ground. "Let's go back to the famous Government Exhibit 673, where your hand is on Mr. Calvaro's shoulder. Are you back there with me?"

"Sure."

"Do you remember saying anything to him?"

"I do."

"What?"

"I said, 'Thank you for keeping your promises.'"

"And he said?"

"He said, 'I always do, Senator, I always do.'"

"How often have you seen him since then?"

"I can't recall."

"When was the last time you talked to him?"

"I can't recall."

"Do you sign quarterly reports of income and expenses for your presidential committee?"

"I do. That's what the law requires."

"And above your signature the printed words say you are telling the truth in all the figures on the thirty pages and thousands of numbers on the reports, is that right?"

"Yes, Ms. Rematti. I don't have the ability to understand thousands of numbers. I do sign them. The reality is I have to rely on what people I trust put on the forms. I'm only human, Ms. Rematti. Just human."

CHAPTER 31

RAQUEL HAD A tremendous sense of relief forged by years of experience. Even though it was Angelina Baldesteri's decision to testify—it was *her* right and all a lawyer could do on the issue was recommend, warn, or suggest—it was Raquel who did have the right to select the approach to the questioning and do the best that was possible to make the Senator likable and convincing. Raquel also knew she wanted the jurors to have an aerial view of Senator Angelina Baldesteri. It would be a mistake to have Angelina "hack around in the weeds" by looking at the Federal Election Campaign reports line by line, category by category. It would also have been a mistake to have Angelina even glance at the hundreds of bank statements of her campaign that Decker's assistant lawyers had introduced as evidence through government accountants who tried to convey to the jurors that the bank statements contained gaps and inconsistencies or were deliberately obscure in order to veil the real source of the money and how and where it was spent. The jurors, as Raquel had observed, were profoundly bored by those documents and that testimony.

Less is more was an Ernest Hemingway adage she shared with her Columbia students. As Senator Baldesteri remained in the witness seat after Raquel announced, "No further questions," she momentarily felt relief for another reason. It was three thirty on a Friday afternoon. For decades Naomi Goldstein had suspended her trials at three thirty on Fridays. She was an observant Jew who lived from her birth in the largely Jewish neighborhood in the peaceful old-world area of Manhattan's West End Avenue from West 79th Street to 96th Street. For every Friday of her seventy-five years she had always observed the Friday Sabbath that made it essential that she not travel by car, subway, or any other means after the setting of the Lord's sun.

So Raquel was surprised when she heard Naomi Goldstein say, "Mr. Decker, I assume you have questions. You may start now."

Hunter Decker had many skills, even though like all experienced lawyers, he was capable of mistakes. One thing he sensed for certain was that Senator Baldesteri—carefully controlled by Raquel Rematti—had created a swift and favorable impression on the jurors. Another truism among trial lawyers is that a witness who left a good impression at the end of a trial week gained the benefit of having the jurors reflect during the weekend that the witness was *nice*.

But the flip side was also true. A closing Friday witness who conveyed annoyance, menace, hostility, unjustified pride, arrogance, or falsehood left those smoldering traces for the weekend, too, and they festered to become perceived realities.

Hunter Decker had just been handed a gift by Naomi Goldstein—at least thirty minutes to begin the work of degrading the image of Senator Angelina Baldesteri before the weekend break.

"Good afternoon, Ms. Baldesteri."

"Good afternoon."

"We've never spoken before, have we?"

"I introduced myself to you, Mr. Decker, at the start of the trial. You said hello but refused to shake my hand. That's the extent of the communication we had."

Decker ignored that: he was a lawyer, not a politician. He had never won a single vote; Angelina Baldesteri had won millions of votes. She had that endearing Southern accent; she had been the First Lady of the United States. Her assassinated husband's popularity was almost astronomical at the time he was killed.

But Decker knew other things about this highly attractive woman. Hundreds of people—FBI agents, Assistant U.S. Attorneys, informants—had worked for him for months to dig for her vulnerabilities. No one was perfect. Certainly, as he knew, Angelina Baldesteri wasn't perfect, not by a long shot.

"Ms. Baldesteri, you just answered Ms. Rematti's questions about Robert Calvaro, you remember that, don't you?"

"Certainly, I remember that, Mr. Decker. It just happened."

"And you told the jury you couldn't remember meeting with Mr. Calvaro after that picture which has been marked Government Exhibit 673?"

"I may have talked to Mr. Calvaro by cell phone a few times after. I can't rule that out."

"You're lying," Decker said.

Angelina, unfazed, immediately answered, "Is that a question? If it is a question, you are even more of a charlatan than I thought."

Hunter was above insult or challenge. He asked, "You're staying while this trial is going on at the Waldorf Astoria, correct?"

Angelina Baldesteri's coolness was disarming. In her past, that coolness and calm had frightened many people. But it had impressed many thousands. It had also confused many. She said, calmly leaning forward to the slender microphone and staring steadily at Decker, "The Waldorf was where President Young and I stayed when we were in New York. And now it is the hotel that is about eight blocks away from my lawyer's office. I don't own or rent an apartment in New York City. The Waldorf is familiar to me and convenient for me and Ms. Rematti. So, yes, I've been staying there."

"How long has this trial been underway, Ms. Baldesteri?"

"Five and a half weeks. Almost forty days, Mr. Decker."

"And how many of the nights during this trial has Mr. Calvaro spent with you at your suite in the Waldorf?"

"None, Mr. Decker. None. Mr. Calvaro put a distance between himself and me when you and the President and the Attorney General you work for decided to indict me for no reason other than political vengeance. You wanted to isolate and dehumanize me and alienate me from people."

"Why don't you turn your attention," Decker smoothly said, "to the computer screens."

Identical images illuminated the large and small computer screens throughout the courtroom. The first was a precisely delineated silent surveillance recording of a man in an oversize baseball cap and wearing a Waldorf Astoria janitor's uniform as he used a card key to open the door of Room 801. His left profile was partially visible. The surveillance footage bore distinct and legible words and numbers revealing that it was recorded at 7:01 p.m. on the first day of the trial.

Raquel, knowing it would be futile to do so because Naomi Goldstein would rebuff her effort at an objection in the jury's presence, sat silently as the fifteen-second scene unfolded.

"Ms. Baldesteri, isn't it true," Decker asked, "that on the first several nights of the trial you stayed in Room 801 of the Waldorf?"

"I did."

"Do you see the man depicted on the video?"

"I do."

"Who is he?"

"He looks like a hotel employee, a janitor."

"Isn't it true that the man in the Waldorf uniform and baseball cap is Robert Calvaro?"

"Not as far as I can see."

"Do you see three Secret Service agents near the door to Room 801?"

"I see them, I know them."

"Is it part of the training of Secret Service agents to simply let janitors enter your room in the middle of the night?"

"I don't train Secret Service agents. As I recall it, the air-conditioning was malfunctioning and I had asked one of the agents to call for a handyman."

"Is Robert Calvaro a handyman?"

"I don't answer stupid questions. That man in the work uniform fixed the air-conditioning."

"And that took him all night?"

"Please, sir, don't play silly games with me."

"Next image," Decker instructed seamlessly. The screens then were illuminated with the image of the same man in the Waldorf uniform. The words on the footage stated in white letters that the film was recorded the next morning at 6:37. Emerging from Room 801, the man in the recording for five seconds was not wearing the baseball cap. His full face as he glanced casually down the eighth-floor hallway was on the screen. He then pulled the brown Waldorf baseball cap from his rear pocket and tugged it tightly over his head, lowering the front brim so that its outer edge was well below his eyes. There were three different Secret Service agents near the door to Room 801. The agents paid no attention to him.

"Isn't it a fact, Ms. Baldesteri, that the man we just saw on the surveillance tapes is Robert Calvaro?"

As she gazed at her client, Raquel remained seated, her expression as reassuring as she always tried to maintain it while watching one of her clients being flayed on the witness stand. There was no point in objecting. Goldstein undoubtedly would have overruled it.

Decker, holding a computer wand, had the screens throughout the courtroom display the image of Robert Calvaro in Government Exhibit 673 alongside the face of the man on the surveillance footage.

"Do you see those two photographs side by side, Ms. Baldesteri?"

Transfixed, every juror was staring at the computer screen image.

Angelina Baldesteri said, "I see them."

There was a long pause. In absolute silence, everyone in the courtroom gazed at the parallel images.

Finally, Hunter Decker asked, "Where is Mr. Calvaro now?"

"I have no idea."

Decker looked at the judge. "Your Honor, the Government asks to resume the cross-examination on Monday morning."

"Certainly, sir."

CHAPTER 32

LYDIA GUZMAN COULDN'T remember a day in her twenty-five years when she had enjoyed herself so much, and she was a young woman who was determined to live out the message of the Cyndi Lauper song, first popular long before Lydia was born,

Girls, girls just wanna have fun.

Early on that Saturday morning, even before dawn, Hugo Salazar arrived in a Mercedes limousine in front of her apartment building on Tremont Avenue in the Bronx. The driver—one of the blond men with the zigzag symbol engraved into his short hair who had walked with Raquel Rematti a few days earlier as she crossed 72nd Street at Madison Avenue before they were joined by another well-dressed man with the identical zigzag marking—left the Mercedes to ring the buzzer to Lydia's apartment. She was in the back seat of the luxurious car within three minutes.

Just after dawn they were on the spotless yacht in the marina on the bay near LaGuardia Airport. The yacht, all gleaming white with burnished fittings and on the yacht's prow an American flag snapping brightly in the clean and refreshing morning breeze, was named the *Golden Seahorse*. Acres of tall salt grass swayed in the freshening dawn breeze on the marina's shores. A bright sliver of moon still gleamed in the deep blue expanse of the sky. An early-arriving jet made its graceful, almost noiseless descent into LaGuardia.

Lydia had never been on a private yacht. Hugo gracefully held her hand as he guided her through the gently rocking *Golden Seahorse*. She saw a linen-draped table with breakfast food covered by silver platters at the top of the galley that led to the yacht's interior. There was a blond man with shorn hair, smiling and dressed in a white tuxedo, who waited for Hugo and Lydia. He was the other man who a few days earlier had walked alongside Raquel Rematti on Madison Avenue. Both of these men were completely unknown to Lydia, who was impressed by the fact that two blond men worked as a driver and waiter for Hugh Salazar. She paid no attention to the zigzag images engraved in their close-cropped hair. In her experience almost all men under the age of forty had distinctive tattoos, and for her the zigzags were nothing more than a unique form of tattoo, a body ornament.

As she and Hugo ate, the *Golden Seahorse* made its steady way from the marina. Its massive engine was virtually soundless. Within minutes the skyline of Manhattan in the early morning rose over the horizon like the Emerald City, an otherworldly spectacle. The heights of the legendary buildings glinted in multiple bright colors. The top of the Chrysler Building, which had always looked to Lydia like melting ice cream on a cone, was blue, green, and silver in the dawn light, and the pinnacle of the Empire State Building was a startling blue against the blue sky. Farther downtown, barely visible beyond the skyscrapers, was the upward-pointing spear of the new World Trade Center building.

By early afternoon the yacht passed under the two-mile span of the Verrazano-Narrows Bridge connecting Brooklyn and Staten Island. Gloriously and brazenly naked, Lydia lay on the *Golden*

Seahorse's white deck. Hugo, a man with the body of an Olympic decathlon champion, lay beside her, wearing only a taut black bathing suit. He held her hand, almost chastely. The Statue of Liberty, Governor's Island, Ellis Island, and the Battery all passed by, as if in slow motion. The huge yacht rolled gently on the calm waters of New York Harbor and the Hudson River.

It was two in the afternoon when Lydia happily said, "Hey, Hugo, let's do a few lines of coke." Still naked, Lydia, in all her physical glory, walked down the galley, unconcerned about the two blond men who discreetly watched her. Eager and swift-footed, Hugo followed her. The cocaine, in a silver chalice, had pride of place on the coffee table. She inhaled through a silver spoon. She settled deeply into a suede sofa. Her smile deepened, she held her nostrils closed, and her eyes luxuriantly widened as if she were suddenly viewing a world of verdant upland pastures. She patted the sofa. "Sit down, man, next to me. Come on."

Lydia used the tiny silver spoon to renew the cocaine's profound loosening of her muscles, nerves, brain, vagina. By four, as the boat was returning to the marina, Hugo and Lydia were watching a *Jason Bourne* movie with Matt Damon on the flat-screen television.

Still naked, she said, "Baby, forget all this boom-boom, shoot-it-up shit. You know, I never saw that movie with that Linda Lovelace broad. *Deep Mouth? Deep Throat? Deep Shit?*" She was laughing; her laugh was honest, infectious. Hugo played ten minutes of the grainy, low-tech, too brightly colored *Deep Throat*. For Lydia, the film had a silly plot, which took too long to unfold before Linda Lovelace unfastened the anonymous man's pants. Lydia said in Spanish, "That lady doesn't know how to do it. I do."

And she took Hugo Salazar's heavy penis from the slender bathing suit he wore. Within fifteen seconds, her lips, tongue, and mouth made him fully erect. The rest was magic.

CHAPTER 33

THEY HAD DINNER in his penthouse apartment: pinto beans, green salad, filet mignon. Lydia was not a heavy drinker, but she joined Hugo when he sipped Pinch Scotch, without ice, from a crystal Cartier glass.

More often than he would have expected, but not enough to concern him, Lydia went to the marble bathroom near the dining room. Each time, as Hugo knew, she was inhaling a line or two of cocaine. She was, as she had been all day, happy, energized. Hugo had actually come, over time, to enjoy her: she was sexy, playful, a little haughty, but also attentive to him, wanting to be sure he was comfortable and well satisfied.

At nine, after Lydia had volunteered to clear the dining room table and put the dirty dishes and glasses in the gleaming, state-of-the-art kitchen, Hugo sat on the sofa in the living room. He didn't turn on the television set or the music system. It was quiet. The penthouse was thirty floors above Manhattan's busy Saturday night traffic. As he waited for her, he stared out the immaculate windows that encircled the living room. Millions of lights gleamed and glittered everywhere throughout the great city. *Here I am*, he thought, as if unimaginable wonders had happened in his life. He had been raised in a village in Mexico that had no electricity. His family's cinderblock house, painted all pink, had no internal toilet. There was running water in the faucets, but it was never heated. Chickens lived in the shallow basement; their pungent odor permeated the small house. The only ornaments were a crucifix and colorized photographs of Jesus and John F. Kennedy.

"Lydia?" It had been thirty minutes since he had last seen her when she carried the dishes to the kitchen. He walked there to tell her that one of the maids would arrive at ten the next morning to finish the cleaning.

Lydia wasn't in the kitchen. "Lydia," he said again. Just casually curious, he went to the bedroom. She was not there either. He noticed that the door to the bathroom was closed.

Despite the fact that he was a highly skilled killer, there was a strange, gentlemanly delicacy to Hugo Salazar. When he first crossed the border into the United States, he slept on a deflated air mattress in a two-room apartment in East Harlem that he shared with seven other men, most of whom worked at the car wash on First Avenue and 108th Street. Hugo, then using the name Juan Suarez, worked on the graveyard shift as a dishwasher at a Chinese restaurant on Second Avenue and 89th Street. He spent his days watching an old television that wasn't linked to a cable but did have an out-of-date DVR machine and, incongruously, a leftover stack of old Cary Grant movies. Watching the movies again and again taught him some oddly aristocratic English and also a repertoire of the mannerisms of the fluid-gestured gentleman Grant always enacted.

Now, in this penthouse apartment, he hesitated, as he imagined Cary Grant would if he were about to knock on the door to a room in which Eva Marie Saint might be combing her radiant hair.

Hugo finally knocked, discreetly, with the joint of his bent right index finger, the finger that was the most useful of the multiple ways he wielded knives and machetes. "Lydia," he gently said. "You okay, *amor*?"

No answer.

Hugo turned the knob. The door was unlocked, and he opened it.

Lydia Guzman was sprawled facedown on the marble floor. She was fully dressed.

Hugo knelt beside her. He stroked her neck and shoulders. In Spanish he said, "Wake up, sweetheart."

There was no movement, there was no pulse.

Gently Hugo turned her gorgeous body over. He looked at her face.

Hugo had killed so many people, and had seen so many dead men and women, that he instantly recognized by a glance at her utterly relaxed and faintly blue face that Lydia Guzman was dead.

The drugs had overwhelmed her.

* * *

Hugo calmly walked through the apartment. He took out the expensive leather garment bag he used whenever he knew he would bring Lydia to the apartment, where he did not in fact live. He put in his garment bag the few personal items, such as a change of clothes, cologne, and shaving equipment that he carried back and forth to the apartment when Oscar Caliente told him to use it.

Hugo then found the expensive Chanel bag Lydia had bought at Saks with three thousand dollars he had given her two weeks earlier. She had treasured the bag. He emptied it out on the kitchen counter and spread out the contents: lipstick, makeup, keys, aspirin, a condom packet, and sixteen one-hundred-dollar bills. He took all the cash. He tossed the rest of the contents back into the Chanel bag.

Her new diamond-studded iPhone was on the dining room table. He slipped it into his pocket, knowing that he would soon crush it on the street and throw the pieces into a series of public trash cans. He wanted no traces of himself or Lydia anywhere. Oscar Caliente had arranged for one of his technical experts to insert a sliver of a chip in each cell phone that would at all times track their movements and locations.

It was yet again time for Hugo Salazar to disappear into another life and another name.

CHAPTER 34

BEFORE DAWN ON Monday morning, Raquel Rematti routinely tapped the icons on her iPad for the *New York Times,* the *New York Post,* and the *New York Daily News.* Checking the headlines had become part of her morning ritual, like brushing her teeth, even before she made her Spartan breakfast of hard-boiled eggs, toast, and coffee. Her months with Hayes Smith had imbued her with that habit.

The perfectly illuminated iconography of the front pages of both the *Post* and the *Daily News* displayed almost identical headlines, and they instantly arrested her attention. From the *Post*: *Angie Juror Dead on Coke OD.* And from the *News*: *Juror 12 OD.* Raquel then turned on the two local all-news stations, WCBS and WINS, which she normally avoided like a plague because of their merciless, loud, and repetitive advertising, instead of her usual NPR station.

As she ate, showered, and dressed, she heard the stream of excited, clashing announcers' voices and recurrent words: *"A Hispanic juror... a woman, a Bronx beautician found dead on Sunday morning in the bathroom of a luxurious penthouse in Midtown... NYPD detectives and FBI agents investigating..."*

Several times she tried, with no success, to reach Angelina Baldesteri. Everything Raquel sent had gone unanswered: voice mails, text messages, emails, messenger notifications on the private messenger screen on Facebook. She had even gone to the reception desk at the Waldorf, where she was told by the hotel's security staff that information as to the Senator couldn't be released. "But I'm her lawyer," Raquel had said. And in response they gave her a wordless, implacable smile.

In reaching out to Angelina, Raquel had several purposes—a tongue-lashing about the blatant lies regarding Robert Calvaro's nights at the Waldorf, a speech about the unspeakable stupidity of carrying on a relationship with Calvaro in the first place, a loud reminder as to how Angelina's wiseass arrogance led her to take the stand in the first place, and a lecture on how, from Raquel's standpoint after years in this very arcane and difficult business, Angelina would likely have won the case without putting on any kind of defense since, in Raquel's view, there was no proof beyond a reasonable doubt that the Senator had given directions to anyone to divert money, to mask the source of funds, or to sign intentionally false filings. Raquel privately believed all of that was true and that the Senator had in fact done all those things, but proof beyond a reasonable doubt was altogether a different issue.

And now Raquel had the urgent need to talk about the overdose death of the exotic Lydia Guzman. And the bribery.

Raquel had even taken her pristine and rarely used black Porsche—her gift to herself after she was miraculously told she was at last free of cancer—from the parking garage on the far West Side across 96th Street to the glittering Triboro Bridge on the East Side. Guided by the voice on the GPS unit of the powerful car, she drove north off the first exit of the bridge to the New York State Thruway. It was only a fifteen-minute drive to Larchmont. Raquel drove through the bucolic suburban streets to 45 Forrest Avenue. The Tudor-style house that was the Senator's official, but illusory, New York residence was empty.

Normally not a news junkie, Raquel listened for hours to multiple sources of information. She talked to no one. She returned none of the dozens of messages she received by email, cell phone, and text. She would only respond to the Senator if she ever made contact.

She was riveted by only one item of information. "We believe," the FBI director for the New York region said in an interview on WCBS, "that Ms. Guzman was a frequent user of cocaine. But we are not yet identifying this as a drug overdose. That is because preliminary reports indicate that the lethal substance ricin was interlaced in the cocaine in her body."

* * *

It was eight thirty on Monday morning when Raquel next saw Angelina Baldesteri, and it happened in the courtroom. Naomi Goldstein's young, efficient law clerk, whose job was to make sure that the judge had the papers and water and other things she might need, had the email addresses in case of an emergency of all the lawyers, the jurors, and Angelina. Goldstein, old-fashioned as she was, but alert enough to be drawn somewhat into the digital world, had arranged to send out through her law clerk a message that she would like the lawyers and the Senator in her courtroom thirty minutes earlier than the jurors were expected to arrive.

Raquel was seated alone at eight fifteen at the defense table when she heard behind her the sharp clicking of Angelina's high heels accompanied by the soft shuffle of the Secret Service agents' comfortable rubber-soled shoes.

Raquel did not turn to look at her client. She simply waited for the Senator to take the wooden seat beside her. Angelina didn't say good morning. Nor did Raquel. They didn't even glance at each other.

Raquel, pretending to make notes on a pad, spoke first. "Where were you this weekend?"

"What do you mean?"

"I reached out to you in every possible way. You never got back to me."

"I was busy. There were many campaign issues I had to deal with."

Still staring at the almost hieroglyphic markings on her pad, and without looking up, Raquel said, "Your campaign? Tell me: Are you in this world?"

"You have only one world, Raquel. I have many."

"Do you mean to tell me that you don't know that the twelfth juror, Lydia Guzman, died of an overdose?"

"I know that."

"And didn't you think we might have things we needed to discuss? There are no more alternate jurors. This is unprecedented, it raises dangerous issues."

"We have enough time to talk now," Angelina said.

"No, we don't. Goldstein will be calling us all—Decker, the other prosecutors, you, me—into her chambers soon." Irritation in her expression, she finally glanced at Angelina. "And besides, as you can see, I've got notes in front of me for a letter I have to write to another judge for another client. *All* my clients are equally important to me. *You* are not my Alpha and Omega."

The Senator abruptly stood up and walked to the courtroom windows overlooking the bright, sun-glinting surface of the East River. She said nothing as Hunter Decker and his six assistants entered the courtroom like a platoon of well-disciplined, grim soldiers.

Cyrus Johnson, the massive bailiff, signaled all of them by banging on the door with his boxer's palm to follow him to the judge's chambers.

In her chambers, the never-changing Naomi Goldstein, always in a simple black dress, was already seated at the head of her immense table covered with orderly files from this and other cases. Decker and his staff knew they were expected to sit at her right. Raquel and Angelina were in the chairs at her left. Just behind the judge was the court reporter.

"Good morning, ladies and gentlemen," Goldstein began.

There was a responsive murmur of voices, barely audible. Angelina didn't say a word.

Goldstein glanced at the mute court reporter, who began to type as soon as the judge said, "We are on the record in *United States v. Angelina Baldesteri*. Present in chambers are the defendant, together with her attorney Raquel Rematti, and Hunter Decker, the United States Attorney for the Southern District of New York, together with six of his prosecuting assistants."

Goldstein referenced words on a sheet of paper in front of her. "It has been brought to my attention that the last of the twelve jurors, Lydia Guzman, died over the weekend. Mr. Decker, is that information correct?"

"It is."

"Let me be clear," Goldstein said. "It is not the court's concern as to how Ms. Guzman died, although, of course, I have sympathy for her family and friends. Instead, my concern is that death's impact on this trial. When we selected a jury, there were eighteen men and women seated and sworn as jurors. In other words, there were six alternate jurors. My concern at the time, as in all criminal trials, was that there were seated jurors who might have to be excused as the long trial progressed. And in fact, as it turned out, we had six jurors who had to be excused for a variety of legitimate reasons, such as illness. All of those reasons for excusals were set forth on the record at the time they happened. I just want to say, possibly unnecessarily, that in all my years on the bench I have never had more than six alternate jurors for a criminal trial. It is not and never has been my practice to excuse any seated juror for anything less than compelling reasons."

No one else spoke. Raquel knew that even Naomi Goldstein, as a federal judge with tenure for life, was protecting herself. She was building what lawyers called a "record." Even judges needed a record if there were appeals because no trial judge was happy with a reversal from the appeals court.

Goldstein continued, "The Senator, like all defendants, is absolutely entitled to a jury of twelve of her peers. And the law also gives her the right to require that the Government prove her guilt beyond a reasonable doubt to all of those twelve jurors. If even a single juror is *not* persuaded of her guilt beyond a reasonable doubt, then Ms. Baldesteri cannot be convicted." She stopped briefly. "But you all know that."

Angelina, who was behind Raquel and so not visible to her, made a soft groan of exasperation, as though this whole process, and even this moment, were distractions to her. Only Raquel heard the groan and only Raquel, after months of exposure to this difficult chameleon woman, understood her client's mood.

Goldstein continued, "I have never been confronted in any of my criminal cases with this situation before. But the law does allow the defendant to elect to proceed with a jury of eleven if the twelfth juror is disqualified, becomes unavailable, or dies.

"The defendant, if he or she makes that decision, continues to enjoy all his or her constitutional rights: the presumption of innocence, the right to have guilt proven beyond any reasonable doubt, the right to cross-examine witnesses, the right to a jury of her peers—without the loss of any other constitutional rights."

Goldstein glanced at the Senator. Raquel could not see the old judge's expression and detected simply by registering Goldstein's reaction that Angelina was in Sphinx mode, without expression, impassive.

The judge said, "So the only issue now, simply put, is how the defendant elects to proceed. She has two alternatives. One is to exercise her right to a full jury of twelve. If she makes that election, then there must be a mistrial, and then we start this process all over again as if the last five or six weeks never happened. I would then schedule a new trial, with a panel of twenty-two seated jurors, only twelve of whom will at the end be randomly designated the final twelve actual jurors who will decide the case."

Raquel said, "Obviously, Judge, the Senator will need time to consult with me and probably others. That will take time."

"How much time?"

"Two days."

"That long?"

"At least."

"Mr. Decker, is there anything you want to say?"

"Nothing except that the remaining jurors will have to be excused for a day or two while the defendant decides. I'm concerned, too, that one or more of the remaining jurors will be intimidated, or fearful, or concerned that Lydia Guzman's death was somehow related to her presence among the jurors."

Staring without even blinking at Decker, the judge said, "I'm not going to require you to answer this because judges don't investigate deaths or any kind of potential crime. But can you tell me what caused Ms. Guzman's death? That might help me more fully understand what concerns you think the other jury members might have."

"I can't answer that in detail for a host of reasons. But Ms. Guzman was a drug addict. She died in the apartment of a man whose picture has appeared in an exhibit at this trial and whose name has been mentioned several times at the trial, Hugo Salazar.

The FBI and the NYPD are conducting the investigation. There are suggestions she may have known Hugo Salazar before the trial, but under a different name or a fictitious one. Law enforcement officials are searching for the man who was with her in the apartment, the man whose picture we showed at trial and whose name the jurors have heard. We believe Lydia Guzman saw him many times during the course of the trial. He left the apartment either before or after she died. We know from the staff at the building, and from the building's surveillance system, that he had arrived with her and five hours later left alone."

Goldstein said, "That's enough for my purposes. I will tell the jurors on the record when they arrive that a tragedy has taken place and that Ms. Guzman is dead, which I'm sure they already know. And that they should return to court at noon tomorrow for more guidance about the direction of the trial."

Raquel was surprised, even angry. "So the Senator has slightly more than twenty-four hours to make this important decision?"

Goldstein stared at her. "I have to take your skills and the Senator's skill and experience into account. Both of you are experienced and intelligent. That's more than adequate time to decide. The jurors, on the other hand, are making sacrifices of time and emotion. And my job is to give the Senator due process, not a perfect world for herself."

"Your Honor," Decker said, "we would ask that as soon as the eleven remaining jurors leave the courthouse they be assigned security details of four agents each and sequestered in hotel rooms."

Normally utterly impassive, Naomi Goldstein said, "Early on, Mr. Decker, you asked me to have the jury completely sequestered. Ms. Rematti made a very effective argument against that, emphasizing that to do so would at least unconsciously lead the jurors to believe the Senator was guilty or had dangerous people under her control. I ruled against you. Now, in effect, you are asking for the same thing. I'm not inclined to change my mind."

"Circumstances have changed, Judge."

"How so?"

"Lydia Guzman was a rogue juror."

"You claimed that just a week ago, Mr. Decker. Out of respect for your office, for the position you hold, I brought her in here. I examined her. She was, I admit, tough." Almost smiling, she glanced at Raquel. "I liked that in her."

"This is different, Judge," Decker persisted.

"Tell me how?"

"Preliminary toxicology reports suggest it was not just a cocaine overdose. Traces of the deadly poison ricin were found in her bloodstream as well as the cocaine."

Naomi Goldstein leaned back in her uncomfortable-looking wooden chair. Raquel had always thought that as people aged their faces became more and more set like masks, unreadable. Did Goldstein now look angry, concerned, unconvinced? The mask had loosened, yet its message was not clear.

But her words made clear she was irritated with Decker. "No, no, no."

"Will you at least remind them that they should talk to no one about the trial?"

"I say that every day."

"And they shouldn't listen to anything about the Guzman death?"

"I'll say that."

"And will you instruct Ms. Rematti or anyone associated with her not to speak to the jurors?"

"That," Goldstein said, "is completely unnecessary, Mr. Decker. She is one of the most experienced lawyers I've ever had in my courtroom. She knows she can't do that. I'm not going to order her to do something she would not do."

Decker said, "You might have forgotten the photographs we gave you, Judge, just before we let you know our concerns about Lydia Guzman's being bribed and corruptly influenced."

"I remember the photos," Goldstein said.

"But you're busy, Judge, so you may not have completely focused on the one that shows Guzman and the man named we think Hugo Salazar, an associate of the person known as Robert Calvaro, recently standing in a tight trio with Raquel Rematti."

Raquel, quickly and powerfully standing, pushed the chair in which she had been seated so forcefully that it fell on its side on the floor. "Decker," she shouted, "you know that picture is a fake, a total phony. We've talked about this. You're lying. I'm going to make you wish you had never set foot in a court."

Raquel reached across the wide table toward Hunter Decker. She was a tall, powerful woman. When she was a blossoming young teenager in Lawrence, her father, a failed semi-professional boxer, had said, "Boys are going to look at you in ways I don't like. I can't be with you to protect you all the time. So I'm going to teach you things about how to hurt men." And he did. "And after you kick them in the balls and knock them down," he had said, "you never let them get up. Use a garbage can or anything you can find to beat them down and keep them down. Word will get out—don't even think about fucking around with Tony Rematti's daughter."

The Lawrence Girl: there was a part of her that still treasured the Lawrence Girl, the street brawler, and not all the years at Ivy League colleges and law schools had ever taken that internal core from her even though she had never had to use it after the age of fifteen. It was what she had sensed, and admired, about Lydia Guzman when Lydia had been brought into Goldstein's chamber.

Hunter Decker could not control his stunned surprise and even fear. He thought Raquel was setting herself in a position to lunge at his eyes. And then, although no one spoke or moved, Raquel simply stopped. She picked up the chair and, still standing, pushed the chair into its place. She remained standing.

Goldstein, without ever once expressing it, respected Raquel and she knew after all her years that long intense trials aroused passions and even irrationality in the most seasoned lawyers such as Raquel. Trials, Goldstein often commented, were not for the fainthearted.

Goldstein finally and without emotion said, "I think we've covered enough ground here. These are, I know, difficult circumstances for everyone. Even for me. I will see you all in the courtroom in ten minutes so that I can speak, as I've indicated, to the jurors. And I will then see all of you here in my chambers at nine tomorrow morning to learn the defendant's decision and move on from there. And, Mr. Decker, I will tell the jurors they are free to return home. Your motions regarding them and Ms. Rematti are denied."

CHAPTER 35

As HAD HAPPENED so often in his life, Hugo Salazar had only one objective: to survive. At the moment he recognized that Lydia Guzman was dead, he realized, too, that Oscar Caliente would order his death. In the years he'd known Caliente, he had developed a sixth sense as to the man's lunatic ways of thinking, planning, and irrationally giving irrevocable orders. Caliente detested failure to carry out his orders.

Thousands of dollars had already been spent, both in cash and cocaine, on Lydia Guzman. She was supposed to live to perform her assignment—to vote for the acquittal of Angelina Baldesteri. All that money was now wasted. And Lydia had died while with Hugo. It was a unique one-person assignment. It wouldn't matter that Hugo had succeeded in seducing Lydia Guzman: "She's a slut and a cokehead," Robert Calvaro had said when Hugo first told him Lydia agreed to take the money and the cocaine in exchange for her vote. "How could you miss?"

Nor would it matter that Hugo had converted Lydia into his girl-friend. Her emotional and physical attachment to him was insurance that the deal would be kept. And Lydia had another important virtue: she was street-smart and knew that if she failed to deliver on her promise, Hugo's men would inevitably punish her. She was bound to him by money, drugs, sex, affection, and fear.

Above all, Hugo recognized that Oscar Caliente not only did not tolerate failure but never allowed anyone to be left in a position to tell secrets. Men who knew his secrets were men who needed to be watched, controlled, or made silent forever. Everyone could be replaced, including Hugo Salazar.

After leaving the penthouse apartment—which for three years was rented at $25,000 each month by the Polo Grounds, LLC, but used only six times by Robert Calvaro, for five weeks by Hugo and was otherwise empty—Hugo went to the apartment he had rented, under the name Hugo Cortes, on York Avenue at 88th Street. It was a spare, neat, one-bedroom apartment in an immense but nondescript building that had a British-sounding name, the Oxford. Hugo was popular there with the uniformed doormen and the small army of porters and handymen. All of them spoke Spanish. They admired Señor Cortes. He dressed each day in tastefully tailored British suits, he was an executive, he traveled often, and it seemed that almost every night he was home he came through the lobby with different women, all gorgeous, most of them blond. The doormen admired Hugo as if he were a famous baseball player, a modern conqueror. He had never brought Lydia Guzman to this building.

Hurriedly and methodically, he packed three leather suitcases with his most expensive clothing and also with the kinds of clothes he had worn when he worked years earlier as a dishwasher at a Chinese restaurant—blue jeans, tee shirts printed with the names of the Mets and the Yankees, and the almost inflexible and oversize baseball caps that were worn with the stiff bills pulled to the right or left side of his head like a teenager who was already in a gang or aspiring to a gang membership. Hugo also carefully packed supple, four-thousand-dollar dress shoes with wooden shoe trees in them. Finally, he took from the safe drilled into the back of one of the closets $225,000 in cash, two pistols, bullets, a switchblade, and his favorite weapon, a machete. He also removed the three passports from Brazil, Colombia, and Argentina, three drivers' licenses from New York, California, and Florida, and six American Express cards. The passports, credit cards, and licenses all had his pictures and the names Ramon Alvarez, Gustavo Lopez, and Raul Escribano. The credit limits on each card were unrestricted.

Hugo stacked his locked leather suitcases and bags just inside the apartment door. After a ride with a woman and her tiny child in the opulent elevator, he strolled through the lobby. Instead of retrieving his new Lexus sports car from the garage in the building's basement, he turned left on York Avenue in the direction of a Hertz rental garage on 91st Street, only a few blocks away. Discreetly, he took his gold-plated iPhone from the left pocket of his sports jacket and Lydia's diamond-encrusted iPhone and, unnoticed by anyone in the cool night, ground both of them under the heel of his right shoe as if he were extinguishing a cigarette. He was a strong man in every possible way: the cell phones were flattened to pieces. He quickly picked the fragments up and, with surprising ease, ripped the flattened phones into pieces. He dropped each of the unidentifiable pieces into separate trash cans as he walked to the Hertz garage.

He was now, he knew, untethered: Robert Calvaro and the ever-changing cast of men who did his bidding could not find him any time they wished through the unique signal from the cell phones.

At the Hertz counter he decided to use the license and American Express card of Raul Escribano. He ordered a Chevrolet four-by-four rather than the Lincoln Navigator the woman at the counter urged on him at the same price, as if she thought the black Lincoln was the ornament that a man as attractive as Raul Escribano should have.

Hugo parked the car one block from his apartment building rather than in its underground garage. Instead of the lobby, he re-entered the building through the service entrance and took one of the wheeled luggage carts in the worn service elevator to his apartment. He loaded the luggage cart and, after tossing the apartment keys on the floor, wheeled the loaded cart back to the service elevator and out of the building to the nearby street where the Chevy was parked. Once he loaded the car, he used the handle of his pistol to smash the GPS screen and the dashboard buttons of the car's navigation system.

CHAPTER 36

FIFTEEN MINUTES LATER, he was driving on the upper reaches of the West Side Highway. He had decided to travel to Canada. In the world in which he had so long lived, he'd learned that the border between the United States and Canada was porous even in the years after 9/11. To his left were the black waters of the Hudson River. There were moving points of light from barges and tugboats on the dark surface of the river. The New Jersey Palisades loomed high over the river's western shore. The walls of the Palisades were a cliff. At the top of the cliffs were towering apartment buildings, all alight. Ahead of him was the expanse of the George Washington Bridge outlined against the night sky by strings of lights. And to his right were the mossy black trees, shrubs, and boulders of Riverside Park.

The north-flowing traffic on the highway was sparse. Hugo intended to drive four hours to the north before stopping at any random chain motel he could find when he reached that four-hour point. He drove carefully, slightly below the speed limit. He was surprised, then, when a black unmarked patrol car in the vicinity of West 128th Street began flashing its lights, signaling for him to stop.

All along the West Side Highway were multiple areas where vehicles could pull over. Most of the cutoffs were large enough for only one, two, or three cars. They had originally been designed for unobstructed views and pictures of the majestic Hudson River and in the farther distance the cliffs of the New Jersey Palisades. Now Hugo knew them only as places where suburbanites at night made quick stops to buy cheap bags of coke or five or six joints before speeding away. Sometimes the cut-out areas held abandoned, stolen, or burned-out cars.

Hugo eased his car into one of the cutouts within fifteen seconds of the start of the flashing lights. He stopped far enough to leave room for the black cruiser to have space behind him. In the rearview mirror, he saw two men leave the cruiser, one from the driver's side and the other from the passenger side. They were dressed in black. They moved quickly.

Hugo instinctively understood what was happening and who they were even though he could see only black silhouettes. In a series of fluid movements, Hugo turned off the lights in his car, took the switchblade from the inside pocket of his cashmere sports coat, and leaped outside. As intermittent traffic swept by, he stabbed the driver in the heart and, two seconds later, plunged the long blade into the other man's stomach, swirling the blade so as to eviscerate him. They were the blond men who had served him and Lydia Guzman on the yacht, the same men who had followed Raquel Rematti on Madison Avenue. They had the zigzag symbols on their scalps.

Hugo quickly leaned into the black car. Using his elbow, he turned off the car's flashing lights and all of its other lights. With a paper towel, he switched off the ignition key and put the key in his pocket. The driver's-side door had been left open and he pushed it closed with his elbow. He didn't have to touch anything and he would toss the key out the window eighty miles north of the city into a rural field.

As he walked away from the black cruiser, he heard moans from the man he had stabbed in the stomach. There was no need for Hugo to do another thing to the man who was groaning; he was only seconds away from death, as Hugo Salazar well knew. He was, after all, *The Blade of the Hamptons.*

CHAPTER 37

KEN'S BROOME STREET Bar, at the corner of Broome Street and West Broadway, was an old-fashioned saloon. In the three decades Raquel Rematti had lived in Manhattan, the bar had never changed. Despite all the cheesy gentrification of SoHo over the years, Ken's remained what it always had been. The bar dated from the late 1800s, the tables and chairs were still all old wood—many of the tables had carved on their surfaces names and initials that must have been etched there as long ago as half a century—and the waiters were still old and surly.

Raquel had loved the place since she first set foot in it in 1985, three weeks after she graduated from law school. She had long ago forgotten the Waspish name of the young partner from Sullivan & Cromwell, where she spent two boring years immediately after leaving Harvard with her *magna cum laude* law degree. Although she'd long ago forgotten the man's name—he had picked Ken's bar because it was then so out of the mainstream that he was sure none of the more senior partners at the stuffy, genteel firm would ever be there to see a junior partner with a gorgeous new associate, a violation of the firm's then-unwritten but iron code of conduct—Raquel had for years cherished the seedy, never-changing saloon. She could, when she needed to isolate herself in order to relax, sit for two hours at the long counter that ran along the windows and gaze out at the parades of downtown walkers. The surface of the street was made of smooth white brick.

Ken's had other advantages for Raquel. For years she had known well the three successive managers and through them she could arrange the use of the small private party rooms, about which very few customers seemed to know. It was difficult for Raquel to imagine a more private place in Manhattan, other than someone's apartment, to have a secret meeting. She certainly was not going to have a meeting with Angelina Baldesteri at her own apartment on Riverside Drive or at her office on Park Avenue or at the Waldorf Astoria. So she had called Irish-accented Tommy Bond, the bar's manager for the last six years, to ask him to let her use one of the small private rooms for two hours.

"For you, Councilor, anything your little heart desires. How many other revelers will you have with you?" Tommy had asked.

"Just one. But people will recognize her. I'd really appreciate it if you could rush her in as soon as she walks into the front door."

"Ain't Angelina Jolie now, is it?"

"Close, Tommy, but no cigar."

One virtue of Angelina Baldesteri was that she was always on time. Raquel sat in the private room, with a mug of coffee, for only a few minutes when she heard a slight commotion just outside the closed door. When it opened, Raquel caught a glimpse of three Secret Service agents in business suits. They closed the door as soon as Angelina entered the room.

Angelina sat down. "This is quite a dump," she said.

"I like it. Lots of privacy. And, lady, do we need privacy."

"What do you think?" Angelina asked.

"That's the first time you've asked me that question about anything," Raquel answered.

"I asked you a question."

"Well," Raquel said, "obviously having eleven jurors increases the chances of conviction. That's simple math. That's what I think."

Angelina was three feet away from Raquel on the other side of the table. They stared into each other's eyes. Absolute hostility. The mutual locked-in gaze of true anger, fear, and naked hatred of warriors.

Angelina said, "That's not a particularly insightful comment. I could get that point from a sixth grader, not from America's greatest female defense lawyer."

"Thanks for the compliment, such as it is." Raquel took a sip of her lukewarm coffee. "I've been around jurors for years. Ninety-nine-point-five percent of them are inscrutable. But Lydia Guzman liked you. Nothing inscrutable about her."

"I felt the same way about her," Angelina said.

Slowly, deliberately, Raquel said, "There's a cardinal rule of life, Senator: don't bullshit a bullshitter. You didn't *feel* she liked you. You knew she would never vote to convict. Personally, I don't think she cared whether you lived or died, whether you were a President or a janitor's girlfriend."

"Why are we talking about a dead junkie?"

"Why not? Who are you going to have bribed next?"

"You can't be that stupid. I wouldn't bribe anyone."

"Where's Calvaro? Or should I say Caliente?"

"I don't know. But I do know one thing. I regret the day I laid eyes on you." She waited, unblinking, and staring at Raquel.

Raquel said, "Senator, right now we're sisters. Right now, we can't disown each other. And you want to know something? I can't ask you any questions if the trial goes on and you get back on the witness stand."

"You think so? I call that malpractice."

"Funny, I call what you did lying. Do you think anybody was fooled when you denied that janitor was Calvaro? Do you think I can have a client on the stand who I know is a liar?"

"Are you calling me a liar?"

"It's a simple, single word that has only one meaning. If I go along with the charade of asking you questions to which the answers will be lies—and I know that from you, by the way—I'll have my license pulled."

"That's the last thing you should be worried about. I can make it happen that you'll wind up in a Bronx courthouse chasing clients for traffic cases."

"I doubt that."

"Don't doubt it."

"I also doubt that Calvaro can get to any of the other jurors. Salazar could pull pearls out of an oyster in five seconds as he did with Guzman—"

"Just like he did with you, by the way," Angelina interrupted.

"But not with any of the others. And if he did, I'd have to report you. We can talk confidentially about anything illegal you did in the past, but I have a duty to go to the prosecutors if I believe you and others are planning to break the law in the future or are in the process of doing it. That's not me speaking from the holy mountain, that's basic ethics."

"What do you know about ethics?" Angelina asked.

"Without a doubt, more than you."

Angelina's eyes narrowed. There was a slyness in her expression. "What about the ethics of sleeping with Hayes Smith while you were defending me?"

"Nothing unethical about that. I can sleep with anyone. You do."

Angelina Baldesteri said, "You need to know something. I slept with Hayes Smith. Even while he was sleeping with you and telling you that *you* were his love forever and anon. He was quite good. In fact, I was sleeping with him right up to the time the trial started. And you, Ms. Confidentiality, were having pillow talk with him about everything I told you. So please don't *you* bullshit a bullshitter."

A freezing wave of jealousy, hatred, betrayal, and the urgent need to cry washed through Raquel's entire system. She hoped desperately that this stone-cold woman didn't detect her feelings or sense that freezing, all-engulfing internal wave.

"Are there any more questions," Raquel said, "that you want to ask me about the decision Naomi Goldstein wants you to make?"

"One of those things about Hayes," Angelina persisted, "was that when his dick was fully erect he had that birthmark on the shaft that somehow resembled a cross. It was like having sex with Jesus."

"I can tell you that if you go back on that stand you are going to wind up being indicted for perjury and obstruction of justice. Or, to put it in a more lawyer-like fashion, you'll be pulled to pieces, flayed. In other words, convicted."

"I told you when we met that I wanted to get this trial over quickly so that I can clear the path for my campaign."

"And I told you that politics didn't concern me at all, that my job as a lawyer was to avoid a conviction."

"No, your job was to get an acquittal, not a mistrial, not a conviction."

"That might have been the job you had in mind, Senator, but I live on this planet. A world without guarantees. You thought you had a guarantee with Guzman." She paused, hoping that the tape recorder function in the iPhone in her bag next to her Ruger was still running. "And in your world of guarantees," Raquel said, "you or Calvaro or someone got it into your head that bribing a pathetic drug addict like Lydia Guzman was one sure way to get a guaranteed acquittal."

"That's interesting, Ms. Rematti, very interesting."

"Except that there are no guarantees, particularly when your guarantee is from a junkie. Junkies forget their promises. And many of them die before they can keep their promises."

"You know, I've heard you talk about bribing Guzman before. And the last thing I am, Ms. Rematti, is naïve. Whenever you talk about bribery, you make it clear you want to lay it at my feet."

"Obviously there are people in the government who think she was being bribed, and now she's dead."

"Think about this: What if people were to say that it was you who arranged to bribe her? What if I went to Hunter Decker to tell him I just learned that you and your former client—Suarez or Vaz or Salazar or whatever his name was—and Robert Calvaro arranged to bribe her?"

"Nobody would believe you."

"Really? You always seem to lose sight of who I am. I have power. You don't. Imagine what it would do for your career if you had been able to get a former First Lady, a sitting Senator, and a presidential candidate acquitted. The great gods Clarence Darrow, Atticus Finch, and Johnnie Cochran would have to make room for you on the throne."

"Let me take you back to the world of the living, Senator. You are a woman in immense trouble. You need to make a decision by nine tomorrow morning. Do you take your chances with eleven jurors? What was the Clint Eastwood movie where he said, *Are you feeling lucky today, punk?* Wasn't it *Dirty Harry*?"

"Maybe when you're disbarred you can become a movie critic," Angelina said.

And Raquel responded, "We know your get-out-of-jail-free card—the card dealt to Lydia Guzman—is off the table."

Angelina stared at Raquel. "First *Casablanca*, now *Dirty Harry*. I've talked to other lawyers. It's amazing to me, but it shouldn't come as a surprise given what I know about the world, that you're in a backbiting profession. Let me tell you something, Ms. Rematti. Most of the lawyers have criticized your performance up and down. Some have said you were never any good, that luck and good public relations and political correctness all combined to give you an out-of-size reputation you never deserved." She stopped, waiting for a reaction from Raquel, who showed none. "Do you know what? One or two of these lawyers—and they are people who don't like you—think I am in a good place, that I now know what the Government's case is, and that you did a solid, simple, succinct job when I testified about Gordon Hughes and how I had too much to do with the overall strategy of the campaign to be held responsible for the details of how it was financed. So, they say, go with the eleven."

"Do what you want. The jury thinks you're a liar. And I know you're a liar. And don't forget: if you go on with the trial, there's more cross-examination."

"I'm much smarter than Hunter Decker."

"Really? That somehow escaped my attention when he made it clear to the world, if not to you, that you were lying about Calvaro's nocturnal visits."

"We live in the modern world, Ms. Rematti. You just said it yourself. So did Guzman. So do the jurors: a woman is entitled to have male visitors and to deny it."

"And to lie about it? The judge, like any judge, will instruct the jurors that if they find any witness lied about one thing they're entitled to believe the witness lied about other things or everything."

"No matter what I decide to do, you are, and I want you to understand this, a woman with no future."

"Are you threatening me?"

"Of course not. You're out of business. Take that any way you like. No one has ever pissed me off as much as you have."

"What a privilege. Now stand up and get the fuck out of this room. I'll see you at nine tomorrow morning."

CHAPTER 38

A GENTLE, REFRESHING rain was falling, almost a mist from the nearby Hudson River, when Raquel left Ken's Broome Street Bar fifteen minutes after Angelina opened the door to the private room and waited for the Secret Service agents to surround her and leave the building. Although it was only five in the afternoon as Raquel walked on the street of rounded, glistening cobblestones, it was inordinately dark. Broome Street was practically empty. There were just a few other walkers, almost all of them in their twenties.

She welcomed the rain. The coolness settled her. Although she had taken an Uber car from her apartment building on Riverside Drive, she decided to walk the ancient wet streets to the station for the number 1 subway train at Franklin Street just to the south of Canal Street. Even though she rarely used them now, she had always found subway rides soothing, even when they were still graffiti-scratched and legendarily dangerous in the mid-1980s at the time she had first arrived in the city and had to use the intricate, rigid grid of subways because she couldn't afford taxis. The comfort she found in subways must have stemmed, she believed, from the presence of other people despite their absolute, self-protective silence and the rhythm of the passage from station to station.

Just as she reached the subway entrance, she felt her cell phone vibrate. She stopped under the frail awning at the front of a dreary Korean grocery store on ancient Franklin Street. Rainwater poured through slits in the awning, but she found enough protection so that her cell phone wouldn't get soaked when she retrieved it from her bag.

What had caused the vibration was a text message from Willis Jordan. *Can I c u at ur apartment for a few minutes tonight? WJ.*

Slowly, using only her right thumb, she typed: *Sure. 7:30 – 728 Riverside Drive between 83 and 84. RR*

* * *

In the two hours she spent after reaching her apartment before Willis arrived, she kept active to fend off what she recognized as her anxiety. She peeled off her rain-drenched clothes and stuffed them into the nylon bag that she would leave in her building's lobby the next morning for the dry cleaner's weekly pickup. Naked, she spent half an hour making sure her always orderly apartment was completely neat. She showered, washing her hair. She emptied the clean dishes, glasses, and utensils from the dishwasher and carefully stacked them in the kitchen cabinets. She opened a bottle of white wine when she saw that, even after all of her activity, she had another half hour to wait before Willis arrived. Never more than a casual drinker, she surprised herself by pouring the expensive wine into a water glass and quickly drinking half the glass. She felt the warmth, the pleasant numbness, suffuse her body.

Like all the people Raquel knew in the television business, Willis was always on time. He lived in a world of deadlines. When she opened the door for him at precisely 7:30, Willis—a large and powerful black man—spread his arms and embraced her, chastely, like a brother. She'd last seen him six weeks before Hayes was killed. As she disengaged from his hug, she closed the door. She turned to look at him fully. His suits were always perfectly tailored, even for his huge size. She had always seen him in a suit in an industry where his mentors were ghosts and role models such as Edward R. Murrow, Walter Cronkite, and Tom Brokaw who always wore suits, as their producers and news writers did. Over the last twenty years, the new style at the level below broadcaster and anchors began to transform to the geek style. Those younger people were talented, fun, willing to devote long hours to news-gathering through computers and technology, but they never emulated Willis' inherited old-fashioned style. Even though he was only in his forties, Willis knew he was a relic. He liked that. Raquel had always felt respect for, and trust in, Willis Jordan. She said, "I can't believe you don't have an umbrella. You're soaking wet."

There were beads of dissolving wetness on the blue British suit that covered his shoulders and chest.

He smiled. "What's a little rain to a Georgia peanut farmer?" he asked.

There it was: that mellifluous, formal, articulate voice. Had it been just slightly deeper, he, too, could have been a broadcaster. But he never wanted that. He enjoyed the power of control and command, as he learned in his two years at Harvard Business School. He never desired to read the news in the isolation of a television studio. He savored making decisions as to the news to be broadcast or not, not to broadcast it himself.

"I should have seen you face-to-face before this, Raquel. It was remiss of me." There it was again, the subtle surprises in the words Willis used. Raquel had never in a private conversation heard the word *remiss*.

"You called, Willis, after it happened. That was really all you could do. We're both busy."

"I did ask to see you right away today, Raquel, not just out of a lingering sense I'd failed to do the honorable thing. I have another reason."

She surveyed him. She had nothing to fear from him. How many friends did she have in the world? *None*, she thought, *except him*. "It's fine, Willis. I've been overwhelmed with the trial."

"You didn't pick an easy line of work."

"I think," she said, "we should sit in the kitchen. Do you want coffee?"

"No, thanks."

"How about some wine?"

"Thanks, but I don't drink." He hesitated. "I wish," he said, "that we had had a memorial service for him."

"The brothers were adamant, as I told you. The irony is that Hayes hadn't been in touch with them for years, possibly ten. But they were in control. Who knows? They may never have looked at Google. They knew nothing about me, I assume."

"Did it hurt? Not having a memorial?"

"No. It was enough that we loved each other." She looked into Willis' eyes and decided to say nothing about Angelina's profoundly wounding disorienting words about Hayes: the truth was shattering. "But you want to talk to me, Willis, about something else. Come on, let's go to the kitchen. Are you sure you don't want coffee?"

"No, Raquel, we just need to talk."

Jordan filled one of the kitchen chairs with his football player's bulk. Abruptly he said, "Two men were killed last night on one of those cutoff areas on the West Side Highway, not far from here. They had knife wounds, expertly delivered. They were both big men, with years of military training. They never had a chance to resist. Their guns were still in their shoulder holsters. The killer had the speed of a jaguar."

"Why are you telling me this, Willis?"

"NBC News, no matter what some people may think of it, is still a powerful news-gathering organization. One of our local reporters was immediately assigned to the story. We assumed the two dead men were plainclothes police officers, and the cold-blooded assassination of police is always big news these days. Every dead police officer is a hero."

"And weren't they police officers?"

"No, or I wouldn't be here except for a simple family-style visit."

"What is it, Willis?"

"It took only a few hours to put it together, but the two dead men were members of the guard team NBC sent with Hayes to Lesbos."

Raquel stood up from the kitchen table and began searching through her bag on the kitchen counter. She took out her cell phone and scrolled through the phone's icons as she returned to the table. She tapped the icon for photographs. It took only seconds to find the three photos she had taken of the men who stopped her on Madison Avenue.

Willis sat patiently. He was a skillful listener.

"I want to ask you something," she said. "Are these the two men?"

She pushed her cell phone in front of Willis. He made no effort to conceal his surprise. Using his own phone, he placed a call. "Victor," he said, "send me as soon as you can—right now, in fact— pictures of the two dead men."

Within ten seconds, his cell phone vibrated. He opened the incoming email and its attachments. As though moving chess pieces, he slid the two phones, side by side, to Raquel.

"These two men," Raquel said, "are the same two men who stopped me a few days ago on Madison Avenue. They told me they were FBI agents."

"I came here," he said, "to bring you information I thought you should know. And now you are giving me extraordinary information our reporters need to know."

"I even have the business cards they gave me."

"You do?"

"Didn't you know, Willis, that FBI agents love to hand out their business cards?"

"I didn't."

"I'll give you the cards in a second. But the names on the cards were *Curnin* and *Giordano*. Do your people know the names of these two dead men?"

"Yes, we think so. Curnin and Giordano. They had business cards."

"Have you asked the NYPD or the Medical Examiner who they really are?"

"I'm not following. They're Curnin and Giordano."

"No, they're not."

Confused, Willis stared at her. "I'm not sure what you are telling me."

"They aren't," Raquel said, "Curnin and Giordano."

Willis repeated, "I'm not sure what you are telling me."

He moved the two cell phones to his side of the table again. He stared at the pictures. Even though the photos on his cell phone were less distinct and lacked the clarity of the pictures on Raquel's phone—the pictures on Willis' phone were, after all, pictures of two recently dead men—there was no doubt in his mind they were the same people. "It's odd," Willis quietly said. "The FBI took possession of the bodies immediately, not the NYPD or the New York City Medical Examiner's Office. We're trying to find out why."

"What about the car they were driving?"

"Our reporters do know sources who have told us it's a United States Government–owned vehicle and not an unmarked New York City police car."

Raquel again sipped her wine. "I have to tell you, Willis, something I almost never say out loud to anyone."

He stared at her. "What?"

"I'm afraid."

Willis' eyes were absolutely black. They were reassuring. "We can help," he said. "You lost a man you loved. We lost a man we cherished. We have resources at NBC that you don't have. And you have a resource we don't have." He stopped for two seconds. "Courage."

"Really, Willis? I wonder. It's the desperation of isolation. When I had breast cancer a few years ago, and a year of treatment, the only people I saw or spoke with were my doctors and nurses and therapists. No one else ever called or visited. I'd had a twenty-year career by then of representing everyone from Oliver North to Michael Jackson. They worshipped me, or my skills. Their families and friends adored me. I had hundreds of students who flocked to my courses. I had lovers. But none of my friends called me. You and Hayes didn't know me. I'm grateful for your friendship now and wish I had it then."

Motionless, staring steadily at her, Willis said, "Cancer is a frightening disease, Raquel. It scares others away. They fear, irrationally, about their own fate."

"It's sweet of you to say that, Willis. But, in that awful, lonely year I realized I had never done anything to develop genuine friends. I'd been surrounded by people for years. Clients, their families, my students, judges, other lawyers, law school professors, television producers and anchors. I had thought of myself as open and accessible. And then for a year, in my late forties, I saw myself as dying, alone."

"Did you ever," he asked, "think of calling anyone?"

"I did think of that. But I didn't have that kind of special courage: the courage to ask for help."

Willis said, "This is all surprising to me. When Hayes introduced us to you, you seemed the most accessible person we had met. He wanted to marry you."

She thought again about Angelina's spear-sharpened, poisoned words about Hayes. Only a woman who had made love to him would know about Hayes Smith's intriguing birthmark, unless somebody else had mentioned it to Angelina in the often-lurid world of gossip of famous women who sometimes collected lovers in the same way professional basketball players gathered women. "Willis, Hayes was never going to marry me."

"Well, there are different states of togetherness other than marriage."

"Sweet man you are, Willis. But that wasn't going to happen either. I'm a realist. And one reality I do know is that I loved him. He did not love me."

He folded his big hands on the kitchen table and said nothing. An acute observer, Raquel saw that his huge knuckles were almost white, like the calluses on a boxer's hands.

"I'll say it again even though you don't like it. We can offer you protection. I have room in my budget for that. You're afraid. A woman of courage is afraid."

"No, Willis, my father taught me how to protect myself. I grew up in a tough factory town. He made me a street fighter."

"The swordsman who took out these two guys—the two guys who tracked you on Madison Avenue of all places—is not a street brawler. He is an expert in the art of killing."

"I want to be open with you, Willis. The man who did the stabbing—and I just feel this by instinct—was a man whose name was mentioned several times at the Senator's trial. Hugo Salazar, that associate of the elusive Robert Calvaro."

Willis exhaled. "Why do you think that?"

"Come on, Willis. You've followed my career. Hugo Salazar is the first man I represented when I came back from the dead. I knew him as Juan Suarez. *The Blade of the Hamptons.*"

"How can that be? He was deported on immigration violations after he was acquitted."

"Don't you think a man who knows how to kill so skillfully could slip through any immigration barriers, even Trump's proposed Mexican wall, especially when men like Suarez, or Salazar, or Harry Houdini work for men with enormous dark power?"

"Like Robert Calvaro?"

"No, Willis. Oscar Caliente. Robert Calvaro is Oscar Caliente. I never met Caliente, but I saw lots of surveillance tapes of him when I did the murder trial in the Hamptons." She looked more intently at him. "And I'm going to break one of the cardinal rules of my business. My client in that case—*The Blade of the Hamptons*—told me that Caliente is a prince of the Sinaloa cartel. There, I've just broken commandment one. I've told a reporter—you—what a client told me."

"And can you tell me this, Raquel? When you recognized that Salazar was your former client during the Baldesteri trial, why didn't you tell anyone?"

"The real reason?"

"Yes, that one." He smiled, gently.

"Because I broke commandment number two of my profession. I had fallen in love with him during the Hamptons trial. I've missed him ever since. You know that old Willie Nelson song? 'Always on My Mind'? Like a lot of corny popular songs, it has been uncannily on target."

"That was crazy, Raquel."

"I know. But I convinced myself of something else. I am, as much as I wish it weren't so, the lawyer for Angelina Baldesteri. I was her lawyer, obviously, when it became clear as day to me that Calvaro was Caliente and Salazar was Juan Suarez, Anibal Vaz, or any of the varieties of identities he has, the one constant of which was that he was a murderer called *The Blade of the Hamptons*."

"And?"

"Think it through. I am in the middle of the Senator's trial. I see that men who are close to my client, for whatever reasons she has, and even if she has no idea who these people are, are flat-out criminals. I take my role as a lawyer seriously—it's the quaint old-fashioned lady in me. If I took what I know to Decker, I would then become an informant for the Government against my client. I'm giving the Government evidence against my client. My loyalty is to my client, as despicable as she is. There are so many subtleties in this profession. But some things are clear—I can't become a handmaiden to the prosecution. I have to protect my client."

Willis was a reporter, of course. As a reporter, he asked, "Did you mention this to the Senator?"

"You know my answer. I can't tell you."

"I have a different question, then," Willis said. "Does she know?"

"That is a different question. *She knows now.* I have no idea when she first knew. I can't tell you about what we say to each other. But I can tell you I never asked the question of when she first knew, and she never said anything about that."

Willis leaned back in his chair. He exhaled deeply, as though he had just run a hundred-yard dash. "Raquel, I do want some coffee. Do you mind?"

"Of course not. I need some, too. I have more I want to say, because, while I don't want your protection, I need your help, and I can help you. I can give you leads."

Raquel did not turn to look at Willis as she poured water into the gleaming coffee maker, ground the coffee beans, and waited for the coffee to brew. She heard behind her the clicking sound of Willis typing quickly, like an agile teenage girl, on his iPhone.

"How do you take your coffee, Willis?"

"Black," he said.

Raquel put the coffee mug in front of Willis. She took her seat. She said, "Here's a lead, Willis. The dead men were definitely not FBI agents. They were not Curnin and Giordano."

"How do you know that?"

"Hunter Decker told me."

"He did?"

"Have one of your reporters call him. Use my name. He has the pictures you have. They are not, he admitted to me a few days ago, Giordano or Curnin. They were strangers to him, or so he claimed. He said he would find out who they are. I think Decker was lying to me."

"Meaning what?"

"Meaning that Decker already knew who those men were."

Deftly, Willis sent another message on his cell phone. "One of our people will reach out to him."

"He will deny it, of course. But I can give you a boost."

"How?"

"I recorded the conversation with Decker. These smartphones are miraculous. I'll forward the recording to you now, and you can relay it to your reporter."

Willis smiled. "You're a shady lady."

"Let me ask you this, Willis."

"Shoot. Although that sounds like one of your lawyer questions is coming." He had a bright, engaging smile.

"You said the two dead men were hired by NBC to shield Hayes. You must have known who they are."

"We had names, resumes, and recommendations for them. Social Security numbers." He sipped the hot coffee. "They were all fake, falsified. We learned that an hour ago."

"Why am I not surprised?"

Willis said nothing.

* * *

Raquel knew nothing about Willis other than the fact that he had been Hayes Smith's longtime producer, that he had been devoted to Hayes, that he was raised in rural Georgia, and that he was, Raquel instinctively sensed, a friend.

She said quietly, almost demurely, "Can you stay the night?"

"If you want that," he said slowly.

"I do. In my bedroom. On the bed. With me."

"Raquel," he said calmly, "I'm gay. I can comfort you. But nothing else."

"I need your warmth." She thought about Theresa Bui, murdered with a single gunshot from the foggy dunes at Raquel's house in Montauk. She had wanted Theresa's warmth, just as she had treasured Hayes' warmth. And, when Hayes was killed, the warmth of another human had been taken away from her: death's awful finality.

In her dark, comfortable bedroom, she and Willis undressed entirely. In the darkness she could barely see the features of his body, just his muscular black silhouette. She lay down on her left side under the fragrant blankets. He stretched out behind her, draped his arm over her shoulders, and lodged his penis against her lower back. It never stirred.

They slept for eight hours.

CHAPTER 39

IT WAS PRECISELY nine in the morning. Angelina Baldesteri and Raquel Rematti, in the five minutes before Naomi Goldstein took her seat on the bench, did not even glance at each other. Every seat in the gallery behind them was filled. There was a murmur of voices and a rustling of paper since most of the seats were occupied by reporters from all over the world. But there was no clicking of computer keys. Naomi Goldstein banned from the spectators in the courtroom all electronic equipment—no iPhones, no iPads, no cameras, no laptops.

Impassive as always, Goldstein switched on the small, useless reading lamp on her bench, the signal that she was about to start.

"Very well, ladies and gentlemen. I want the record to reflect that the defendant and her attorney are present. Mr. Decker and his assistants are present for the Government. The remaining jurors are all in the jury room. They are prepared to proceed." She looked at Raquel. "Ms. Rematti, are you prepared to proceed?"

Raquel stood. "That, Your Honor, is a question only my client can answer."

"I take it you've spoken to your client about this?"

"I have. But she knows the answer to your question. I don't."

Shifting her gaze to the Senator, Goldstein said, "Ms. Baldesteri, the issue, as you know, is whether you elect to proceed with a jury of eleven and to waive your right to a jury of twelve. As I explained to you yesterday, all your constitutional rights are preserved with a jury of eleven—guilt must be found beyond a reasonable doubt, you preserve the presumption of innocence. You understand all of that, Ms. Baldesteri, do you not?"

"I do."

"And you understand that if you decide to adhere to a jury of twelve, which is your right, I will declare a mistrial?"

"I understand."

"And that I will, if the Government insists on retrying you, schedule a prompt retrial?"

"I understand."

"What is your decision?"

"I want a jury of twelve."

The gallery was startled into movement and anticipation.

Naomi Goldstein was all efficiency. "Very well. I declare a mistrial. Before I call the jurors in to thank them for their service, I want to ask the Government if it intends to retry the defendant?"

Hunter Decker stood. "Without a doubt we do. Yes."

"I've looked at my calendar. The retrial will start thirty-two days from today, August 28."

"That date," Decker said, "is fine with the Government, Judge."

"Fine or not, Mr. Decker, that's the date."

Angelina Baldesteri spoke out firmly. "Excuse me, but that's impossible for me."

"That does not matter, Ms. Baldesteri."

"That leaves no time to prepare."

"Ms. Rematti is familiar with the case."

"I've fired Ms. Rematti. She is no longer my lawyer."

"That, Ms. Baldesteri, is no concern of mine. There are many competent lawyers who can prepare themselves adequately in thirty-two days."

"I have no reason to believe that."

"What you believe or do not believe is not a concern of mine," Goldstein said.

"Judge Goldstein," the Senator said in the same authoritative tone she used when she herself was examining witnesses at a Senate hearing, "this is profoundly unfair. I've fired Ms. Rematti because she has an impossible conflict of interest."

"Ms. Baldesteri, I ask that you sit down."

"No. When I do my work as a Senator, I insure that a record is complete. Ms. Rematti's conflict is that she is herself the target of a grand jury investigation for the bribery of Lydia Guzman, the dead juror."

"That's enough, Ms. Baldesteri. That has nothing to do with this process." Her voice rising, Naomi Goldstein was genuinely angry. "This is my courtroom, Ms. Baldesteri. I control it. You don't. Sit down now or I will hold you in contempt."

Angelina, stone cold, sat down. Raquel, always a proud woman, was rigid, stunned, furious: every television station, every blog, every newspaper in the world would immediately broadcast the news that a grand jury was investigating her for the bribery of a now-dead juror and that she had been fired by a United States Senator. Despite years of high-profile trials, notorious clients, tense contacts with prosecutors and others, no one had ever questioned her integrity. There had been anonymous bloggers who made cutting, often illiterate statements about her, usually after one of her television appearances. There were those who made anonymous posts commenting on her legs when she wore short dresses and sat on a couch during a televised interview. There were creeps out there in the world who posted sites called "Upskirt," which broadcast on the Internet views of her when she crossed and recrossed her legs. She pretended that these things amused her; in fact, they annoyed her.

But most of the hundreds of entries about her on Google, Yahoo, and Bing were flattering. And she took pride in the fact that no client had ever sued or criticized her, that no disciplinary committee had ever investigated her, that no one, at least in public, had ever faulted her work.

But now, in one gratuitous sentence, one of the most powerful women in the world had said in public that Raquel had been fired *and* was the target of a grand jury investigation for the bribery of a dead woman. Raquel felt as though her face had been slashed, leaving irreparable scars.

"Mr. Decker," Judge Goldstein said, "I will expect to see you on August 28, ready to select a jury."

"Yes, ma'am."

"And, Ms. Baldesteri, you will be here at the same time and ready to pick a jury."

"That's impossible, Judge, and not fair."

"You can always represent yourself. Or you can be here with a new lawyer."

Raquel stood. "Your Honor, I have a motion."

Judge Goldstein stared at her for five seconds. "Ordinarily I expect motions to be made in writing, Ms. Rematti. What is it?"

"I move for leave to withdraw as counsel to the defendant, on the basis of the statements made this morning by her. I do not want any further responsibility for this client."

"Mr. Decker, do you have any reason to oppose that motion?"

"None."

Angelina stood. Goldstein looked surprised, even upset, saying, "What is it, Ms. Baldesteri? Do you oppose the motion? Like any other lawyer who has appeared for any client in any case, he or she continues as the client's lawyer unless and until a judge signs an order relieving the lawyer. Those are the rules. Do you oppose Ms. Rematti's motion?"

"Ms. Rematti received half a million dollars to represent me. I want that money returned."

"Ms. Baldesteri, that is not a concern of mine either. That is between you and Ms. Rematti. Do you have a substantive reason?"

"I'm not even sure I know what that means. The reason I gave is a substantive one."

"Ms. Baldesteri, you are trying my patience. Given what you said a few minutes ago, I cannot imagine you have a substantive reason for opposing the motion."

"I want her withdrawal granted, but only on the condition that she return the money she received."

"That's nonsense. It is, in any event, a private civil issue between you and Ms. Rematti." She appeared to wait for a moment before her words registered with the Senator. And then Goldstein said, "Ms. Rematti's motion is granted. And as of this moment."

Acting deliberately, as always, even though nothing like this had ever before happened to her, Raquel locked her two bags, stood, and left the courtroom. Dozens of reporters followed her into the marble hallway.

Raquel answered none of the shouted questions, which she heard as if the voices were submerged. She was making a transition, she recognized, into a new world. It was the same sensation she experienced several years earlier when three doctors told her she had breast cancer.

CHAPTER 40

As Raquel emerged from the revolving door of the courthouse, she recognized that three Secret Service agents—two men and a woman she had come to know quite well and liked—had already been told that Raquel was *persona non grata*. The agents, who stood near the four black SUVs in the clear sunlight, turned to face the street, making no effort to open any door for her. They were under orders not to drive her anywhere.

Raquel was followed from the moment she left the courtroom by many reporters. She said repeatedly, "No comment," but knew that wouldn't deter any of them from pursuing her.

As she stepped briskly from the sidewalk to the street, she had only two choices for a way to return to her office: a taxi or a subway. Across Centre Street was a nondescript plaza with the entrance to the number 6, 5, and 4 subway trains, all of which had stops two blocks from her office. But the reporters, she knew, would follow her.

As she waited for the light to change so that she could cross Centre Street, a yellow taxi suddenly materialized from the left. She nodded and the driver stopped. Raquel opened the rear door, saying, "Good morning, sir. Fifty-Seventh and Park."

The reporters were stranded on the sidewalk. There were no other cabs in sight. Raquel laughed: she thought about the *Road Runner* cartoon and the bewildered expression on Wile E. Coyote's face when the Road Runner always made his or her miraculous escape.

For the first time in seven months, the orange police cones had been removed from the parking spaces on Park Avenue in front of her office building. Ordinary civilian cars were already parked there. There were many reporters on the sidewalk. She moved through them without speaking. None of them would be able to enter the elevator with her since the security system and staff in her office building were rigorous about controlling who was allowed through the turnstiles leading to the elevators; that was true even before Angelina Baldesteri came into her life and would stay true now that she had passed.

It was only when she sat down alone in her sun-filled office that, breathing in and breathing out deeply, she started to take account of where she now was in her life. She had managed to live in total independence or, as she sometimes thought, in total isolation. Even when she was with Hayes, she really had not believed, although at times she had hoped, that she had found a companion for life. In any event, she now knew that any hope of a lifetime with Hayes was certainly an illusion even if he had not been killed. She remembered that she made no effort to learn where Hayes' cell phone was, for she had always been worried about the secrets it might contain, and she didn't doubt for a second the hurtful words about Hayes Angelina had spoken.

And her isolation as of this moment went beyond that. Hayes was gone. She had just been publicly humiliated. Like a wicked seer, Angelina had said she had the power to do that and she did it. Raquel had spent virtually all of her career as a darling of the media, and now there were reporters everywhere wanting to ask her questions about a grand jury investigating her for the bribery of Lydia Guzman. No matter what Raquel might say, and even if she said nothing, there must already be stories flooding the Internet in which her public humiliation was proclaimed to the world. She resisted the temptation to type her name into a Google search where she would see the most recent postings about her. By now, even though it was only an hour after she'd left the courtroom, she was certain that Reuters, the Associated Press, Bloomberg, and others had already distributed articles about the mistrial and, of course, about her. The bloggers, she knew, would be in full rant. Project "Upskirt" would seem to be the trivial nonsense it was.

And there was another issue, another sense that her life had suddenly crossed a dangerous line. Raquel now, for the first time in her career, had no work to do. For months she had dedicated her life to the former First Lady of the United States. The world of potential clients appeared to be aware of that. For six months, only two or three men and women—wealthy people suddenly in trouble for insider trading or tax evasion—had approached her. They were all told that, while she appreciated the overture, she was completely engaged with the Senator's trial and the preparation for it.

And then another thing made her hands involuntarily tremble: money and the precarious sense of not having enough. She hadn't looked at her bank account for many weeks. Tapping the icon on her cell phone that gave her access to weeks of transactions in her main Citibank account, she felt as if the floor were collapsing under her. The account into which she had placed the infamous $500,000 fee now had less than $100,000.

By scrolling through several months of transactions, she focused for the first time on the fact that she had paid from the account more than $150,000 in fees to accounting and other experts whom she, as a careful lawyer, thought might be necessary for the trial. In addition, many thousands of dollars had been paid out for her expensive office and salaries for the two young lawyers and two paralegals on her staff, one of whom had her authority to sign checks. Paying the court reporters for daily copies of the trial testimony accounted for more than $50,000. She had expected to be ultimately reimbursed for these huge outlays, but it was a certainty of her life now that that was never going to happen. She'd forgotten, as she looked at the electronic bank statements, one of the key adages of the profession of criminal defense lawyers: *Be careful; your first check will be your last.* It was one of those adages that had never applied in her career until now.

Another old adage now haunted her: *In this line of work, your clients are at your feet at first and later at your throat.*

Angelina Baldesteri—always arrogant and always with a sense of entitlement—had never really sat in worship at Raquel's feet. But now she was at Raquel's throat, and not about to let go. In Angelina Baldesteri's world, if anything ever went wrong, someone else had to be sacrificed.

Snap out of this, Raquel thought, almost speaking the words aloud. *Take action.*

* * *

Michael O'Keefe, even at seventy-eight, was still one of the most attractive men whom Raquel had ever seen. His full head of hair was blond with a sprinkling of white. His face, almost completely unlined, resembled JFK's but was better structured. His wire-rimmed glasses were barely visible. His suits were all an immaculate deep blue.

Michael O'Keefe was also in the same rarefied league as Raquel, except that he had entered that league long before Raquel became its informal dean. Fresh out of the Boalt Hall law school at Berkeley, he had been picked by the wily, wild-haired William Kunstler as one of the lawyers representing the defendants at the trial of the Chicago Seven in 1970. Like the defiant, brilliant Kunstler and all the other defense lawyers, Michael had been held in contempt of court by the edgy, bad-tempered, almost insane Julius Hoffman, the Captain Queeg of federal judges. The contempt citation, which could have derailed O'Keefe's career at its outset, was vacated by the appeals court in Chicago. He was now the last surviving defense lawyer from that legendary trial. The contempt citation had long ago become a badge of honor, the Silver Star of courtroom battles. During his long career he had represented Bobby Seale; Jimmy Carter's derelict brother; Ivan Boesky; and Michael Milken. He had also been Oliver North's lead defense lawyer in the Iran-Contra trial of the late 1980s, the trial in which he had added the young Raquel Rematti as one of the defense lawyers.

Rising from his chair in his office on Fifth Avenue, he gave her a quick, warm embrace as soon as she walked through the door. "My Lord," he said in that soft, endearing Irish brogue he typically reserved for trials, "you look as beautiful as ever."

They hadn't seen each other since before she had been stricken with cancer. He said, "Let's sit on the sofa. I don't want to speak to you over the desk."

"Thanks for seeing me, Michael, on such short notice." She had called him only an hour earlier. She had left her office building through the service elevator and service exit in order to avoid the large group of reporters in the building's main lobby and on the Park Avenue sidewalk. Just as she had expected, there were reporters at the service exit on 58th Street, but only five or six of them. Some were people from CNN and the *New York Post*, with whom she had spoken freely and often for years, but not now. Once again, a taxi instantly appeared, as if by prearrangement, and she quickly slipped into the back seat without saying a word. Michael's office was only four blocks from hers, but she had dreaded walking to Michael's office with a horde of reporters surrounding her. The readily available taxi had again saved her from that.

Only two feet separated her from Michael as they settled into the large office sofa. Michael's ability to put people at ease was astounding.

"Do you know what's happening?" she asked.

"I do, Raquel. It is, unfortunately, all over the news. And reporters have been calling me for comment about the mistrial and you. I've said, 'No comment.'"

"I need your help," she said. After a lifetime of self-reliance, she seemed to be asking for help, any help, from others.

"There's no one," Michael answered, "in God's world I'd rather help."

"People have been whispering to me for weeks that I'm the target of a grand jury investigation. You know me; I asked Decker point-blank a week ago if that was true."

"And Hunter didn't answer you. He once briefly worked for me, you know, before he went over to the dark side."

"I know."

"Who told you about the investigation?"

"Two men. They said they were FBI agents. They gave me their cards. Curnin and Giordano."

"Well, that's chilling," Michael said.

"Even more chilling than you might think. They weren't Curnin and Giordano. They were the two men who were murdered on the West Side Highway last night."

Michael O'Keefe said, "My God, Raquel. You need to tell me everything."

Raquel did tell Michael everything, except for the existence of the Ruger. Unburdening herself gave her comfort. Michael was a great listener, and he ended the conversation by saying, "Let me think through all you've said, Raquel, and I'll get back to you with a strategy."

He gave her all of his cell phone numbers and email addresses.

CHAPTER 41

IT WAS ALMOST midnight. Hugo Salazar had driven deeply into upstate New York, a grim area he had never seen. Dreary farmland, fields, and forests swept by him as he drove steadily on a highway called the Northway. There were miles-long stretches of dark road where he saw no other cars or trucks; it was as though he were driving on the surface of the moon. Occasionally, in the distance to the east and west, there were isolated lights in run-down farmhouses. *How*, he wondered, *could anyone live in places like this?*

When he passed a sign that read "Glens Falls, 2 Miles," he was relieved to see clusters of lights gradually emerge from the darkness. At first there were gas station signs on extremely tall poles—Exxon, Shell, Sunoco. And then beyond the gas station signs were the huge illuminated symbols of McDonalds, Burger King, and Roy Rogers outlets. The road on which Hugo drove was no longer the four-lane highway divided by a median strip but a strip-mall street, with many stop-and-go lights, that led into downtown Glens Falls.

It was the ugliest city he had ever seen in the United States. Most of the storefronts were boarded up with plywood and apparently had been for years. There was an abandoned movie theater on whose marquee only the letters *M*, *Z*, and *A* were suspended at awkward angles, an incomprehensible rendering of the title of the theater's last film. The only people on the Main Street were young men, most wearing loose hoodies, who were gathered, smoking, in front of a bar. They were all white, their shoulders hunched over. Even at night, Hugo saw that they all had tattoos on their scrawny arms.

He drove into the entryway of a Holiday Inn Express. There were only a few other vehicles scattered through the parking lot, no two side by side, many of them battered and rusting pickup trucks. He continued to the doors that opened into the reception area. When he stood at the registration desk, a brightly smiling local girl, probably not older than eighteen, politely asked, "How long will you all be staying with us, sir?"

He gave her his ravishing smile. "Just tonight."

She asked for his license and credit card. He used the Raul Escribano ones.

She gave him the key and asked him to park farther down the row of empty parking spaces. In the absolute darkness, he carried every one of the four elegant pieces of luggage from the Chevy into the room.

An impeccably neat man, Hugo carefully hung the clothes he had been wearing in the open closet with no doors next to the entrance. He examined his sport jacket, white shirt, and slacks. There were no blood splatters on his clothes. He was an expert at knifing, like a matador who never let a charging bull's horns tear his clothes or cape.

Exhausted and naked, he sprawled on the bed without disturbing the bed clothes. His last thought was that he would easily reach Canada the next day. And then on to Chile. He had more than enough money for the trip to Chile. A man with his skills could make money anywhere and travel the world.

*   *   *

Hugo Salazar was abruptly awakened at some point in the dark room. He was startled. Regaining his focus almost instantly, he reached to his left for the long knife he had unsheathed before he fell asleep. The knife wasn't there.

Only the faint fluorescent light above the door at the entrance was on. Hugo sat up in the bed, his feet on the floor. He was completely immobile, still naked. There were at least four men in the room. In Spanish, Hugo asked, "Who the hell are you?"

In English one of the men—in silhouette, like the others—said, "Shut the fuck up. And stay where you are."

Suddenly the door opened and Hugo recognized the slender man who slipped into the room, quickly pulling the door closed behind him and latching it with the silver security chain so fragile and aged that a twelve-year-old could have broken it.

Robert Calvaro said, in Spanish, "You didn't really think you'd get away from me, did you?"

Hugo remained silent. The leather travel bag in which he had placed more knives, a machete, and three handguns was in the small closet to Calvaro's right. The closet was at least five long paces from where Hugo sat. He would be dead, he knew, as soon as he stood up.

Calvaro snapped on the bathroom light. It was fluorescent and he stood in the white glare. He was dressed as always in a suit. "Don't look around the room," Calvaro said. "I don't want you to recognize anyone. Seven hours ago, you saw two important men who worked for me. And you killed them. That was a terrible mistake. All they wanted to do was talk to you, to give you instructions from me. What do you think? Do you think I have an endless supply of men? Do you think it's simple to get two new men to work for me? Two ex-Marines? That costs a lot of money, much more than you do."

In a firm voice, Hugo said, "And how could I know that?"

"You've worked for me a long time, my friend. By now you know how I operate. If I wanted you dead then, they would have shot you while you were driving. They trained as sharpshooters. That's why they cost me so much money. So, since you know me, you should have known they wanted to talk to you. You're a smart man."

Remaining motionless on the bed, Hugo concentrated on Caliente's soft hands. Hugo didn't speak.

"You know, I could have these men cut your balls off."

Hugo was utterly calm: he had been in the presence of the prelude to killing many times. He said, "But, Oscar, you'd have to walk out into the hallway. You're like a little girl. Afraid of blood."

Robert Calvaro stepped forward, with the swiftness of a cat. His slender outline was now entirely black against the unnatural white lighting behind him. He slapped Hugo Salazar's face several times before drawing a thin trace of blood from a small cut above his eyebrow. "See, my friend," Calvaro said, "blood doesn't bother me."

Hugo laughed. The other men for the first time moved, but just slightly, as if making themselves taut before jumping on him. Hugo was a strategist for moments like this: his plan now was to make an explosive charge at Calvaro, who was six inches shorter than Hugo, and to toss him violently around in the dark room. In the confusion, Hugo envisioned rolling on the floor to the closet in which the leather bag containing the knives, the machete, and the guns was lodged. He calculated he had almost no chance of survival, but in his earliest years, as a street brawler in Mexico, he long ago pledged to himself that he would never die without fighting back.

At that moment, Calvaro spoke as if reading Hugo's mind. "Hold onto yourself before you do anything stupid. The two men you killed really were, at least for the time being, going to talk to you.

Hugo, my friend, you got edgy. Don't get edgy now. That's not like you. And it's not healthy for you."

"I fucked up when Lydia died. You told me to keep her safe."

"We all make mistakes."

Hugo said nothing. The room slipped into silence except for a hum of the forced hot-air radiator. It was almost completely incapable of warming the room. In the silence, Hugo began to feel cold. But he would never ask for a blanket or some other relief from discomfort. The Mexican years had taught him never to appear grateful. Gratitude was a symbol of weakness.

Calvaro said, "Do you want to listen to me? Or should I just have them kill you?"

"All right, Señor Caliente, I'm listening."

"And you'll pay attention?"

"Always."

When Oscar began speaking quietly in Spanish, his voice almost muffled, Hugo noticed for the first time that the other men in the room were blond men who were not likely to understand Spanish even if they could hear the subdued intensity of Oscar's voice. "I'm going to do something for you I've never done for anyone, my friend. You're getting a second chance. There are two people I want you to kill. And then I never want to see you again."

Hugo remained motionless.

Oscar Caliente, who had made it a habit to punctuate his encounters with people by humiliating them, picked up Hugo's black, tight-fitting underwear from the floor and tossed it at Hugo's face. Hugo didn't flinch. "Get dressed. The two people I want you to get will be easy to find and kill. They know more about Angelina than anyone else in the world. Without them, there will never be another trial for her."

"I know who they are," Hugo said.

But Oscar continued. "One of them played me for a fool. He lied to me. That's despicable. He thinks he's untouchable. It's a game for him. I can't allow that."

"Just let me know where he lives," Hugo said.

"And the other one I just hate. She loves you, and you'll have no trouble finding her and taking her out."

"Doesn't matter who it is. You know that."

Whispering, Oscar said, "That's what I've always liked about you. And it's why you're still alive."

* * *

As they walked down the mildew-smelling corridor, Hugo saw that the clumsily concealed, 1980s-style bulky security cameras had already been smashed, probably when Oscar and his crew first entered the revolving lobby door. There were no hidden modern security cameras since the dingy entrance had not been modernized in thirty years.

While Hugo moved through the carpeted corridor, he noticed for the first time the zigzag symbol etched in the hair of the four men with crew cuts. They were the same markings as the two men who had served him and Lydia on the yacht on the day she died; he had killed those two men. It was obvious to him now that these four men meant to kill him but would not attempt that until after Hugo had carried out Oscar Caliente's orders.

Hugo also saw, but was not surprised, by the sight of the youthful, acne-scarred young woman who had eagerly checked him into the motel hours earlier. She was on the floor behind the counter. She was motionless. She was dead.

CHAPTER 42

HUNTER DECKER WAS an exceptional swimmer. He was in the Olympic-size pool near the huge Tudor house that he inherited at thirty-three when his father and mother died as their private jet crashed on its approach to their summer home on Nantucket. When Hunter married the beautiful Carolyn Whitehouse two years later, she had supervised the renovation of the manor house's exterior and interior, restoring them to the original condition of the building as constructed by Hunter's great-grandfather, who had commissioned McKim, Meade & White to design it. The fifty acres surrounding the mansion were the landscape creation of Frederick Law Olmsted's talented sons. The older Olmsted had envisioned and created Central Park, and his sons had learned well some of their father's astounding visionary skills. All the estate's open grounds had massive, rustling trees like those on the quads of many famous old New England colleges.

In the midst of all that privacy—and the fact that the house was empty because Carolyn and their live-in nanny had taken the nine-year-old twins and their six-month-old girl to nearby Connecticut for a Little League game on this limpid summer afternoon—Hunter was naked as he swam. How long had it been, he wondered, since his still gorgeous blond wife had been naked in the swimming pool with him? Probably since shortly after the twin boys' birth almost a decade ago. As the water flowed by his hips, Hunter felt a slight arousal in his groin since this pool had once been the scene of intensely erotic lovemaking with Carolyn.

Even by this point in their marriage, he believed he loved his wife, although it troubled him that now he had only memories of sex with her in the pool outside the huge Tudor house. She was passionate then, far less so now. The thought of divorcing her sometimes crossed his mind, but not often enough for him to act on it. For four generations, divorce among the Decker clan was rare, as were affairs. The WASP social circle in which he and Carolyn moved was small enough and closed enough that his wife would soon learn about any affair. Hunter wanted to spare her from that. Her father, whose name was part of an old and highly respected investment firm, had left her mother when Carolyn was only eight. She still bore the strains and resentment her father's abrupt and highly publicized abandonment of her mother and her had caused. He had died twenty years later, long after Carolyn graduated from Vassar. She had never seen him again, or taken any of his telephone calls, or answered any of his fervent, guilt-ridden letters, or cashed any of the checks he sent her. Hunter didn't want to hurt her in the same way her father had.

As he dove under the surface of the pool water near one of its walls and pushed outward from the wall with his legs, his mind wandered to the question of when it was that he started his regular visits to prostitutes. Probably three years earlier, he thought, at about the time he was named United States Attorney for the Southern District of New York. There were women for whom he paid two thousand or four thousand in cash for each afternoon they spent with him. There was some chance, he knew, that he might be recognized, unmasked to the public. But not likely, since even as the lead attorney for the United States in New York, he was on television infrequently, usually with six or seven other law-enforcement men and women. He was not a widely known person except in legal circles, and he could feel somewhat secure in his anonymity.

Everything about his frequent use of prostitutes had worked out, or so he thought. If any of the sophisticated young women knew who he was, no one ever let on. The names and identities of their clients clearly were of no interest to them; their interest was cash. Since all of his transactions were in cash, the agency had no record of his name. He had a code name with the agency that employed these women, *Billy the Kidd*. His only reputation for special status in that world was that he had picked up a reputation for never using a condom. The original Billy the Kid was reckless in 19th-century America. So was Hunter Decker as Billy the Kidd in the 21st century.

To rest after intense laps in his pool, he floated on his back. In the deepening and darkening blue of the evening sky—an almost full moon was reflected on the refracting waters of the pool's surface—he felt aroused again, this time not by the memory of the long-ago swimming with Carolyn in this pool but by the weeklong memory of Lori in the afternoon at the new, chic Ailo Hotel on Greenwich Street, in the old warehouse district now completely renovated into expensive apartments inside the structures of the century-old warehouses.

Lori was black. Hunter Decker had discovered a special liking for black women.

As the pool water lapped at his ears and caressed his neck and shoulders, he recognized yet again how fortunate he had been in life. Born to wealth and an adoring mother and father, treated like young royalty at Choate and Yale, privileged as soon as he left law school by a clerkship with Antonin Scalia, endowed with a partnership at one of the city's oldest firms, and then anointed by President Spellman as the U.S. Attorney for the Southern District of New York, he thought of himself now as the *fortunate son*. He had even been fortunate in carrying out his multiple encounters with young prostitutes, which he knew was risky but well worth it for him. He sensed he was the *fortunate son* not with a sense of self-satisfaction or pride, but with a sense of gratitude. Tremendous athletes like the Jamaican sprinter Usain Bolt are born with power and grace and go forward in life to fulfill that gift of birth. Hunter Decker was born to become a kind of great athlete of a life widely admired.

Except for rare moments, he had managed to forget the long-ago visit from Robert Calvaro or, to the extent he ever thought about the visit now, he saw it as a ruse or a gambit by Calvaro and Baldesteri that failed. Instead, he focused on the joyfulness of life.

CHAPTER 43

MONTHS EARLIER, NOT long after the announcement of Senator Baldesteri's indictment, one of his assistants surprised him when she said, "Robert Calvaro wants to meet you. Should we ignore him?"

"No," Hunter Decker had answered. "Call him and ask him when he would like to meet."

Robert Calvaro arranged to meet Hunter in the fortress-like building in Lower Manhattan that housed the U.S. Attorney's Office for the Southern District of New York. All that Hunter knew about Robert Calvaro at that point, although Hunter learned far more later, was that Calvaro was the central money man collecting and disbursing funds for Angelina Baldesteri through the recently formed super PAC *America Renewed*.

Decker was intrigued by the fact that Calvaro wanted to see him so soon after the Senator's indictment. Like any skilled prosecutor, he thought it was important to keep his door open to people like Calvaro if they knocked on it. They might have information, and information and evidence were the coin of the realm for prosecutors. And sometimes people like Calvaro wanted to turn on their partners, associates, friends, and at times family members in exchange for leniency. Decker was prepared to listen. In fact, his appetite was whetted by the key connections he knew Calvaro had with the Senator.

Calvaro had conditions to the meeting. No one else could be present, no recordings made, no interruptions allowed, no checking of anything he carried, no security scanning or pat-downs performed on him, no notes taken. Always confident, Decker told his assistants to agree to the conditions. Given what he then knew of Calvaro, he had no reason to fear him. After all, Calvaro was the son of an old, wealthy Jewish South American family; he was a graduate of St. Paul's and Yale; he had made a fortune in the South American oil business; he was a naturalized United States citizen; and he owned and operated a hedge fund. He was a vocal advocate of left-leaning causes.

From the beginning, Decker knew that Calvaro and *America Renewed* were at the heart of the case against Baldesterl. Vast amounts of money had passed into *America Renewed* from anonymous donors; much of the money was traceable, through intricate accounting by Government experts, to prohibited foreign sources. Calvaro was not only the Chief Executive Officer but he was also in effect the *alter ego* of *America Renewed*. He had managed to attract prominent names of company executives to the Board of Directors, which never met, and, for an annual *honorarium* of $150,000, to appoint the legendary Leon Stanski as the "Chair" of *America Renewed*.

What Hunter didn't then know was that Robert Calvaro in his real life was Oscar Caliente. Despite its sprawling reach, the Government had never been able to locate measurable and accurate samples of the DNA of the wily Oscar Caliente or his doppelganger, Robert Calvaro. But eventually there would be old-fashioned investigation work that established it.

It might be, Hunter told his assistants, that Calvaro wanted to cooperate, to "spill his guts," so as to avoid a future indictment.

Turning Calvaro against Baldesteri would make it *one, two, three* work to convict the Senator.

When Calvaro entered Hunter's huge office, with its windows overlooking the glittering waters of the East River and the 19th-century grandeur of the ornate Brooklyn Bridge, Hunter was struck by how much Calvaro had the appearance and mannerisms, even with his South American nuances, of the adult versions of the boys who were Hunter's classmates at Choate.

Calvaro sat at one of the wooden chairs facing Hunter's desk. He balanced on his knees the slim Hermes briefcase that he had carried into the office. "I'm glad," Calvaro said, "that you were willing to see me."

"I don't meet often, Señor Calvaro, with people who want to see me. They're first vetted by my assistants and security people. But you are, after all, Robert Calvaro, a financial wizard and frankly from my standpoint a benefactor of Angelina Baldesteri. All of which makes you very interesting to me."

"And all of that is very gracious for you to say, Mr. Decker. But I need to get to the point. You must either drop the case against Senator Baldesteri or lose the trial."

Calmly and steadily, Hunter said, "Do you understand who I am?"

"Certainly, I do. You can decide over the next few months that there is insufficient evidence to proceed against her or, if there is a trial, withdraw the case midway by announcing that the evidence, as it turns out, can't support a conviction. That you in good conscience can't allow the case to reach the jury."

At that moment, Hunter sensed the stirrings of anger, concern, fear, amazement. It struck him that this slender, well-dressed man wearing flesh-colored glasses for which he plainly had no need, never touched the doorknob, the chair in which he sat, or anything else. It was obvious he was avoiding coming into contact with anything from which his DNA could be isolated.

"Did Baldesteri send you here?"

"Nobody ever tells me what to do."

"So this stupidity is all your idea?"

Almost daintily crossing his legs, Calvaro said, "I never do anything stupid." He paused, staring at Hunter without blinking: his eyes were green, startlingly so. "But you do stupid things, Mr. Decker."

"Let me tell you something, Mr. Calvaro, that you don't understand. Right now you are committing a crime. Telling me to drop a criminal case or throw a trial is obstruction of justice. It's a felony. I could have you arrested now."

"Is that right? Well, I need to show you something that makes it clear there are two people in this room who commit crimes."

"You need to leave now. Or I'll have my Marshals drag you out by the heels."

"You know Lori Givens?"

Hunter Decker froze. "No, I don't," he lied.

"She's the $5,000 a night hooker you prefer."

"You're out of your mind."

"And do the names Gail Abernathy, Veronica Silva, Maia Alexander ring a bell?"

"Whoever they are," Hunter said, his voice with a faint tremor, "they are as crazy as you are. By the way, who *are* you really?"

Calvaro ignored him. He took from his valise an iPad. He placed it carefully in his lap, saying, "Take out your cell phone. I know your private email address. In a second you will receive a gallery of pictures featuring you. And, in each one, a different young woman."

Hesitantly, Decker removed his iPhone from the interior pocket of his suit jacket. He saw a new *Inbox* entry from *Americarenewed@ Americare-wed.com*. He pressed the icon.

There on the vivid screen was a gallery of pictures with him un-dressed and with naked women, some of them obviously as young as sixteen.

"This is extortion," Hunter said.

"No, no," Calvaro answered. "It's information. The information may give you time to think about the wisdom of dropping the in-dictment or throwing the trial. Not just your beautiful wife would be interested in these pictures. So would the world."

"How did you get these?"

"I take an interest in owning large parts of many businesses that interest me: polo horses, brokerage houses, restaurants, casinos, classy hotels. And I own the escort service you prefer."

"You're sick."

"And what are you? Several of these girls are as young as sixteen. You are a man headed for disgrace, Mr. Decker, or worse, such as statutory rape, if you ignore me."

"Just leave before I have you thrown out."

Calvaro snapped his iPad shut and slipped it into his valise. He said, "You've really impressed me and the Senator in one way. For a WASP, you are remarkably well endowed. Congratulations on joining my club. The women were all impressed by you, they all told me that."

*   *   *

Hunter Decker dropped his iPhone into the Tiffany pitcher of water on his desk, and within seconds the phone was ruined. Then he put his personal iPad and laptop into the classically scuffed leather litigation briefcase he always carried. There was a dump not far from the Harrison estate where he would throw them away that evening. The iMac computer on his desk was programmed to re-ceive and send only Government emails.

* * *

Two weeks later, and still several months before the Baldesteri trial started, Curnin and Giordano reported to him that there was indeed a Robert Calvaro. He was born in 1965 and so was roughly the same age as the Robert Calvaro who had visited Hunter's office with the revealing iPad pictures, about which Hunter said nothing to anyone. According to Giordano, Robert Calvaro had come from a wealthy Argentinian family. He had attended St. Paul's and graduated from Yale and was from age twenty a member of the New York Athletic Club, a legacy member since his grandfather and father had been lifetime members. Giordano and Curnin showed Hunter an old Polaroid photo of Robert Calvaro, at age twenty-eight, bare-chested and his features clearly visible as he handled ropes on a classic sailboat off the coast of Maine. Ocean waters and small pine islands shimmered in sunlight on the Atlantic behind the joyful, vigorous young man. Years had passed, but that young man with a body and vigor of youth, had, in Hunter's eyes, grown essentially into the Robert Calvaro he had recently seen.

But the real Robert Calvaro had died in 1989 while climbing the sheer wall of a high mountain in the Himalayas. His body was never found.

There was not a trace of the DNA or fingerprints of the dead Robert Calvaro, or of the Robert Calvaro who had sat so carefully in Hunter Decker's office.

Curnin asked, "Want us to arrest him?"

"No."

CHAPTER 44

WHILE STILL ON his back and resting on the gentle swells of the water, Hunter for the first time noticed the man standing on the edge of the pool. He was in silhouette, entirely in black, in the darkening, gentle air. Because the man's face was shadowed by the swiftly oncoming night, Hunter didn't recognize him.

His first reaction, as he floated on his back with his chest and naked loins exposed, was embarrassment. And then anger at the brazen intrusion. And then utter vulnerability.

"What's up, Jack?" Hunter asked, raising his voice, trying to sound angry and commanding.

"One name I've never had, Señor Decker, is Jack." He had a steady baritone voice, tinged with a Spanish accent. Hunter recognized that he was not Robert Calvaro, whose voice was reedy, almost effeminate. The only time Hunter had ever been in Calvaro's presence was months earlier, at the unsettling meeting in the U.S. Attorney's office. Hunter had, except for a few unpredictable moments on those rare occasions when he forgot the good fortunes of his life, remembered Calvaro and the distinct pictures on Calvaro's iPad. During those lapses, Hunter sometimes thought the encounter with Calvaro was a ruse or an illusion or even a rare bad dream. He once looked at the rigorously maintained log book of his visitors: there was no record of anyone named Robert Calvaro who had ever visited him. In fact, on that day, the log revealed no visitors. Calvaro was a phantom. And Hunter had utterly destroyed the photographs Calvaro had forwarded to his electronic objects.

In the pool, Hunter lowered his long legs and torso below the surface of the water, peering at the unfamiliar silhouette of the powerfully built man towering above him as if on a museum pedestal.

Hunter asked, panting slightly from his long vigorous swim and his treading movements in the water, "Who are you?"

"A friend of Señor Calvaro. You haven't forgotten Señor Calvaro, have you?"

Hunter, still gazing upward, a position of acute disadvantage, didn't speak.

The man standing at the edge of the pool glanced briefly to the leafy trees and shrubbery that separated the pool from the mansion. "Jesus, you live really well, Señor Decker, I mean, really well."

Hunter continued to tread water, only his shoulders and head above the surface. "How the hell did you get in here?"

"Let's just say I'm a ghost. I pass through walls, gates, trees."

Hunter then had a flash of recognition. The man, he now knew, was Hugo Salazar, or Juan Suarez, or another elusive pseudonym. Hunter had never seen this man in person, only in photographs and surveillance tapes, usually with the man Hunter knew as Robert Calvaro and, more recently, as in Government Exhibit 673, as the man talking to Angelina Baldesteri. Hugo's dense black hair, drawn into a sleek ponytail, was unmistakable. It was his signature. Hunter was able to see it because Hugo inexplicably again stared at the carefully maintained shrubbery, as if he recognized something or someone impossible to see clearly.

"Did you know we have a few things in common, Señor Decker? Did you know that?" It was a soothingly calm voice, even though its message made Hunter's submerged groin tighten with fear.

"You need to leave. And now."

"One of the things we have in common," Hugo Salazar said as if speaking confidentially, "is making love to women. As many as possible. Except I don't have to pay for it."

"I need you to leave. Don't forget who I am. I can have you arrested any time I want. And I always have guards. You see them in the bushes right now, don't you? They have you in their sights. Their work is to protect me."

Again, Hugo bypassed Hunter's words. "Another thing we have in common, Señor Decker, is the foolish hope that we can ever outrun Oscar Caliente."

Hunter said, "I don't take orders from Robert Calvaro or Oscar Caliente or whoever that faggot is."

"You met with him, my friend, remember? Señor Caliente told you what to do. You didn't do it. That's not healthy. You may not take anything seriously—look, Señor Decker, at the way you live; men who live like you never do take anything seriously except maybe losing a fraction of their money—but Oscar Caliente always takes things seriously and seriously punishes disobedience. He told you to find a way to let Baldesteri go. And you didn't. And now you say you won't. And you're humiliating Señor Calvaro. That does not please him. That's not healthy."

"As I said, I don't take orders from Robert Calvaro or Oscar Caliente imitating Robert Calvaro. And did you know Robert Calvaro died years ago?"

"Oscar Caliente, Señor Decker, has been many people. So have I."

Hunter said, "But you are a nobody. You're nothing."

Night had come on rapidly. In his black clothing, Hugo Salazar was almost invisible. The underwater lights that illuminated the pool suddenly spread their attractive glow precisely when the automatic timer sensed the right level of darkness. When the lights rose through the water, shimmering, they shone on Hunter Decker's naked body. He was very pale underwater.

From the darkness Hugo finally said, ignoring the insult, "Señor Caliente knows you enjoy giving orders. Just the same way he does."

"He's a creep. I'm not. He knows nothing about me."

"He knows that you had Lydia Guzman killed by your people."

"That's bullshit, Jack."

Hugo said, "And you tried to have me killed, too. Who did you have put ricin in the coke I gave Lydia? I was supposed to take care of her, and you had her killed when I was supposed to be taking care of her. Señor Caliente was, and still is, really angry with me. Your people killed Lydia. And now his people intend to kill me. So you, Señor Decker, are putting me in danger."

"Ricin? You people are crazy. I don't like that."

"It was the men with the zigzag marks in their hair, wasn't it? You sent them into my life, Señor Decker, and they killed her so that she couldn't set Baldesteri free. And you tricked Señor Caliente into believing the zigzag men worked for him. That was very magical work by you, Señor Decker. Really. I don't know anyone who ever came close to tricking Señor Caliente. You almost did. The zigzag men showed their complete allegiance to Señor Caliente by killing that gigolo, Hayes Smith, so that Raquel Rematti would be painfully hurt and think the killers were coming for her, too. And lose the trial."

Hunter began to swim from the center of the Olympic-size pool toward the aluminum ladder. "I'm not listening to any more of this," he said. For the first time in his life, this man of privilege and fortune was genuinely afraid.

"Slow down," Hugo said steadily. "You're never leaving that pool, Señor Decker. Ever."

With his entire body and head under the surface of the water, Hunter continued swimming toward the ladder. As he gripped the first submerged rung, his head rose into the cool air.

Then Hunter saw two other men emerge from the darkness in the carefully tended shrubbery. In the faint upward illumination from the underwater lights, he recognized Curnin and Giordano. As his muscular arms gripped the railing, Hunter said, "You've made huge mistakes, Salazar or Suarez. These men are going to arrest you. They take my orders."

* * *

Hunter Decker's last moment of life was the recognition that Curnin and Giordano were aiming black pistols at him. The sharp, brief burst of gunfire resonated for two seconds above the pool and then abruptly subsided. In only twenty seconds the water of the pool was permeated with red. Hunter Decker, spread-eagled and eerily floating, drifted gently downward through the depths of the illuminated water.

* * *

Hugo Salazar would need only five minutes to nail and tape to the walls of the house's main hallway twenty-one pictures of Hunter Decker, naked, having sex with fifteen different women. Oscar Caliente had told him that the pictures should be the first things that Hunter Decker's wife and kids saw when they entered the house that night even before they looked for Hunter.

CHAPTER 45

CURNIN AND GIORDANO had spent enough time by now with Hugo Salazar to know how powerful he was because of his connections to Caliente. They also knew how erratic Salazar was and how intricately unpredictable Caliente was. They said nothing as they stood in the house's grand entrance while Hugo tacked and taped to the walls a vast montage of pictures of the naked Hunter Decker with so many different young women. The pictures would be the first things Carolyn Whitehouse and the children would see when they walked into the mansion to begin to wait for their loving husband and father to greet them when they returned from the Little League game.

As he carefully secured the multitude of photographs to the walls, Hugo said, "I used my cell phone to film you shooting Decker. I've already sent it to Señor Caliente and wrote in Spanish that you did a great job. He wrote back and told me to say *Good work* to you."

Without answering, Curnin and Giordano simply left the house as Hugo continued with his posting of the photographs. While they walked on the long pathway to the smoothly graveled area where the two cars were parked, Giordano and Curnin didn't speak. They both realized that Oscar Caliente now completely ruled their lives: he had a film of them killing the U.S. Attorney for the Southern

District of New York. The video could easily be posted on the
Internet and viewed by millions of people, including the Director
and other officials of the FBI, from which Curnin and Giordano
had permanently and secretly removed themselves because of the
lure of the vast reservoirs of cash Oscar Caliente had already arranged to deliver to them and promised to continue to deliver so
long as they maintained the façade of active FBI agents. That en-
abled them to feed the Sinaloa cartel with invaluable information.

As they waited uneasily for Hugo Salazar to finish his work,
Giordano quietly said, "How long is it going to take for that crazy
motherfucker to tape up his little display?"

"What's the difference?" Curnin said. "I mean, what could be the
difference after all the sick shit we've done? Let him take as long as
he wants. Maybe he'll choke on the tape."

After two more minutes, Hugo stepped onto the veranda. He
pulled the oak door shut behind him and, not speaking but leading
them, casually walked past them. His Chevy and the black SUV in
which Curnin and Giordano had arrived were parked side by side in
a dark culvert near the long driveway's entrance.

Hugo waited for them. As they came closer, Hugo said, "I'll see
Señor Caliente soon. I know him. He's generous. He'll give you a
bonus when I show him again the film of what you did to Decker."

The remote area where the vehicles were parked was even darker
than the surrounding air because of the thick, enveloping shrubs.

Neither Curnin nor Giordano answered him. They despised
him. Since the cars were side by side, the men were both within the
range of Hugo Salazar. Like a magician whose movements were all
sleight-of-hand, Salazar plunged a long blade into Curnin's neck
and with the same blade into the heart of the terrified, immobilized Giordano.

Hugo had one more assignment, and after that he would use his chameleon skills to elude Oscar Caliente forever. Hugo knew to a certainty that Caliente, despite his promise at the sleazy motel to let Hugo slip away into the world after murdering Hunter Decker and Raquel Rematti, had no intention of allowing him to live. But Hugo wanted to live, and there were many places in the world to live.

CHAPTER 46

IT WAS A wondrous night in Riverside Park. A slight breeze from off the Hudson River rustled through the myriad leaves of the park's ancient trees. On the walkways lined by British-style lampposts, dozens of men, women, and children strolled. In the nighttime cloudless sky, a bright half-moon—the same moon that shed its lunar glow on the lifeless, steadily bloating body of Hunter Decker at the bottom of the pool thirty miles north of the city—was intense enough to create the shadow of Raquel Rematti as she ran toward the esplanade along the river's shore.

Ever since her happy, successful years in college, Raquel, although not a flawless runner, had always found in exercise a way to unravel the knots of anxiety and fear that sometimes—but not often—seized her thoughts and muscles. Even when she had cancer, there were days or nights when, with a white turban wrapped around her bald scalp, she was able to stride for two or three miles in her running clothes through the familiar park. At that point, she sometimes found herself wondering whether that particular time would be the final one she'd envelop herself in the lushness of the park.

Tonight, when she reached the esplanade, she turned north, in the direction of the awe-inspiring immensity of the George Washington Bridge. She already sensed some of the anxiety that had come to beset her drain away from her consciousness and her body. She thought for a moment that she might be able to run to the esplanade directly under the bridge, which would loom above her, with traffic roaring overhead. But that was at least four miles away, and then four miles to return, and she knew that would be too much distance since, during the weeks of the Baldesteri trial, she hadn't found the time to exercise consistently.

In an oversize pouch strapped to her waist, she carried identification cards, the Ruger, and her cell phone. After half an hour of slow movement uptown, with steady river traffic of cargo ships and tugboats flowing down the Hudson to New York Harbor, she felt her cell phone vibrate. From habit, she stopped at a green bench facing the river and the New Jersey Palisades. She found the phone and on its screen appeared Michael O'Keefe's name.

She pressed the *Accept* icon, and Michael's voice emerged. "Raquel, my dear, where are you?"

"Michael, I'm running along the Hudson River, believe it or not." She laughed ruefully and said, "Trying to forget my troubles."

Michael, usually circumspect so as to calm clients, was blunt. "Your troubles are deeper now."

Involuntarily, even in the warm and benign night air, she began to shake. "Why?"

"Hunter Decker is dead."

"What?"

"He was swimming in his pool in Harrison. About two hours ago, two men shot him."

"My God, how do you know this, Michael?"

"He has a younger brother, Gordon, a lawyer, who also worked briefly for me. He left the law. He wasn't cut out for it. But he stayed close to me. He calls me Uncle Mike. Hunter disliked that. But Gordon was, because of their grandfather and father, as wealthy as

Hunter. Gordon lives less than a mile away from Hunter. Gordon called me even before the local police arrived."

Raquel spread her hand over her face. "How awful, how awful." And then she said, "How did Gordon find out so soon?"

"Hunter was married to Carolyn Whitehouse. Carolyn had been away all afternoon at a Little League game for their twin nine-year-olds. She also had the baby girl with her. The first call she placed was to Gordon Decker. Gordon and Hunter were estranged. But Carolyn treated Gordon as a brother."

"So Hunter's wife found her husband dead in the pool?"

Michael O'Keefe inhaled and blew out a stream of pained breath. "Not right away, not right away."

"How?" Despite Raquel's shock and her involuntary quaking, the question was motivated by the lawyer in her, that need to know. "So how did she find him?"

"We're in a business with hard truths, Raquel. And here is a hard one. When she returned to their house, it was already dark. The front of the house—it's a mansion, Raquel—was illuminated. She opened the front door. The boys ran in ahead of her, shouting for their daddy. The boys were still in their uniforms. They had won the game."

"And they couldn't find their father because he was already dead in the pool?"

"Not quite that."

"Then what?"

"Taped to the walls and bannisters were arrays of photographs of their father, naked, having sex with young women. Many young women. He was obviously obsessed. He had a secret life."

"What did Carolyn do?"

"As soon as she saw the lurid pictures, she took the boys and the little girl upstairs to their rooms. There was a nanny with them. One of the women in the pictures turned out, in fact, to be the nanny."

"This, Michael, is far beyond anything I can understand. And I thought I understood everything."

"Carolyn ran outside. Carolyn did know that Hunter, who was very fit, often did laps in the pool, which even in the winter was heated, but on a warm summer evening like now was perfect in every way. She immediately saw that the water in the pool was reddish. When she looked down into the water, she saw Decker at the bottom of the pool. His head and chest were, she said, like pulp from the gunshot wounds."

"Good God. What then?"

"She called her brother-in-law. Gordon ran to her house. He saw the pictures in the hallway and then found Carolyn upstairs with the kids and the nanny. Gordon called me. I told him to contact the local police and the FBI. Even old radicals like me know when you need the police."

Driven by anxiety and shock, Raquel stood up and leaned against the iron railing that separated the esplanade from the black, glittering waters of the fast-moving Hudson. "Have the police found the killers?"

"They did."

"Was it a robbery gone badly? Hunter and his wife must have had expensive antiques in the house."

"It wasn't a robbery gone badly. There were two men who deliberately did the killing, Raquel. Their guns still had that telltale smell of cordite. The two men who did the killing, Raquel, were Giordano and Curnin."

"I learned as a good Catholic girl not to hate. But I hate them. Are they under arrest?"

"They would wish they were. They're dead."

"What?"

"They were stabbed in the same way the two men with the zigzag hair markings were killed on the West Side Highway."

One hand squeezing the curved iron railing, Raquel gazed across the Hudson to the heights of the brightly lit apartment buildings atop the Palisades on the New Jersey shore. "I'm certain those were the same two men who stalked me on Madison Avenue a few days ago."

"My guess," Michael answered, "is you're right."

"Michael," she said, utter conviction in her voice, "I know who has done these things."

"Raquel, my instincts all tell me I do, too. It's the man you told me you once loved. Juan Suarez, Hugo Salazar, or what was he known as? *The Blade of the Hamptons*?"

"He's a serial killer, Michael."

Quietly Michael O'Keefe said, "Raquel, dear, he's coming for you. Fifty years in this business have taught me to understand the rare men like this. It's dark outside. Most killings take place at night. Go to your apartment. I'll meet you there. We will pack everything you need tonight: clothes, food, your precious high heels. I'll have a driver—I'm too old to safely drive myself—take you to Maine, tonight. I have a house I rarely use in Maine. It's on the coast, next to Bath, the Maine village, on a peninsula called Orr's Island. You'll be safer there than anywhere else in the world. And as inept as the FBI is, when it comes to their own agents, even agents who were as thoroughly corrupted as Curnin and Giordano, they have an uncanny ability to find the killer. He will never find you on Orr's Island. The house rests on a granite promontory at the very end of the peninsula."

"Michael, my daddy taught me never to run. Instead, he taught me how to fight."

"Your daddy was wrong, Raquel. You're now engulfed by a class of professional warriors. This is not a street fight on Main Street in Lawrence, Massachusetts. You were exquisitely brave enough to battle and overcome cancer. As courageous and resourceful as you are, you're not likely to escape this one. Let me be blunt because I love and admire you. The man you were candid enough to tell me you loved during the Richardson trial is a man I came to know in another context—as a potential coconspirator in a Sinaloa investigation of several people after the Richardson trial. He had quickly and easily slipped back into the country after he was deported. There was never an indictment then because the FBI and the U.S. Attorney's Office ran into a stone wall when they couldn't coerce any of the targets to testify against any of the others."

"Are you telling me, Michael, that you met and know this man, this Suarez, Salazar, whoever he is?"

"I do. He was the worst of the worst. And the most resourceful."

Raquel said, "Why didn't you tell me this when we met? I told you all I knew about him. It sounds, Michael, like a betrayal."

"Raquel, if I sound now like an old man with wisdom, bear with me. I said at the end of our meeting that I wanted to develop a strategy to help you. Once upon a time, I acted, sometimes impulsively, on instinct. Maturity has taught me to pause and think. Was there a way, I wondered, for me to use my once-upon-a-time knowledge of him and, more important, of the people he worked for and guarded in every way, to help you? These crazy men think they owe me a favor for saving them from an indictment and jail."

Raquel watched a big, brightly lit boat, crowded on three decks with partygoers, cruise steadily north against the relentless, seaward currents of the Hudson. At last she said, "That's a kind offer about the house in Maine. Let me think about it."

"Raquel, dear, dear, you don't have time to think about it. There's a serial killer on the streets of Manhattan. It's no secret where you live. He's like Dracula tonight. There is no end to the amount of blood he needs."

"Michael, I live in a safe building. There are always two doormen in the lobby. There are porters at the service entrance. And, believe it or not, the two elevators aren't automatic. They each always have an elevator operator who uses a handle to take you to your floor. And the gates are those iron-mesh, accordion-style gates."

"Let me tell you something. For a man like Suarez or Salazar, access to a building like that is as easy as taking ice cream from a kid."

"I don't believe that. The building is a turn-of-the-century fortress."

"Well," Michael said, "things are happening quickly—events could overwhelm you. At least let me come to your apartment later tonight. As I said, I'll have one of my BMWs and the driver wait in front of your building for the drive to Maine if you decide to do it. I can help you choose what you will need for Maine because I know how well stocked the house is and what the weather is like in this season."

She glanced at the surface of the cell phone. It was not yet eight. She needed time to think. She said, "Michael, can I call you later? An hour or so? I'll let you know then."

"There isn't much time, Raquel." Michael's words were blunt and direct. They didn't now have that soothing, reassuring Irish brogue that was Michael O'Keefe's trademark.

CHAPTER 47

RAQUEL TURNED FROM the Hudson River railing and saw that the only people on the esplanade were the runners, walkers, and bicyclists. All of them were, she was certain, harmless. She recognized none of them. In just a few running strides she was in the dense foliage of Riverside Park, feeling secure in its enveloping darkness.

When she reached the bright lobby of her building, both uniformed doormen greeted her with their usual smiling decorum. One said, "Looks as though you enjoyed your run, Ms. Rematti." She knew there was a gleaming sheen of sweat on her forehead. Like all doormen in Manhattan, they never asked anything but pleasant questions and they kept secrets about the people who lived in the buildings and the strangers who visited them. If the doormen knew anything about all the negative public comments, often insulting and painfully derogatory, now being made about her in the press and on the Internet, they didn't convey it. But they certainly knew. Just as they knew she had been a loyal, kind, and generous tenant for years.

To her surprise, since he ordinarily worked the graveyard shift from eleven p.m. to seven a.m., Jose, her favorite staff member in the building, was operating the old-world elevator. As they rose slowly from floor to floor, with the chains and ropes straining above them, Jose said, "Julio called in sick today. So I get to substitute." Julio ordinarily operated the elevator at this time of the evening. "But, you know, Ms. Rematti, I don't mind the overtime."

They stared at each other in the elevator's confines. Unexpectedly, he said, "I'm sorry, Ms. Rematti, that you are going through so much now."

She smiled. "Jose, thank you. But I've been through worse and I'm still on my feet. You are a good man."

"If you need anything, I'll be here all night."

* * *

Inside her apartment, she took the Ruger from her commodious running pouch and walked through every room, opening all the closets. She was alone. She returned the Ruger to the pouch. She then stripped off all her damp running clothes, and, just as she was walking naked toward the bathroom for her shower, Raquel was seized by an unexpected impulse. Her computer was on a desk not far from the bathroom door. She sat on the chair in front of the computer, turned it on, and waited for the screen to emerge from its somnolence. Adroitly she typed in Google maps and then Orr's Island.

Exactly as Michael had described it, Orr's Island was a stony peninsula jutting into the waters of the Atlantic. She brought the peninsula, by hitting the *zoom* icon, so sharply into focus that it was as if she were flying over it in a helicopter in clear daylight. A big, windswept stone house—Michael's house exactly as he had described it—occupied the outermost granite formation that extended into the white-capped, windswept ocean. The inner areas of Orr's Island, connected only by a stone bridge to the slightly larger Bailey Island that in turn was joined to the mainland in Bath, had twenty houses on it. There were piers, lobster cabins, and lobster traps stacked along the water's edge. Small harbors and inlets were everywhere.

For some reason she typed into the Google search engine *Residents of Orr's Island*. She carefully looked down the lists of old English names such as Redwine, Coursen, and Pierce adjacent to each house, together with the dates the properties were purchased. The stone house on the property at the peninsula's end was owned by James Honeycutt; it was purchased by his great-grandfather in 1888.

There were no O'Keefes on Orr's Island.

*   *   *

Startled and unsettled, Raquel pressed further. Returning to the Google search window, she typed in the name *Hunter Decker*. Instantly his face appeared in an official Government photograph in front of an unfurled American flag. Below that was a brief Wikipedia article about him. She read it three times. Scion of a wealthy 19th-century industrialist family, graduate of Choate and Yale, and now the United States Attorney for the Southern District of New York. Widely considered as a potential candidate for United States Senator from New York. His parents died when he was thirty-three years old in the crash of their Cessna off the coast of Nantucket where they owned a vacation home. He had inherited approximately forty million dollars.

And Hunter Decker never had any brothers or sisters.

*   *   *

Raquel immediately sent a text message to Michael O'Keefe: *Why did you lie to me?*

He never responded.

CHAPTER 48

RAO'S WAS ON First Avenue and 114th Street, an old-style Italian restaurant still in the heart of the never-rejuvenated and steadily decaying East Harlem. There was an era a century to seventy-five years earlier when East Harlem was a neighborhood crowded with new Italian immigrants, utterly safe because the Mafia controlled the streets. Then gradually, incrementally, after the Second World War the area from East 96th Street on the south and East 127th Street on the north and from upper Fifth Avenue to First Avenue in the 1950s and 1960s became known as Spanish Harlem. For the last several decades, it was known simply and neutrally as East Harlem, its geographically correct location in Manhattan.

But Rao's had outlived these profound changes. To the north and south were rows of bodegas, candy shops, secondhand clothing and furniture stores, laundromats, tattered gas stations with signs on which were written "Flats Fixed" and one that read "Fats Fixed," and storefront evangelical churches with neon signs announcing *Jesus Saves* in Spanish. Many of the places near Rao's had through the years been looted or burned or defaced with meaningless graffiti.

But never Rao's. Through some type of unwritten code or fear or enduring Mafia protection, Rao's had a pristine storefront and awning, which had never changed for decades. The name *Rao's* was still imprinted on the two windows flanking the main entrance. There was not a trace of damage anywhere on or in the restaurant.

Every night of the week, SUVs and black limousines were parked three deep on the street as drivers in black suits waited for their passengers while they ate and drank inside. There were many nights when Bill and Hillary Clinton ate there, as did actors, writers, and politicians. None of the vehicles was ever ticketed by the police, for even the Police Commissioner and the Mayor often ate there.

Oscar Caliente had started visiting Rao's when he first arrived in Manhattan. Even then he knew it was a sacred place where no one was ever harassed. It was a sanctuary for politicians, for Italian dons, for well-dressed street gang leaders, for overlords of the drug trade. In fact, there had never been an arrest at or near Rao's.

In time, as Oscar Caliente methodically and ruthlessly came to dominate drug distribution in Manhattan, Rao's became ever more familiar and comfortable to him. He became one of the many prized patrons. Nobody ever discussed what he did for a living. He was simply Señor Caliente, as if that were a status in and of itself.

There were times when, to reward Hugo Salazar for an exceptional assignment or kill, Oscar took him and several other people, including two United States Congressmen, to supper at Rao's. Hugo Salazar was so handsome, so charismatic, so obviously close to Oscar Caliente, that the drivers waiting on the street and sidewalk who were on Oscar Caliente's payroll and who not only drove his entourage but served as his bodyguards, thought nothing of the fact that Hugo Salazar, obviously late for dinner, arrived in a yellow taxi. He walked quickly over the sidewalk, among the bored drivers, and into Rao's.

Oscar Caliente's customary table was a big circular one near the entrance. He never had dinner alone. Some of his guests were famous men and women, but always at least two men at the table had the sole task to protect him.

Dressed in his customary black, Hugo Salazar moved rapidly toward Oscar's back. Hugo was utterly concentrated on the rear of Caliente's head, where his carefully trimmed brown hair met the sleek collar of his silk shirt.

Caliente, about to slip a raw oyster into his mouth, detected a sudden look of alarm in the bodyguards' expressions. He began to turn in the direction of the door. He never completed the motion and never tasted the oyster whose shell he held in his hand because Salazar's razor sharp, sword-like machete entered Caliente's skull effortlessly and its tip almost instantly emerged from Caliente's throat as did gushes of projectile blood.

Hugo Salazar pulled the blade out of the still-quivering Oscar Caliente. He wiped the blood from the blade with two of Rao's red-checked cloth napkins, and confidently left the fragrant restaurant. He strode along the sidewalk where the drivers languidly stood or leaned against their vehicles. Within ten seconds of plunging a sword into Oscar Caliente's head and neck, Hugo Salazar was in a taxi at the corner of First Avenue and 114th Street. *No one*, he said aloud to the small, baffled Muslim driver, *will ever kill me. I don't give a fuck whoever he thinks he is.* The driver, reacting as though he had a typical Manhattan maniac in the car, glanced once in the rearview mirror and then continued the trip to Riverside Drive.

CHAPTER 49

WHEN SHE HEARD the scraping noise behind the service door in her kitchen, Raquel was startled awake from the sleep she had managed to achieve after sitting for hours on the sofa in her living room. She glanced at her cell phone. Just as she had been while at the computer, she was still naked. She had managed to cover herself in a thin wool blanket that was usually folded neatly on the sofa.

It was two a.m., a time of night when Jose went from floor to floor in the service elevator to collect the trash from the bins on each floor. A considerate man, Jose was usually as quiet as a phantom.

Not so tonight. The scraping at the lock to the service door, very noisy at first, stopped when a distinct click sounded as the lock sharply snapped open. She heard the door swing. That had never happened before, something Jose had never done.

From the sofa she asked, "Jose?"

A familiar voice answered, laughing, "Jose? Jose is on a coffee break with Jesus Christ."

Instantly she recognized the voice. And at that moment, she saw Juan Suarez. In the hundreds of times she had been near him before and during *The Blade of the Hamptons* trial and then that final time in the federal prison in Brooklyn as he was awaiting deportation,

this was the only time when bars didn't divide them or guards separate them.

She covered her breasts with her arms. "How did you get in here?"
she asked, trying to conceal both fear and anger.

"Don't be worried," he answered. "I'm not going to hurt you."

"How did you get in here?"

"What does it matter? A man named Jose had the keys I need. I
took them from him."

"Did you kill him?"

"I let him know you were one of my oldest and best friends and
that I was passing through the city and you wanted to see me. He
said he would call you on the intercom. I said you'd be happier if I
just surprised you. He said no. He was not cooperating with me. So
I had to take his keys."

"Is he dead?"

"I have the keys. He would not let them go."

"He has a wife and three children."

"He didn't mention that. He should have thought about them
when I asked for the keys."

"You killed a sweet, innocent man."

"Raquel, I only do the things I have to do. And to people who
deserve it. You don't."

His voice had a soothing, almost simplistic tone. It was that
voice—so low, so straightforward, so essentially seductive—that
had first arrested her attention when she met him in prison before
the East Hampton murder trial. She had found herself meeting
with him so often both before and during the trial because of that
voice's inherent beauty and his compelling presence.

He walked calmly, as if gliding on velvet slippers, into her living
room as she remained under the blanket on the sofa. He sat down
almost casually on a nearby Eames chair.

"I never thanked you for saving my life."

She said, "Would you please leave?"

"Do you know this is the first time we have ever met when we were just alone? We have never been able to speak freely until now."

"I don't have anything to say to you, except please leave."

"You loved me, and I never touched you. If I touch you in the ways I know how, you'll love me even more. You'll be a very happy, happy woman."

"That is not going to happen."

He leaned back in the chair, looking utterly relaxed. "You are missing out on something you'd love, I promise."

"I'm not interested. I never was."

"You're lying to yourself, Raquel."

"No."

"I'm going to kiss you. All the time we saw each other, we never had a chance to kiss. We both wanted that. You know it. I know it."

"There won't be any kisses. There won't be anything."

"I never forced myself on any woman, Raquel. And I'm not going to do that with you. I'm not a rapist—the other way around, women come to me." He smiled at her, confidence dominating his every elegant, Cary Grant–like gesture and word. "You wanted to come to me. You do now. You know that."

Fear was accelerating through her. Under the blanket her naked body began to quake. For only the second time in her life—the first was when she learned she was stricken with cancer—she was in the presence of a killer, and she was again uncertain she had any defense.

"Raquel, listen to me. You have no life now. Everything you have," he said, waving a hand at the objects in the room, "will disappear soon. Baldesteri, Michael O'Keefe, and everybody you knew—all of them are in the process of ruining you. You'll have no reputation, no money, no friends, no place where you would want to live. You're a proud woman, Raquel, and even as we speak here together, the Internet is swarming with stories about what a lousy lawyer you are, a charlatan, a woman who wins cases by bribing jurors. There are already pictures of you, Lydia Guzman, and me on the Internet two weeks ago. We were a happy group."

"That picture is a hoax. You know that."

"I know that, Raquel. But that was not my doing. Nobody but nobody will believe you."

"Whose idea was it, creating a fake picture to ruin me?"

"I can't say. I need to stay alive."

"Was it Decker's idea?"

"Decker had too many ideas, Raquel. And, besides, he had so many ideas he is dead. So he has run out of ideas. He deserved to die."

"Did you kill him?"

"No."

"Who did?"

"That doesn't matter. They were people you know, who wanted to hurt you, too. Now they can never hurt you. I protected you. I owed you that. Now, you owe me."

"What happened to the men who killed Decker?"

"I made them dead."

"That's a strange way to speak. You killed them?"

"I was with them when they died."

Raquel knew, and had for a long time known, that this man was wildly unpredictable, a beguiling charmer; alluringly odd, opaque, but also, at all times, a dedicated, enthusiastic killer. Not all the physical beauty and attractiveness of this man, even his moments of extraordinary grace, could alter all that.

I have to save myself, she thought. *Only I can do that.*

"Do you know what a euphemism is, Juan?"

"No, but I understand what you mean. I was with Decker when he died. I gave that order, because I was ordered to do it. So even though I was there, I didn't murder him." He leaned forward, confident, reassuring, even affectionate. "We can leave together. I know places to go with you. I have money, more than enough, for us. You must have some money, too. Your life has all fallen down, and can't be put together again. I can do that. No one can touch us."

"Stop that, Juan. You're here to kill me. So why not? Caliente assigned you to do that long ago."

"He did. And I didn't."

"So why not now?"

"Caliente died before he could slip an oyster into his mouth. He called oysters his Viagra."

"Caliente is dead? When?"

"Two, three hours ago, just before I came here. You're alive and strikingly beautiful with your clothes off. Just as I dreamed." He bestowed on her one of his beguiling smiles. "Caliente can't do another thing."

"Did you kill him?"

"Sure. He planned to have me wasted. But I reached out to him first. I couldn't stand him from the minute he picked me out of a crowd and took me away from washing filthy dishes at the miserable Chinese restaurant on Second Avenue. And I needed to save you, too. Three days ago, he gave me orders again to kill you."

"He was a busy man."

"He had a lot on his mind. He had to be a different person all the time. Robert Calvaro was only one version of him. There were so many others."

Raquel had dealt for years with men and women who were criminals. They shared one trait, no matter who they were, whether they were insider traders in securities, or powerful men who habitually used their positions to seduce women who wanted to be actresses or television personalities, or politicians. Criminals, she knew, never changed. They carried with them forever, by instinct or genetics, the impulse to exercise the powers they had. Juan Suarez was a killer. He would, she knew, kill her this night no matter how many kind or engaging words he used. Like a drug addict, he loved his drug of choice above all else; and in his case, his drug of choice was to make people die.

Even under extreme pressure, Raquel was resourceful. She somehow had to grab the pouch she had used on her run and had dropped on her dining room table. It still contained her Ruger. *Humor him for as long as you can*, she thought, *until you get the Ruger and use it.*

She said, "The truth is from the moment I first saw you I wondered what it would be like to kiss you."

"Let me show you."

Trembling, she slipped the soft wool blanket off her entire body. She remained on the sofa, fully exposed. She had never doubted her own beauty. She detected an odor of sweat intermixed with perfume on her entire body. She hadn't showered since her sweat-inducing run.

He was a large man, although slim, muscular, and powerfully built. But Raquel, a profoundly sensual woman who spent a lifetime since age seventeen in many sexual encounters with many different kinds of men, was repelled by Juan Suarez' long-desired kiss. He loomed over her, carefully holding the sides of her head, pressing his warm lips against hers, and sweeping his tasteful tongue around her tongue. As she sat naked on the sofa under him, her eyes slightly open and struck by his glamorous face, hair, and body, she felt like vomiting.

And yet through years of experience, she knew how to kiss and touch as if in passion even at those times when she lacked anything genuine. She knew by instinct that her chance of living depended on seducing and deceiving him in the most basic sense: to make him, as crazy as he was, believe that erotic kisses and touches would gradually and ineluctably lead to her bedroom and hours of various lovemaking positions. That passionate movement to the bedroom would lead them close to the pouch in which her Ruger was concealed. It might be that this man, a man with climacteric passions, might be so focused on the thought of entering her that he wouldn't react quickly enough as she seized the pouch and unzipped it to get the Ruger. As she knew, Juan was extraordinarily fast in his reactions, but, as she also knew, men's lusts were deeply self-absorbed, stripping away all thoughts other than the touch of their naked bodies in bed, their experienced tongue in the folds of her vagina.

Like a willing lover, she laced her fingers through his and simulated pleasure with a low moan after he kissed her again. Clutching her fingers, he led her in the direction of the bedroom.

The dining room table, messily covered with the remnants of her day, running clothes, her wallet with her IDs, her keys, crumpled cash, and the runner's pouch, was within reach of her free hand as she passed it. She was terrified that somewhere in Juan's black, Zorro-like clothing was one of his hidden knives. She knew how to fight—her father's legacy—but she didn't know anything about how to exceed the speed of a trained swordsman.

Before she could make the crucial, life-threatening decision as to whether to lunge for the running pouch, an utterly unexpected sound resonated through the apartment. It was the iron service door through which Juan had entered the apartment. His entrance had been quiet, but this new noise was explosive, the full door striking the adjacent wall.

In the entrance of the service door, she saw Willis Jordan, in one of his beautifully tailored suits, staring at the naked Raquel and the black-clad man. The expression on Willis' normally tranquil face was stunned, confused: Had he intruded on lovers' impassioned movement to a bedroom, the seduction by Raquel of a Latin man she had just met at a downtown club?

And then Raquel shouted, "Run, Willis!"

Willis Jordan was as large as a football lineman, but it was obvious his size was comprised of loose muscle and bone. Visibly frightened, Willis shouted, "Are you all right? I've tried to contact you for hours."

"Is this fat ass your boyfriend?" Juan asked.

Watching Juan but ignoring his words, Willis said, "Raquel, the night porter is dead."

At that point Juan, now concentrated and furious, began to lunge in the direction of Willis.

Raquel simultaneously grabbed the pouch and for an agonizing pulse of a moment had trouble sliding open the zipper. But then it slid just wide enough for her to pull the Ruger out; it had a magazine of bullets locked into its deadly slot.

She had no hesitation. Juan, a blade in his hand, was well within striking distance of the innocent, benevolent Willis Jordan, who was unable to move, completely immobilized by fear.

Raquel's single shot from the Ruger entered Suarez' body precisely where she aimed: the center of his spine. Even in the weapon's explosive, instantaneous din, she heard the crack of his bones. As he fell to the floor, he spun around to see, in the last moments of his life, a naked woman with a black pistol.

Unhurt but stunned, Willis had dropped to the floor on his knees. She saw tears streaming from his eyes and over his cheeks. Still carrying the Ruger, Raquel, entirely calm, walked toward

Salazar's body one foot away from the kneeling, crying Willis Jordan.

When she looked at Hugo, Raquel saw, or imagined she saw, his eyes watching her. He appeared to still be alive. She bent forward, placed the Ruger at his temple, and shot again. The side of his head exploded, blood and fragments of brain splattered over the floor and nearby walls, and on her naked body. She slid the Ruger across the room, away from her and from the dead man.

Raquel then, still naked, knelt down to console the trembling Willis Jordan. They embraced. He was shuddering from a place deep within his massive body. She was not shuddering or shaking.

CHAPTER 50

SEVERAL WEEKS HAD passed since Raquel Rematti had been in a courtroom. She easily made arrangements with the local director of the United States Marshal's Service to gain access to Naomi Goldstein's ornate courtroom as television vans and crews crowded Foley Square on a cool cloudless morning. Courthouses were public buildings, and, once people had waited for an hour to pass through the airport-like security stations, they were in theory free to wander through all the courtrooms.

On this morning, however, there was one courtroom to which there was no free access, and that was Naomi Goldstein's courtroom. Raquel was one of the late arrivals as the hour for Senator Angelina Baldesteri's guilty plea was approaching. Naomi Goldstein would, as ever, prove herself a prompt judge.

Raquel took a seat in the spectator gallery next to Willis Jordan who, as a senior press corps member, had access to the courtroom. Seated at the defense table was Senator Baldesteri, her back turned to Raquel and the rest of the gallery as she waited stoically for Naomi Goldstein to emerge from the judge's door. To the Senator's left was silver-haired Michael O'Keefe. Raquel, accustomed to endless surprises, wasn't surprised to see the legendary Michael O'Keefe, now Angelina Baldesteri's lawyer. As one of Raquel's longtime mentors, Michael O'Keefe had often told her that, in this profession, a lawyer had always to expect the unexpected.

Willis, in a half-whisper, asked, "And how does Michael O'Keefe come to be her lawyer? Seven million of the eight million people who live in New York are lawyers. Why him?"

"To lawyers like Michael O'Keefe, loyalty means nothing. I went to him not long ago to help me with Baldesteri. And now, magically, he is Baldesteri's lawyer. He was also—and I didn't know this when I went to him for help—at one time the lawyer for Salazar and Caliente. I once idolized Michael O'Keefe. He's like Zelig: he changes all the time."

"Zelig," Willis mused. "Our Jewish friends call them Golem."

"Willis, how does a farm boy from Georgia learn what a *Golem* is?"

In the moments of subdued murmuring before Goldstein entered, Raquel whispered to Willis, "How are you?"

"A happy man. No stories on NBC ever gave me more pleasure than the ones where we reported that you were instantly vindicated by self-defense, that you saved my innocent ass, that there was never anything other than an imaginary grand jury investigating you for bribery, and that clients were yet again clamoring for your miraculous services. You survived."

Raquel pressed his fleshy arm. "You know, you're a brave man. Most people would have run for their lives when they saw poor Jose dead in the basement. You didn't have to come up to my apartment. You saved me, Willis. I did not save you. Now, how is that for honesty?"

"No, most men, and certainly every man who knew you, would have done what I did: find you and protect you. And in my case, I just wanted to sleep in your bed again. Just that, just to comfort you."

Suddenly there was a slight commotion at the defense table. While Willis and Raquel were whispering, the Senator for the first time, noticed that Raquel Rematti was in the gallery. Raquel was attuned enough to the all-too-familiar defense table and the sibilance of Baldesteri's voice to hear her say to Michael O'Keefe, "Does that bitch have a right to be here?"

O'Keefe, calm and soothing, whispered, "She does if she wants to waste her time. We have more important things to think about."

At that moment, Cyrus Johnson pounded the judge's door three times, saying, "The court will come to attention in the matter of *United States v. Baldesteri*."

As Naomi Goldstein made her way up the three steps to her bench and switched on her useless reading lamp, everyone in the courtroom stood. The Senator was erect and betrayed none of the tension that must have permeated her as she waited to plead guilty to felonies that were bound to lead to a prison sentence, her immediate expulsion from the Senate, and obviously the end of her presidential campaign.

Stone cold, Raquel thought. *She was always stone cold*.

In her distinct voice, Goldstein began by announcing, "I understand the purpose of this hearing is for the defendant to withdraw her prior pleas of not guilty, and instead to now plead guilty, to certain charges in the indictment while the Government will in exchange move to dismiss the remaining charges. Is that correct?"

A lawyer at the crowded prosecution table stood. She was obviously Hunter Decker's successor. She said, "That's correct."

"Mr. O'Keefe," Goldstein said, "to which counts of the pending indictment does your client intend to plead guilty?"

"Those counts involving perjury and false statements to United States law enforcement officials and conspiracy to obstruct justice."

Goldstein shifted her gaze downward to the new prosecutor. "And what charges does the Government intend to move to dismiss?"

"Conspiracy to defraud the United States," the woman answered. Even in those few words, and even with the brief view of her position and gestures, Raquel recognized, as an experienced baseball manager would recognize in young players the few who would evolve into exceptional professionals, that this young woman had the poise, the necessary intensity, and the focus to become a great trial lawyer.

Goldstein, as always, was unemotionally direct: "Ms. Baldesteri, I ask that you continue to stand so I can pose questions to satisfy myself that you are voluntarily and intelligently prepared to proceed with your guilty pleas. This is, as you know, a serious day for you."

Angelina, a fighter with no tolerance for condescension from anyone, said, "Judge, I do *not* understand how you can even suggest that I don't recognize what is or is not serious."

In the gallery, Raquel whispered into Willis' left ear, "She just added two years to her sentence. Two years for arrogance."

Goldstein impassively said, "Before we proceed, I want everyone to understand that, while the Government and the defendant have signed an agreement contemplating a plea of guilty to certain offenses and a dismissal of other existing counts, I am not bound by that agreement or any aspect of it. For example, the Government and defendant have agreed that the offenses of conviction indicate a range of twenty-four to thirty-six months of imprisonment. That does not bind me. Over the next several weeks I will receive reports from investigators and letters from private citizens who may wish to make comments that are favorable or unfavorable to the defendant, which may lead me to impose a different sentence." She halted, looking at Michael O'Keefe. "Does your client understand that, Mr. O'Keefe?"

"I explained it to her."

"No, no, Mr. O'Keefe. That was not my question. My question was, does she understand that?"

Angelina Baldesteri spoke out. "Yes, obviously, I understand that."

"Ms. Baldesteri, when I address a question to your attorney, *he* answers, not *you*."

Michael O'Keefe, summoning that gentle brogue Raquel Rematti now hated because she saw it as an integral part of the repertoire of a skilled liar, said, "I can assure you the Senator understands."

"Mr. O'Keefe, what is your motion?"

"My client's motion is to withdraw her plea of not guilty to counts one, six, and ten of the superseding indictment and to enter instead a plea of guilty to each of them. These all relate to perjury, bribery, and obstruction of justice."

"And you anticipate that the Government will, if I grant your motion, which I'm not required to do, move to dismiss the eleven remaining counts?"

"That's my understanding."

Goldstein turned her attention to Baldesteri. "I first have to assure myself, from hearing Ms. Baldesteri's own words, that she, in fact, did those acts as to which she is pleading guilty. It's not enough that she says she is guilty as to specific enumerated sections of the law. In other words, I need to hear, in layman's language, what you did, Ms. Baldesteri. For example, I can't have you say you conspired to kidnap the Lindbergh child if you weren't even alive when it happened."

As Raquel knew, nothing—not even a vital moment like this—ever interfered with Angelina Baldesteri's ego.

The Senator said, "I arranged with a man I knew as Robert Calvaro to bribe a juror to vote for my acquittal."

"Who is Mr. Calvaro?" Goldstein asked.

"He's dead."

"No, no, I didn't ask you that. Let me repeat it: Who *is* Mr. Calvaro?"

"Mr. Calvaro told me he was Mr. Calvaro."

"Ms. Baldesteri, I'm at a loss to understand you. Unless you cooperate with me, unless you are honest and thorough with me and not evasive, I can reject your plea agreement. At that point, you can either plead guilty to every one of the counts in the indictment, which carry under the federal guidelines that bind every federal judge a two-hundred-year sentence if you are convicted. Your only other choice, Ms. Baldesteri, is to go to trial with a new jury as if this hearing never happened. Possibly, Ms. Baldesteri, you'll be acquitted. I'm a judge, not Nostradamus." Goldstein then stopped and stared steadily at Baldesteri. "What," she stated, "do you really want to tell me?"

"Robert Calvaro was, or so he told me, a wealthy South American who later became a naturalized United States citizen."

"That tells me nothing more than what you just said. And the sum total of that is nothing."

Raquel Rematti gently pushed Willis Jordan's arm. "This is great," she whispered. "Baldesteri is her own worst enemy."

Goldstein's voice was as loud as she could make it: "You still haven't said a word to flesh out what you did. Are you understanding this process? What crimes did you commit with Mr. Calvaro *and* anyone else? That is what I need to hear."

"Soon after the trial started, Robert Calvaro said he did not believe it was going well for me and that Raquel Rematti was not nearly as effective a lawyer as everyone had claimed. Certainly not, Mr. Calvaro said, a woman worth half a million dollars in legal fees. And so Mr. Calvaro told me he knew of a better way to gain my acquittal. He said he had an associate named Hugo Salazar who would be able to attract and bribe a female juror to vote to acquit me. Calvaro said, as I remember it, that John Gotti was the *Teflon Don* and acquitted three times because a juror in each of those trials had been bribed for a vote of acquittal. Those acquittals were not the work of Gotti's lawyers, they were insurance. Mr. Calvaro called it *American justice* at its best level."

"And tell me more. What did you say or do?"

"I gave him my blessing."

"Your blessing? What does that mean?"

"I said he and Salazar should go ahead."

"How?"

"By Salazar's befriending her, by becoming her lover, *and* by giving her one hundred thousand dollars in cash and cocaine."

"Who was that juror?"

"I'm not sure of her name. Lydia Guzman?"

"Don't mislead me, Ms. Baldesteri. What was her name? You know it and so you must say it."

Defiance in her tone, Angelina Baldesteri said, "Lydia Guzman."

"And she is dead?"

"So I'm told."

"Do you have any reason to believe she is not dead?"

"I never saw her body."

"Don't do that again, Ms. Baldesteri. Even I remember a song from the time I was a cloistered young woman. Play with me and you 'Play with Fire.' Is Lydia Guzman dead?"

"She is."

"Did she ever receive any of these bribe payments?"

"She did."

"Who gave them to her?"

"Calvaro or Salazar, as far as I know."

"Did you?"

"I never saw her outside of this courtroom."

"Did you?" Goldstein persisted.

"Never."

"But you authorized it all, correct?"

"I said that already."

"Ms. Baldesteri, listen carefully. Did you authorize and direct giving Ms. Guzman cash and drugs?"

"Yes."

"You've mentioned Calvaro and Salazar, both of them now dead. Did anyone else know of the conspiracy?"

There was a long, profound, and very tense silence in the courtroom. Willis Jordan's hand squeezed Raquel Rematti's.

Baldesteri said, "Not that I'm aware of."

"Listen to me carefully. Did Raquel Rematti know of or participate in this conspiracy?"

"You would have to ask her."

"No, no, no," Goldstein said, her voice even louder. "Did she? I am asking *you*."

Another profound silence dominated the courtroom. "No, she didn't."

Willis squeezed Raquel's hand even more tightly.

Goldstein leaned back slightly, as if she herself were relieved. Then she glanced at a piece of paper in front of her. "There is yet another charge against you for conspiracy to obstruct justice. And it relates to photographs that appear to show Ms. Rematti, Mr. Salazar, and Ms. Guzman together recently in a dance club. Is there anything you can say about those pictures?"

"Yes."

"What?"

"Mr. Decker, two FBI agents, and Mr. Calvaro—all now dead—arranged to take old photographs and alter them."

"Why?"

"Mr. Decker and his agents wanted to ruin Ms. Rematti."

"How do you know that?"

"The dead agents reported that to me. So did two men whose names I did not know but who had strange markings—like zigzags—etched in their blond hair. They told me they were separately and secretly working for both Mr. Calvaro and Mr. Decker."

"Did you know their names?"

"No."

"Is there anything else you can tell me about them?"

"They were part of a group that murdered Hayes Smith, the television broadcaster, on the island of Lesbos."

"Did they say why?"

"To intimidate Ms. Rematti."

"Do you know where they are now so that I can issue warrants for their arrest?"

"Dead."

"Who ordered them to kill Mr. Smith?"

"Oscar Caliente."

"Who is Oscar Caliente?"

"As I understand it, Oscar Caliente was the real name of Robert Calvaro."

"I didn't ask you that," Goldstein said. "Who is Oscar Caliente?"

"He was the head of the Sinaloa drug cartel in Manhattan and the Hamptons."

"How do you know?"

"He told me that once at a restaurant known as Rao's in Upper Manhattan."

"Did you report that to law enforcement?"

"No."

The faintest look of disgust passed over Naomi Goldstein's otherwise enigmatic face. She said, "There is one other factual issue as to which you plan to plead guilty. Did you perjure yourself to the jury?" She paused.

"I did."

"How?"

"When I said Robert Calvaro did not visit me overnight at the Waldorf Astoria. He, in fact, did, and did so many times." She paused. "And by that time, I knew he was Oscar Caliente."

Still enigmatic, Goldstein said, "You are aware of the fact that if you have lied to me today, you will be indicted for perjury again?"

"I'm well aware of that," Baldesteri said. "Well aware of that."

Naomi Goldstein wrote notes on a sheet of paper in front of her. There was a three-minute pause of complete silence in the courtroom. Raquel continued to clutch Willis Jordan's hand.

"I'm satisfied," Goldstein finally announced, "that the facts to which Ms. Baldesteri has just testified are sufficient to support her pleas of guilty." She glanced at the young woman who had replaced Hunter Decker. "Does the United States have a motion?"

"To dismiss the other counts."

"That's granted."

Judge Goldstein turned slightly to look again at Angelina Baldesteri and Michael O'Keefe. "All that remains now for the moment," Goldstein said, "is the important issue of bail. Under the agreement, Ms. Baldesteri has forfeited her right to appeal. She will be formally sentenced by me in one month. Mr. O'Keefe, is there anything you want to say?"

"The Government and I have agreed that the Senator can be in home confinement and wear an ankle monitor at all times until sentencing. In other words, she will be monitored but otherwise free."

For the first and only time, Naomi Goldstein angrily slapped the bench at which she sat. "No, no, no. What I have heard today is gross misconduct by one of the highest officials in this country. It's a malevolent breach of the public trust. It also reveals that she is a person prepared to condone and plan violence by others. And, given the kinds of people she has willingly associated with, she presents a risk of flight to any country with which the United States does not have an extradition treaty."

Goldstein signaled to the senior member of the ten United States Marshals to her bench and held the microphone under her hand so that no one else in the courtroom could hear her as she spoke. When the Marshal stepped away from the bench, he approached Angelina Baldesteri.

Judge Goldstein said, "There will be no bail. I remand Angelina Baldesteri immediately to the custody of the Justice Department so that she can begin serving the prison sentence I will impose next month after receiving all the reports and comments I need."

Just at that moment, two things happened: a female Marshal placed handcuffs on Angelina Baldesteri's wrists and led her toward the side door, which, through an elevated bridge, connected the courthouse to the nearby prison known as the Metropolitan Correction Center.

And Angelina Baldesteri turned to look directly at Raquel Rematti. "You bitch," she said. "We'll get you."

* * *

On the steps of the grand federal courthouse, in brilliant sunlight, Raquel, accompanied by Willis Jordan, heard many questions, all of them as indistinct as if they came from underwater.

But there was one question that resonated for her. "What's your reaction, Ms. Rematti?"

Raquel Rematti said only, "Justice."

AUTHOR'S NOTE

Raquel Rematti fascinates me, as she has many of the readers of my earlier novel *The Borzoi Killings*. Raquel made her first appearance in that novel as the celebrated lawyer who undertook, for free, to represent a scorned "illegal" immigrant accused of the brutal murder of one of America's wealthiest men at an East Hampton estate.

Although Raquel appears again in *The Warriors*, this novel is not a sequel to *The Borzoi Killings*. They are stand-alone books.

Raquel was chosen for *The Warriors* because of who she is. In the rarefied world of the four or five best criminal defense lawyers in America, she is not only one of them—she is the best. But Raquel is more than that. She is tough, compassionate, an utter realist, a person of remarkable bravery and independence. She is, too, a devoted friend and lover who faces hurt, loss, and betrayal.

Finally, I bring Raquel into a world of top-quality lawyers that has been utterly dominated by men, both fictional and real—Atticus Finch, Clarence Darrow, Johnnie Cochran. We need to know there are women of genius, charisma, bravery, and integrity who can excel in one of the last male-dominated arenas of our world. So, as a reader, I hope that you have concluded that the endlessly various aspects of Raquel Rematti make her not just one of the best bullfighters in the arena—but the best.